THE VAULT

For Debbie
Hope you enjoy this
Kind regards
Kam Long

THE VAULT

THE SECOND ELEANOR RAVEN THRILLER

KAREN LONG

ISBN-13: 9781503142213

For Michael

CHAPTER ONE

Mackenzie Webber was not a man of vision, which was why he had been employed by the Westex Landfill Company, in the capacity of site worker and entry grade sanitation officer. Both job titles were subject to minimum wage and as such required only the vaguest of training. So, when the surface fire started, he ran to find his supervisor Larry Beatman, rather than following recognised protocol. By the time Larry had been tracked down, the fire had consumed half an acre of landfill and was threatening the methane collectors positioned on the west side. Larry, whose wage reflected his greater understanding of Health and Safety procedure, immediately instructed Mackenzie to contact emergency services, whilst he started the mini douser.

The Fire Department rolled up within nine minutes of taking the call from the barely coherent Mackenzie, and after a thorough check, declared the fire extinguished and the site safe. However, what they didn't dismiss so readily was the charred skeleton lolling in a position some would describe as coquettish, its blackened arms crossed demurely over its lap, the head bent forward, and the legs touching at the knees and angled slightly to the right. The fire had been fast and hot, destroying much of the flesh and all of the clothing that might have been attached. This was the most puzzling aspect of the whole event for Fire Officer

Mike Bradshaw, who, after twenty-three years in the service, recognised that this body couldn't have been secreted under anything more substantial than a blanket, or a couple of bin liners. As he dialled Control, Mike stared suspiciously at Mackenzie Webber, whose body language, if not actually signing a confession, was certainly convincing him it was only a matter of time.

Eleanor Raven sat at her desk and stretched her leg out, trying not to wince. It had been six months since she'd had the skin grafted onto her thigh, and despite the regular application of creams and unguents, it remained tortuously tight and raw to the touch. This, according to her consultant, was as good as it was going to get and gratitude for not having lost complete sensation in the leg, or more muscle, should be felt. Gratitude was not what Eleanor Raven felt at this precise moment. Her kidnapping and subsequent torture at the hands of Lee Hughes, had left her with three broken ribs, a punctured lung, fractured collar bone, enforced home rest till today, and compulsory weekly attendance at the 'Serving Officers' Psychiatric Unit'. Gratitude was not a word she used.

From the sudden increase in peripheral noise it was apparent that her boss, Chief Inspector Marty Samuelson, was on his way. A man of height, girth, impatience, and simmering outrage, he encouraged his homicide officers to 'think outside of the box', but to be aware that meticulous practice was the only way to ensure convictions. He'd always given Eleanor Raven a wide degree of latitude when it came to policing, but after nearly losing her on her last case he had decided to be more circumspect, and had insisted on a probationary period for the next three months. The door to Eleanor's office flew open, and Marty barged in with two cups of coffee.

"Sweet Jesus!" he gasped, putting both cups down and dragging the seat over from her partner's notably empty desk. He stared at Eleanor for a second or two, noting the paleness of her skin, and the heavy dark circles under her eyes. Her long, chestnut brown hair was lazily plaited, and her childish sprinkling of freckles made her look considerably younger than her thirty odd years. "You look like shit," he said bluntly, taking a slurp of coffee. "You sure you're ready for this? Take a holiday, go somewhere sunny, and get some colour in your cheeks."

Eleanor sipped her coffee, grimacing at the amount of sugar. Marty noticed. "Get it down you – you need to put on a couple of pounds."

"And my teeth?" she responded.

"No-one died of teeth. Being skinny: every day," he replied, smiling.

"Well you're going to outlive us all then boss," she nodded at his waistline.

He smiled and lifted his coffee mug. "To long life and big coffins."

Eleanor smiled and raised hers too.

With a sigh he leaned back in his seat and lifted his chin questioningly in the direction of her partner Laurence Whitefoot's desk. "Where's Captain America?"

Eleanor shrugged. "It's a mystery."

"First day back and your partner ain't here to welcome you?" said Marty disapprovingly. He scrutinised her expression before carrying on. "Did he tell you that he's applied for a transfer to another precinct?"

Eleanor said nothing. This was news to her and left her feeling strangely flat.

Marty leaned forwards and lowered his voice, "What the fuck's happened between you two? He saved your life, but according to Mo, only visited you twice in hospital. I want to know what's going on before I recommend any transfers."

Eleanor paused for a moment before replying. "I have no idea sir."

Marty was working his jaw, about to launch into an interrogation, but mercifully her phone rang. With ill-mannered speed Eleanor grabbed the receiver and listened, jotting down an address and a couple of names before hanging up. "Sorry sir, I'm on. Skeletal remains have been found on a land fill site over on East." She stood up, hoping that Marty would take the hint, but hinting had no place in Marty Samuelson's world.

"We deal with conflict and mayhem every day Raven, and I won't have that shit in here. I want answers before I let this go, and you two will remain in this 'marriage of convenience' till I do." With that Marty stood up and turned to leave. "You don't work alone any more, and if this turns out to be bigger than a dead hobo you hand it over to Timms."

Eleanor stared at him.

"We on the same page?"

"No question," she replied.

It had become apparent to Eleanor over the years, that once an individual had acquired homicide status, the chances were that he or she would make their way, in a black bin liner, to the Westex Landfill site. Current statistics put the number of victims reclaimed at nine, since the plant opened in the eighties, all but four having been solved and the perpetrators incarcerated. Sadly, two of the bodies were under five years of age and caused untold distress to everyone who had the dubious privilege of working these cases. One of the big plusses to having sealed up a body in a bin liner before having it dumped on the site, was that generally the bag contained sufficient trace evidence to make apprehension not too difficult. Over half of the bags were covered in incriminating fingerprints, generally spousal.

As she approached the security gates of the landfill site, she noticed that the air quality had taken a sudden lunge. Rather than closing the dashboard vents, she drew in the vapours, trying to distinguish those naturally produced by the disposal of thousands of tonnes of household waste and contaminants, and those that might be linked to the cremation of flesh and bone. Seeing Mike Bradshaw, she pulled her Tauris over to the side, and stepped out.

"How you doing Detective Inspector Raven?" he said warmly, as he walked towards her.

"I'm good Mike," she held out her hand. "What we got here?"

Mike slipped off his glove and grabbed her hand, holding it protectively rather than shaking.

"We have a strange, and interesting situation," he said, steering her gently in the direction of the site office. "We were called in at nine twenty-eight am, to tackle a small surface blaze of unknown origin. By the time we arrived, the fire had been controlled and extinguished. We did a detailed check of the area, to make sure there was no threat to deeper layers, and discovered this." Mike stabbed at his phone, and handed it to Eleanor. The image was initially difficult to interpret but by adjusting the depth of field Eleanor could make out a blackened skeleton.

"How hot was the fire Mike?" she asked, skimming through the images.

"Hot, but not cremation hot. There couldn't have been much in the way of flesh beforehand because there'd be more left. Not that that's set in stone, just an opinion." Opening the trunk, she swapped her shoes for a pair of rubber boots and drew a couple of pairs of latex gloves out of a bag.

Eleanor nodded and looked around. Taking his cue, Mike began to walk in the direction of the fire.

"Where'd it start?" she asked, noting that the sooty air felt granular as she drew it in through her nostrils, a sharp stink of volatile chemicals searing her palate as she inhaled. He pointed over to his left.

She wrinkled her nose, and turned to Mike. "You think this was started deliberately?"

Mike raised his eyebrows, and shook his head slightly. "Wouldn't surprise me but it didn't start by the body."

In a natural gesture, Mike took her hand and helped her climb over the sodden mounds of debris that had been forked out when the site was checked. "Steady," he said, as she caught her foot on a length of twisted metal.

The skeleton was leaning against a pile of unidentifiable burned rubbish and was at first difficult to single out, particularly as the wind was picking up a little and twists of smoke were being swept straight towards them, making their eyes water.

"That smells like an accelerant to me," said Mike darkly. "Maybe he did start it."

"Who's he?" asked Eleanor, following Mike's line of sight. A slightly-built man swathed in too large a work suit, hopped nervously outside a small hut.

"That's Mackenzie Webber and he called it in," said Mike turning to the skeleton.

Eleanor looked at Mackenzie for a moment or two and then gave her full attention to the body. The bones were heavily burned and several of the long bones showed signs of heat cracking. She picked at some small fragments of material around the body. Mike peered over her shoulder. "What's that?" he asked.

"Not sure yet but there's a pattern here. Clothing I think," she said, carefully placing it in the position she had collected it from.

"You need to bag that?" asked Mike.

"Crime Scene are on their way. Now might be a good time to go talk to Mr Webber."

Eleanor sat in silence and stared at Mackenzie Webber. He was sweating profusely and kept rubbing a grubby index finger across his forehead, as if trying to massage a convincing response to the barrage of questions that were about to come his way. She had elected to interview Mackenzie in his cramped hut, as it would give her time to assess the man before she heard his story. Of the existence of a story there was no doubt in her mind. The hut was filled with an eclectic collection of objects selected from the landfill. Lamps, a scabrous moose head, a small table, two chairs, and a chaise longue crammed into a corner attested to Mackenzie's commitment to his job. Interestingly, neatly stacked on a small oak table were, what looked like, two dated photograph albums.

She waited, the longer the better in her opinion. But after three minutes Mackenzie crumbled. "I don't know nuffin' about no body," he said, flinging himself back in the seat heavily. The seat groaned ominously. Eleanor raised an eyebrow, conveying her disbelief to Mackenzie. His eyes saccaded to the left and he began to worry a fingernail. "It didn't look like a body," he muttered so quietly that she had to strain to hear.

"How did it appear then?" she responded with interest.

"Like a...a dummy you know. A shop dummy," he replied.

She leaned towards him and smiled, encouraging him to carry on.

"That's what I thought it was...Until the fire and then..." Suddenly he had an idea. "Perhaps that's what it is!" he yelped. "A dummy."

"Mr Webber. What you see out there are the remains of a human being. Perhaps you'd like to explain to me why you thought it was a shop dummy?"

Mackenzie opened his mouth but snapped it tightly closed, as a brisk knock accompanied the hut door being opened.

Eleanor experienced a wave of irritation as she felt the ease of the interrogation pass through her fingers, in no way relieved by seeing that the interruption was due to the arrival of her partner, Detective Laurence Whitefoot. She hadn't seen him for several months and their parting had been anything but pleasant. She greeted him with a curt nod. With a functional smile, he put out a hand to Mackenzie, whose eyes narrowed with suspicion. "This is my partner Detective Whitefoot, Mr Webber. He's here to observe only."

She didn't miss the hardening of Laurence's mouth, as he manoeuvred cautiously between the moose head and Eleanor's seat, and sank into the ill-sprung chaise longue. Turning her attention back to Mackenzie she said warmly, "I'm astonished as to why people throw out so many wonderful things."

Suddenly, Mackenzie was all nods and positive body language. "You ain't wrong there. Look at all this stuff," he flung his hands around expansively. "There's tonnes more. I ain't got room for it all 'ere, but I give it to..."

"These are interesting photographs Mr Webber," said Laurence quietly, from the chaise longue. Eleanor turned and saw that he was leafing through one of the photograph albums. He swivelled it round, so that Eleanor and Mackenzie could see what he was looking at.

"Could you explain who this is?" he said, pointing a finger to a polaroid shot of MacKenzie, with his arms flung round what looked like a fully clothed woman, positioned in practically the identical posture to that of the skeletal remains. What was particularly disturbing about the image was that the woman appeared to have a green patina of mould covering her face and hands. Her hair was mid length and dishevelled, the eyes open and staring vacantly into the distance. Mackenzie leaned possessively into the woman, an idiotic smirk across his face.

"Tell me where and when you found the body," said Eleanor.

"I found her a couple of months ago..."

"Months?" gasped Laurence incredulously.

Mackenzie scowled. "Yeah... months. I was working over on the east side..."

"Working?" asked Laurence, ignoring Eleanor's frown.

Mackenzie stared warily at Laurence. "The trucks bring the garbage in and me and Kev make sure that they're spreadin' it evenly. Kev drives the earthmover and flattens it all, but I check that they're not bringing in too much food waste, 'cos that has to go to another area. The drivers don't give a shit what they dump, they just wanna drop and go."

"So how do you check this?" asked Eleanor, wrestling back control of the interview from Laurence, whose mouth was just opening.

Mackenzie's lip curled, as if this question was too stupid to respond to. "I open up some of the bags!"

"That's how you found the woman?" said Eleanor.

"The shop dummy!" snapped Mackenzie. "Yeah. She wasn't in a bag. I like to give everythin' a good goin' over and when I dug around the top layer I saw a leg. So, I dug it up and bought it back."

"How did you bring her back?"

"In the van. I drive the pick up and thought..." his voice trailed off, as if unable to comprehend just what he had thought.

Eleanor and Laurence waited.

"I thought she'd be company," he said quietly.

Eleanor needed a few moments to digest the implications of what Mackenzie had just said. "Where do you live Mr Webber?"

He looked nervous. "I live here. I do the security here as well." He glanced around at the possessions in the hut. There was a kettle and a small hob tucked into a corner of the room, a chipped enamel jug and bowl neatly placed under the wooden surface. "I don't cost no-one nuffin!" he said, defensively. "I get all my stuff off the site and the wages pay for food. I like it 'ere."

Eleanor nodded. "Who took the photograph of you and the... dummy?"

Laurence cast her a swift look.

"I did," he said proudly. He turned round and opened a cardboard box, gingerly lifting out an old-fashioned Polaroid SX-70 camera. "Found this last year, but couldn't use it 'cos I ain't had no film to put in. But..." he lifted out a half empty, instant film cartridge. "I found this before Christmas and take the odd one to put in my albums. And look!" He gently unhooked the closing mechanism and twisted the camera into operational mode. "See that!" He pointed to the button, his eyes sparkling. "If you twist that to the right, it will give you thirty seconds before it clicks."

Eleanor nodded. "Would you mind if I borrowed this and the remaining film?"

Mackenzie looked worried. "I ain't got no more film other than that."

"I understand and will bring it back to you as soon as I can."

Mackenzie nodded, "Ok."

"So, when you found the..." Eleanor started.

"Della," responded Mackenzie uncomfortably. "I called her Della."

She nodded. "When you found Della, was she wearing the same clothes in this photograph?"

He nodded. "There was a scarf round her neck but I didn't like it." He put his hands back in the cardboard box and brought out a lime green silk scarf. It was dirty and torn along one edge.

"Did anyone else know about Della?"

He shrugged. "No-one comes over here very often. Well not the back bit. I go to the main office. Larry knows I'm 'ere but he don't come over."

Eleanor reached over, picked up the album and pointed to the photograph. "She has a greenish tone in this photograph. Is that accurate or..."

"That's what I told ya!" he said, exasperated. She was mouldy. Like she'd been left outside for a long time and she felt like she was made of plastic. Solid but I wus surprised that she had a drawing on 'er arm. Like a tattoo. It was faint. A faint snake!" he smiled, pleased with the rhythm and rhyme he'd created. "It wus a big snake with a black open mouth. I dunno what sort..." He was beginning to fidget. Eleanor imagined that he'd probably not maintained a conversation for this amount of time, in a good while.

"A black mamba," said Laurence.

Eleanor looked at him. He shrugged his shoulders imperceptibly and turned away from her.

Mackenzie looked baffled, "Maybe..." he said non-committedly.

"Her eyes?"

"What about 'em?" Mackenzie asked, confused.

"Did you look at them?"

His mouth dropped slightly, as if trying to second guess where a confession might take him.

"What were they made of?"

He sighed and looked relieved. "Glass I think. Yeah, glass. No *real* person would have eyes made of glass, would they?"

Eleanor stood up and reached for the photograph albums. She noted the sudden anxious look that passed over his features. "We will need you to come down to station headquarters and be interviewed later on today."

"Am I in trouble?" he said quickly.

"Not unless you're hiding something or refuse to co-operate," she said calmly.

He shook his head vigorously.

By the time Eleanor had finished her interview with Mackenzie, Susan Cheung and her team were organising the retrieval processes. The coroner was just manoeuvring his van between the CSI trucks and Mike Bradshaw was preparing to leave. He waved to Eleanor and Laurence, trotting over to meet them.

"He tell you anything?" asked Mike.

Eleanor shook her head. "Thought it was a shop dummy. Found it a couple of months ago and brought it back here."

"Huh?" said Mike.

Laurence flipped open the photo album and showed Mike the Polaroid.

"Holy fuck! And he thought she was a mannequin? Why?" asked Mike incredulously.

"Gonna have to find that out," said Laurence.

"Well, have fun kids," said Mike, turning to leave.

Eleanor turned to her partner. She hadn't seen him for several months and in that time he seemed to have grown a little older. His dark beard showed flecks of grey and his blue eyes reflected a little less light. She didn't know how to break the ice between them or even if it could be broken. "You got a bag for those?" she indicated the photo albums. He nodded, turned, and walked towards his car.

As she threaded her way across the compounded mounds of charred household waste, Eleanor tried to imagine how a body could have been preserved and then deposited at the waste site. So far she'd only managed to come up with a med school prank or funeral home blunder. She stood at the edge of the taped-off area and stared at the body.

"How the hell are you?" asked Susan Cheung warmly. She pulled the mask away from her face and rested it on her forehead.

"I'm good."

"First day back and you're dealing with this huh?" said Susan, knowing that that was exactly the sort of thing that Eleanor wanted to deal with.

"What have we got here?" asked Eleanor, selecting a pair of plastic bootie covers and slipping them on.

"Hmm. Ok gotta be honest, I really don't know." Susan leaned her face towards the body and using her hand in a scooping action, drew the fumes into her nostrils.

"What do you smell?" asked Eleanor, with growing interest.

"Formaldehyde but I'm not committing to that till I've run chem tests."

"Embalming fluid?"

Susan raised her eyebrows and shook her head slightly. "I really don't know yet. Early days but it's kind of a distinctive smell."

"If... supposing it was, would that have explained why there's so little flesh left on it?"

"It might," said Susan. "Formaldehyde burns hot and hard."

The sound of talking drew Eleanor's attention for a moment. Laurence was chatting to Manny, Susan's tech officer and helping him carry up a collecting box. She turned her attention back to the body. "Is there any flesh left?"

Susan nodded. "The backside has melted into the garbage beneath it. So we're going to take the whole thing in a bag down to the morgue and hope that we can separate the two."

"How long?" said Eleanor.

"Doc Hounslow's in at midday and said if we can get down before twelve she'll do it."

Eleanor nodded.

"You'll text me the autopsy time?" asked Eleanor.

"Will do," replied Susan returning to the task in hand.

The walk back down to the manager's office was uncomfortable and, for the most part, silent. Eleanor took careful footsteps, aware that a slip would involve physical contact with Laurence, which was the last thing she wanted at the moment. Larry Beatman was waiting for them, his face blackened and sweaty from the morning's activity.

"Hey, pleased to meet ya! Larry Beatman, site manager," he drawled. They both shook hands with him.

"I'm DI Raven and this is Detective Laurence Whitefoot," she said curtly. "Tell me what happened Mr Beatman."

"Larry, please. It was a fire, nothing major, happens couple of times a year. We've found a big pile of batteries, probably mercury cells. They have a tendency to short circuit and ignite."

"So you don't suspect arson?" asked Laurence.

"Nah!"

"Uh-huh. That doesn't explain why we've got a partially-cremated skeleton on our hands," said Eleanor. Larry shuffled his feet and massaged his temple with grubby fingers.

"I know it looks bad but Mackenzie ain't the type to go killin' anyone. He's not very bright but totally harmless. He lives on the site 'cos he ain't got nowhere else to go. He thought it was a shop model or some'at," he sighed.

"Did you see the 'shop model' before the fire?" she asked.

He nodded. "Yeah but only from a distance. Mackenzie knows he ain't supposed to take trash from the site but he's curious and lonely. I saw it when I went to see him. Looked like a plastic shop doll to me... Look he ain't done nothing wrong. He's a lonely boy, can't read or write but he does a shitty job. One that we can't get no-one else to do, ok?"

"He says he found it over on the east side. When was that being filled?" she asked.

Larry scratched his head. "Can't say for sure but at least two months ago. We moved round to the north from there."

"We'll need to get a spot on where the body was initially located and send crime scene there."

Larry nodded. "I'll do that now."

There was a pause as Eleanor waited to see if anything more would be forthcoming. When it was clear that Larry had said what he was going to, she handed him her card. "If you know of anything that might help us in this matter please call me on this number at any time. Larry tapped his forehead with the card in salute and then headed off.

"What's the plan boss?" said Laurence, without making eye contact.

Eleanor took her time. "Autopsy's going to be around midday and I want to be there for that. In the meantime I think I'm going to do a bit of research."

"Uh-huh? Care to elaborate?"

"Care to follow?" she said lightly.

Laurence stood next to Eleanor outside 'The Saunders' Family Funeral Parlour', his jaw lolling forward slightly as he absorbed the contents of a framed bulletin propped on a pink and gilt easel in the bay window. It read 'Papa Saunders and family warmly embrace the following guests this week. Lola Andrews, Mama to Rosa and Letitia, and Baby LeToya, an angel.' Two huge photographs of Lola and baby LeToya were positioned above their names and in curling script across the bottom of the bulletin was written, 'Their maker tends to their souls and we tend to their earthly remains'.

"Really?" asked Laurence quietly.

"Really," Eleanor nodded and knocked on the door.

The door was opened by a black youth in his mid-teens, dressed, despite the weather being in the high twenties, in full morning suit, including tie, waistcoat, jacket and high collar. "Sir, Ma'am, how may Saunders be of service to you?" he asked with a combination of surprise, empathy and politeness.

"May I speak with Mr Saunders please?" asked Eleanor.

For a moment what looked like fear passed across the boy's features but he pulled open the door and ushered them in. "Would you mind waiting in the guest room Ma'am?" he asked quietly.

Eleanor nodded. "Tell your father it's DI Eleanor Raven."

The boy's lip twitched but he nodded and left them.

"Why are we here?" whispered Laurence, picking up and scanning one of the many glossy brochures that adorned the mahogany side table. "Do you think the body went missing from here?"

Eleanor raised an eyebrow. "Do you think that likely?"

Before Laurence could offer an opinion the door opened and the boy entered, clearing his throat. "My father is with a guest in the basement. He asked if you'd care to join him."

Titus Saunders, like his son, was dressed in full morning attire and was hovering proprietorially over the corpse of Lola Andrews. The only concession to his work in the basement being a pair of latex gloves, which he pulled off on seeing the detectives and warmly shook their hands. "Well Detective Raven it has been too long. Too long!" his voice still bore traces of a life begun in the southern states.

"You are looking well Titus. And how is Matthew?" asked Eleanor.

Titus' beaming face glowed proudly. "He's just completed his law degree and is applying to take his masters."

Laurence, not wanting to hover on the periphery of yet another Raven dominated interview chirped in. "He intends to practise?"

At this Titus' smile disappeared and all trace of ease evaporated. "No sir, he will *not* be practising!"

"I need your help Titus," butted in Eleanor, extracting the Polaroid photograph and handing it over to Titus still sealed in its plastic evidence bag. Titus changed his glasses and peered at the photograph, shaking his head. "Dear Lord! What is that? That ain't no doll if you're seeking me out."

"Tell me what you can see," she said. "This photograph was taken before a fire."

Titus' mouth grew hard. "How hot and what's left?"

"Fast and hot but not cremation temperature. Autopsy's this afternoon but I want some ideas first."

Titus nodded. "This idiot know what he's got there?" He pointed to Mackenzie's image.

Eleanor shook her head. "He thought it was a mannequin of some flavour."

Titus made a snorting sound, turned to a workbench and focused an illuminated magnifying glass over the photograph. "May I?" he asked slipping on a pair of latex gloves.

Eleanor nodded and peered over his shoulder as Titus removed the Polaroid from the evidence bag and lined it up under the huge glass. He turned to Laurence. "You wanna see this?"

Laurence joined them at the bench. Titus manoeuvred the photograph around, allowing the light and magnification to reveal truths.

"Hmmm, can you give me anything more?"

"Not yet. The body was located under bags of domestic refuge. It was then propped on a box and left outside for a couple of months." she replied quietly.

"It was rigid?" Titus asked. "Plastination and mummification leave a body rigid. Formaldehyde and glycerine is what we use to keep our guests soft; like Mrs Andrews here. Go on touch her hand." He nodded to them both. Eleanor wrapped her hand around the corpse's, which offered some resistance but wasn't entirely solid. "Relatives like to touch their loved ones and they don't want reminding they're dead. Formaldehyde keeps 'em pliable. They used to use formalin, and in older times arsenic to preserve the bodies, when they had to transport them back from battlefields. Nowadays, we got dozens of products to use. Each company has its own formula." He opened a cupboard and showed them neat lines of plastic bottles bearing a company logo and a standard 'biohazard' label. "We use this brand for the embalming fluids but several other companies for make-up and sanitising equipment."

"There was a mould," she stated.

"Maybe the products used weren't in high enough concentration. Formaldehyde works on most fungi, bacteria and viruses but it ain't fool proof. We use mixtures that contain centrimide, which is an ammonium bromide powder and can help, but you need to realise that the human body *wants* to decompose and you are fighting the organisms that achieve that. You said this body was left outside?"

Eleanor nodded.

"Embalming, if that's what this is, is difficult. What I'm doing for Mrs Andrews is slowing down the natural processes, so she can be viewed by her family. I ain't preserving her for time eternal. Look at this..." He reached for a textbook off a shelf and flicked through the pages. "This is little Rosalia Lombardo." The reproduced photograph showed a sepia image of a little girl lying, as if asleep, in a tiny coffin with a glass partition. Blonde curls framed her perfect features and a large silk ribbon sat pertly on her crown. "Rosalia died in 1918 of pneumonia and she was preserved by the master Alfredo Salafia, using a combination of formalin, glycerine, zinc salts and salicylic acid. She is perfect but she isn't exposed to any dampness. " He raised his eyebrows meaningfully. I don't know what you've got there but it must have been professionally done to have been exposed to the elements for a couple of months and remained in that condition."

Eleanor thought for a couple of moments and then nodded. "Thank you Titus, you've been a great help."

Titus carefully replaced the photograph in the evidence bag and handed it back to her. "I'm here if you need further thinking."

"I appreciate that. Thank you."

"So how the fuck did I put my foot in it this time?" asked Laurence tetchily, as they headed for their cars.

"Matthew Benton will never practice law because he's serving two consecutive life sentences for first degree murder… and I put him there."

Laurence stared for a moment, trying to process this information. "How come you're best buddies with his father then?"

"I didn't judge Matthew; I caught him." she replied simply.

CHAPTER TWO

"What strange and exotic mayhem have you brought with you now Detective?" asked Dr Mira Hounslow, as she stared at the blackened remains precariously balanced on an autopsy table. Dr Hounslow was the very antithesis of the chaos she examined. Her hair was always immaculately arranged and her make-up flawless; her manner crisp and decisive.

"Susan has filled me in on the circumstantial details," she said, positioning several x-rays into the illuminated viewer.

"We have a Polaroid of the body prior to its being burnt," replied Eleanor, holding the evidence bag in front of her. Protocol in the autopsy suite demanded that movement and conversation were at Dr Hounslow's discretion only.

"Strange and exotic indeed," she said, beckoning Eleanor and Laurence over to the viewer. "This photograph," she reached for it. "It depicts our gentleman as alive?"

"Gentleman?" asked Eleanor.

Dr Hounslow pointed to the second slide. "That," she said, pointing to the pelvis with a gloved finger. "Is an adult *male* pelvis. The iliac crest is considerably higher and narrower than a woman's and I'm looking at a sub-pubic angle. There is no doubt in *my* mind but if there's some in yours

Detective, then I suggest you run the measurements through the national database." she said, pointedly.

Eleanor smiled and shook her head. "The body was found in this condition under piles of domestic waste at the Westex landfill site." She handed over the Polaroid. "It gave the impression of being a shop mannequin to one of the workers, who photographed it and placed it near to his workplace."

"It must have been fairly hard to the touch to be so convincing. Still, an understandable mistake for anyone to make," replied Dr Hounslow studying the image.

Laurence cleared his throat, a gesture encouraged by Dr Hounslow as a way of seeking, rather than demanding, her attention.

"Yes?"

"What is that?" he pointed to the third x-ray.

"Ah, that's quite a thing isn't it?" she answered, moving closer to the viewer.

"Surely it couldn't have been surgically inserted before death?" he asked.

Eleanor moved over and stared at the opaque cylindrical object wedged into the pelvis.

"Not without causing considerable damage. No, I believe it was a post-mortem addition."

"What is it?" asked Eleanor confused.

"I imagine it was placed there to facilitate access to the poor gentleman," she said brusquely.

"As in sexual access?" said Eleanor moving closer to the viewer. "Will you be able to tell when you open him up?"

"Depends on what's left down there. I don't imagine there will be anything resembling biological evidence, but we'll see. Right, let's to it."

The autopsy took three-and-a-half hours to complete and left Eleanor with a dull thumping pain in her upper back and stabbing pains in her thigh. Her expression must have reflected this, despite her best efforts to the contrary, as both Dr Hounslow and Laurence insisted that she have a coffee and something to eat in D'Angelo's, the 'go to' eatery across from the morgue. Eleanor sat at a corner table and watched Laurence select and purchase pastries and coffee, surreptitiously dry swallowing two painkillers and hoping the coffee would arrive sooner rather than later.

"Ok, you up for a run through?" he asked in a concerned tone.

Eleanor waved her hand dismissively, as she gulped her coffee. "I've just had a text from Susan Cheung. They've identified material from, what appears to be, silicone implants."

"Which means that we have the remains of a transgendered female. Should make it easier to identify as a missing person," Laurence suggested.

"Mmm, but we've no idea when the victim was murdered."

"We even sure that she was murdered?" Laurence mused.

"I'd say that the non-burial and tampering with a human body constitutes a major crime right there. So until we can establish the means of the victim's death, then we proceed as if a homicide took place."

"What's the plan?" asked Laurence devouring a second pastry.

"Without an ID we've got nothing. We don't know whether our victim died a lawful death, was embalmed and stolen before burial or if he was murdered and embalmed by the perp. Once Susan Cheung has run a chem analysis, we can hopefully ascertain whether, or how he was embalmed."

"We're not referring to our victim as 'she' then?" said Laurence playfully.

"Not yet," Eleanor replied thoughtfully.

Laurence raised his eyebrows.

"That pipe was placed inside our victim post mortem. Couldn't the implants have been too?" said Eleanor quietly.

Laurence stopped chewing, "Jeez."

"What have you got?" asked Laurence pulling his chair over to Eleanor's desk and peering at her laptop screen.

"Thirty-eight real possibilities over the past five years."

"Thirty-eight trannies went AWOL over the past..."

"No," she cut in. "Thirty-eight men, between the ages of eighteen and thirty-five, who fall into the right height and racial category and reported as missing in a hundred mile radius. Of those thirty-eight, five were considered to be either living as women or were transgendered. "

"Is that all?" he replied, surprised. "Thought there'd been hundreds."

"There were. Just trying to narrow it down a little."

"Using what criteria?"

"Circumstantial mostly. Look, Ronnie Bennett aged twenty-four," she tapped the screen with her pen. "Missing after heading off for a late night fishing expedition on the Lake. Judged by friends to have been, 'under the influence'. Neither he, nor his boat, was seen again. Not on our list. David Waterston, right age, right height but obese to the tune of two hundred pounds. Not on our list."

Laurence nodded, "What about the thirty-eight?"

Eleanor pointed over to the photocopier. "Want to prioritise them?"

"You betcha," he responded, shoving back his chair and reaching for the pile. "Oh, good news is that Professor Locke is interested in our 'corpus delicti' and is going to give us a 2D reconstruction of the victim's head and face, presenting both as male and female. He's got the original Polaroid, ok?"

Eleanor nodded, "Excellent. What's the turn-round likely to be?"

"He said twenty-four to forty-eight."

Eleanor looked up as the door to their office opened. "Get outta my chair!" snarled Mo to Laurence, who smiled and stood to attention. "Hey Ellie," Mo said warmly, opening his arms and moving towards her. "Which bits am I allowed to hug?"

"All of them," she whispered in his ear, as she embraced her ex-partner, Mo.

"Can any human being be that skinny and still suck air?" he said, looking at her critically.

"Apparently," she replied lightly. "Where have they got you working?" she asked, pulling her own chair over for Mo.

"This week it's mornings only, and I just... I don't know what the fuck I'm doing actually. Bound to be a pile of paperwork that Timms shoved in a back drawer." He smiled and lowered himself onto the proffered chair.

Eleanor looked him over. He'd lost at least four stones in weight after his heart attack a year ago and although unlikely ever to return to active duty, he still liked to potter around homicide dabbling in cases and generally offering the expertise acquired after thirty years of service.

"You interested in looking at this?" she asked, holding her hand out for the papers. She saw Laurence's jaw tighten and his lip twitch, as he held out the sheets to Mo. No-one moved or spoke for the next couple of seconds.

"Going to get a coffee, interested in your thoughts Mo," said Laurence quickly, placing the photocopies in front of him.

"How's that diplomacy course going then?" asked Mo, waiting for the door to close after Laurence.

Eleanor sighed and studied her hands.

Mo threw up his hands in despair then leaned towards her, letting his voice drop to a hiss. "Six months ago you were hanging from a goddamned meat hook, with this much life left in you." He pinched his index finger to his thumb to emphasise. "When Whitefoot kicked his way into that room he had no idea whether Hughes was armed or *even* if he had back-up. He put his life on the line to save yours. So, some recognition that he's here for more than just tea duties might not go amiss."

Mo looked at her intently, willing her to respond. When she remained silent, he leaned closer still. "Is this still about the invasion of your privacy? Your sex life is your own business; not mine, not Whitefoot's. But your safety is. Your partner did everything in his power to respect that, but you were *gone* and we were willing to do anything to get you back. We couldn't have this conversation if Whitefoot hadn't investigated in the way you taught him to. Leave no stone unturned, remember? What you keep under that stone has been respected by both him, me and Timms."

Eleanor opened her mouth but Mo held up a finger. "You didn't listen to him when he came to explain to you in hospital who had turned you over to Hughes. I heard you ask, 'Was it you?'. Who can't you forgive Ellie? Whitefoot... or yourself." Mo sat back in his seat, took a deep sigh and massaged his tightening chest. He looked at her expectantly.

Eleanor felt the airless room choking her. "He's applied for a transfer."

Mo processed this and sighed deeply.

She stood up more quickly than she'd intended, making her head cloud. "Coffee?" she asked, her voice sounding distant to her.

"Love one," he said, turning his attention to the photocopies.

Laurence hadn't quite made it to the coffee station and was taking a call and peering out of the window at the well-stocked bird feeder that the department had installed. Eleanor busied herself with the coffee-making ritual, rummaging through the cupboard for a recognisable coffee mug. The politics of mug ownership and usage in homicide ran dangerously deep. She found her old tin mug lying on its side at the back. Mo's 'Best Dad in the World' mug was on the surface but she had no idea which one belonged to Laurence. Another diplomatic coup she thought wryly. Then she saw a large white mug with a printed image of the head of a black and tan German Shepherd, its tongue lolling to one side and its eyes half closed. The legend below read 'Monster'. Surprised that Laurence would have been inclined to celebrate the ownership of a dog he had clearly loathed, she wondered if perhaps Timms had had it made up for him, as an ironic statement. She poured coffee into the three mugs, clicked several sweeteners into Mo's and shovelled three generous spoons into Laurence's.

"Crystelle Blair," said Mo, waving a photocopied sheet in front of her. "This is where you start." Eleanor stared at the photograph. "I'm not seeing any physical likeness to Mackenzie's Polaroid."

"But Crystelle worked at the 'Good Times' and that's a good place to start."

Eleanor nodded, picked up her partner's coffee and headed over to the window.

The 'Good Times' bar was tucked innocuously into a narrow, ill-lit street off Dundas. With little to indicate its existence, its clientele tended to be those 'in the know'. Laurence pressed the call button, which was answered after a couple of moments by a chirpy, "Who's knocking at this little pig's door?"

"This is Detectives Whitefoot and Raven."

"Ooh, sounds like a stage act," said the voice, giggling theatrically. "Down in a mo!"

The door was opened by an impressively tall man, sporting a beard complete with twirling handlebar moustache and a pink frothy beehive hair-do. His clothing was less visually challenging: sweatpants and a black T-shirt.

"Lovely, come in darlings," he said, standing back and ushering them in. "Now how can I help you two officers?" he asked as he headed up the stairs that lead to the bar.

"Are you the owner of this establishment?" asked Laurence.

"I am for my sins. Madame Angela, aka Phillip Hendry," he giggled holding out his hand.

"Two years ago an employee named Crystelle Blair, was reported as missing," said Eleanor.

"Two years ago is before my time," he replied, putting a thoughtful finger to his lip. "Hang on. Cover your ears." He turned his face away and bellowed in the direction of the bar. "Honey! Honey, I need you for a tiny mo." He turned back to Laurence and Eleanor, ushering them over to a small round table covered in paperwork, receipts and a calculator. "I wasn't here then but Honey was. She might remember. Please ignore the awful mess."

A door opened in the rear of the bar and Honey's head popped through. "What?" came less than honied tones.

"Darling, we have police company and they need your help," cooed Madame Angela.

What sounded like a muttered, 'For fuck's sake', accompanied the arrival of Honey. That and a vicious slapping sound, as she stomped over in pink diamanté flip-flops and hovered over them. Honey was at least sixty plus, with an expression that registered the last fifty years of bad nutrition, nicotine addiction and poor choices in sexual partners.

"What d'ya want?" she hissed.

Madame Angela looked poised to leap in with some mollifying statements, so Eleanor cut in, "Crystelle Blair."

There was a pause as Honey's eyes narrowed and her body language changed. "Uh-huh?"

Eleanor stared at her for several moments and then stood up. "You know where she is," she said.

"That a question?" asked Honey nervously.

"It's a statement. I want to know where she is and why you didn't report your knowledge."

"I don't..."

"...You 'don't', is likely to get you arrested on an obstruction of justice charge."

Honey let out a huge sigh and sank into a chair. "Well I guess I better tell all then," she snapped. "Crystelle Blair isn't dead or missing."

Madame Angela let out a theatrical gasp and placed his chin on his hands, "Oooh, you old gossip."

"Shut up Phil," Honey spat.

In response her partner made a zipping gesture across his lips, his eyes twinkling.

"You know who reported Crystelle as missing, don't you?" said Honey in a defeated tone.

Laurence checked his notes, "Elizabeth Slade."

"That's her daughter. Crystelle had another life, as Roger Slade, and was married with a daughter. She used to come in here before she had the op. Turned out real nice she has. Here you have to live as a woman for about a century before they'll give you surgery. Well she had her tits done and was booked in for the hack and slash but..."

"The what?" asked Laurence, mystified. Honey rolled her eyes.

"You know," said Madame Angela, making several informative gestures around the genital region.

Laurence nodded.

"But turns out she couldn't afford it, especially as the divorce wasn't going well. So, to cut a long story short, she met a guy who would pay for the op, if she came and lived with him as his wife. All very 'happy ever after' shit but Crystelle's ex-wife wants her to stay out of Elizabeth's life. If she would just go walk out of their lives, she'd not claim maintenance. Everyone got what they wanted. No nasty tranny turning up at family Christmases and scaring grandma and Crystelle able to pretend she was born and raised a girl. So everyone gets happy...."

"Except for Elizabeth," said Eleanor.

"Exactly. Kept looking for her dad, thinking he'd been murdered or some shit and me having to lie to her, saying I'd not seen him. Knowing that her dad was living it up with some Mexican down in Puerto Rico and didn't give a shit that he'd hurt his little girl. I ain't got no address or contact details but that's what I know."

"Do you know anyone who does have contact with her, or could corroborate your story?" asked Laurence.

Honey sighed and shook her head. "Dunno. Guess you could open up worm cans and ask the ex-wife." She raised her eyebrows meaningfully. "Anyway why the interest after all this time? You just running through the back catalogue of unsolved?"

"We've found the remains of a male body with what could be silicone implants. It's difficult to ascertain when he was killed."

Honey and Madame Angela exchanged glances.

"Do you recognise this person?" asked Eleanor handing over an enlarged photocopy of the Polaroid, MacKenzie having been cropped from the picture.

Honey put on a pair of glasses that had been dangling around her throat on a chain. After careful deliberation, she shrugged her shoulders and handed it over to her partner. "Can't be sure. You got any better photos?"

Eleanor and Laurence moved forward on their chairs simultaneously. "Who do you think this might be?" asked Eleanor.

"I don't know either," said Madame Angela. "You thinking this might be Giselle?" he asked Honey.

Honey shook her head. "It doesn't look like her."

"Who's Giselle?" asked Laurence.

"Giselle used to come in here for drinks and to 'collect company'," said Madame Angela meaningfully. "About a year-and-a-half ago, maybe less."

"Why do you think this might be her?" asked Eleanor.

"She disappeared, and weirdly so."

"Weirdly?"

"She left a couple of hundred bucks here and never came back for them. Shared a flat with a student from that catering college. She'd pop in here occasionally for a drink or to meet Giselle. Anyway, about a week after we last saw Giselle, the flatmate... Parminder something wasn't it?"

Honey shrugged and checked her nails. "If you say so."

"Mmm, Parminder I think. Indian girl, so I guess kinda odd that she'd be sharing a pad with a tranny like..."

"Get to the *fucking* point!" shrieked Honey.

"Ooh, so grumpy. Well Parminder comes in and asks whether we've seen Giselle because her snake looks hungry and she isn't going to feed it. I don't think she liked the snake."

Honey rolled her eyes and sighed loudly.

"So I recommended that she call up the zoo because some of those snakes can be really nasty."

"Do you know what sort of snake it was?" asked Laurence.

Honey and Madame Angela stared at him in disbelief.

"How the fuck should we know? One that bites ok?" snapped Honey.

Laurence opened his hands in a gesture of defeat.

Eleanor smiled. "Was the snake collected by the zoo?"

"Dunno. Never saw either of 'em again," said Honey decisively.

"Is there any possibility that you would have kept a photograph of Giselle? Maybe one was taken during one of your special events?" Eleanor asked pointing to a large poster advertising 'Heroines of the Silver Screen'. Pinned next to it were numerous flyers, business cards and photographs with cell numbers attached.

"Oh you *must* come along this Friday. I can so see you as Marlene!" Madame Angela cooed, stroking Eleanor's face. "Oh, cheekbones to die for!"

"That's what we need to make the night a complete fucking success. Two detectives asking all and sundry whether they know any dead trannies!" shrieked Honey, who stood up and flumped noisily off in the direction she had come from.

"Thank you Madame Angela. I may just take you up on that offer," said Eleanor warmly, as she selected a couple of the flyers and stood up.

"We'll both be there!" said Laurence, emphatically.

Eleanor stared at him, puzzled for a moment.

"Can you remember where Giselle lived or what her original name was?" said Laurence.

"No sweetheart, I really can't. But I can say that although that photo doesn't look like her, it doesn't look *un*like her. If you get what I mean."

Eleanor nodded and handed her a card. "You'll call if you think of anything?"

"Well I won't have to darlings because you will be here on Friday to add that touch of glamour that the lovely Honey no longer does. But seriously I will."

He began to walk them in the direction of the exit. "Giselle occasionally did a little pole dancing here. Nothing too racy... or skilled for that matter," he giggled. "She'd had the tits done but none of the plumbing and had no intention from what I gathered. There's a good living to be made out of indecision, if you get what I mean." He closed the door behind him, giving them a little wave.

Eleanor waited until they were in the car. "What was that all about?"

"What?" asked Laurence, unconvincingly.

"I don't need either your permission or presence to investigate in my own time."

Laurence's jaw was working. "The cards," he spat out. "I saw you looking at the cards with that sign on it." His jaw was set and his eyes fixed unblinkingly on the road ahead.

"Which cards and what sign?" she asked, confused.

"The ones you pick up when you want a...sexual encounter."

Eleanor felt a wave of anger, undoing in an instant the remorse she'd felt. "You mean that you noticed a card with a yin/yang symbol on it pinned to the board and suspect that I'm going to attend the party, give the number a call, arrange for a sexual encounter of some disapproved of flavour and then get myself kidnapped and murdered. Is that right?"

Laurence said nothing. The already over-heated car was now sweltering. Laurence flipped on the air conditioning.

"Perhaps next time I want to arrange a consensual one night stand I should invite you along to monitor the situation?" she hissed through pinched lips.

"I'm your partner! I care about your safety," he said, embarrassed. "I didn't say that I was judging you," he added lamely.

Eleanor focussed her attention on the city and let the silence settle between them.

CHAPTER THREE

"Listen bru," said Dieter, peering into the vivarium. "Everything you have said so far is correct."

Laurence stood immobilised in front of the glass, staring at the snake's eyes. Eleanor watched him, fascinated to see whether his knowledge of snakes or people would determine Laurence's next move.

"The eyes are predominantly black, with a thin orange iris surrounding... hang on, *almost* surrounding the iris," said Laurence, carefully.

"Cor-*rect*," replied Dieter, pleased.

Laurence took a couple of steps to the left, observing that the one-and-a-half metre green snake followed his movements with its head and top eighteen inches. "That's a white belly... Shit I just can't remember whether green mambas have green or white undersides."

"Problem bru. Problem," replied Dieter sagely. He smirked at Eleanor. His deeply lined and bronzed skin indicated a lifetime of snake hunting in the veldt. "You gotta make a decision man. You want the information? Name the snake and you get it." Dieter was having a fabulous time. Having agreed that he had been to collect the snake from a small apartment near to the college, he refused to further any more information, unless Laurence could correctly identify the green snake that was watching him curiously from the inside of a glass-fronted vivarium, in the back room of Toronto Zoo's reptile house.

"You've narrowed it down to two possibilities, either –" Dieter raised his eyebrows "– it's a Natal green snake: harmless. Or, it's a green mamba, which is listed pretty high on Africa's most deadly list. So which is it?"

Laurence had taken this challenge to a ridiculous level of competitiveness. Eleanor could see what looked like small beads of sweat appearing on his neckline.

With a decisive gesture Eleanor reached for the bolt and drew it, her eyes locked onto Dieter's. It took her less than a second to register his reaction. She then slid opened the glass partition and reached for the snake, gently cupping its head and body with her hands and lifting it out.

"Your partner knows her snakes then," said Dieter admiringly. Laurence had instinctively taken a step back.

"Sorry, I have no idea what type of snake this is," she said, fascinated by the creature's head. "Your pupils told me it was safe."

"They did?" laughed Dieter.

"No dilation. No fear," she said rubbing a finger gently across the snake's back. "And as Head Herpetologist the chances of you endangering anyone's life in a stunt like that were pretty much zero."

Eleanor saw Laurence smile and handed him over the snake.

"Ah man! You are *too* good," he laughed, wagging his finger at Eleanor. He handed her a piece of paper from under an empty coffee mug. It contained an address, contact name and a description of the snake identified as a 'Natal Green Snake'.

"Can you remember entering the apartment?" she asked.

"Well give or take," he said. "Don't be looking for forensic observation here because I tend to focus attention on the scaly stuff, not people or places."

"I understand," Eleanor responded. "Was there anything about the apartment that struck you as interesting or unusual. Apart from the snake of course."

"The girl who'd kept the snake had a couple of skulls in her room." He grimaced and shook his head "They looked pretty old to me but I'm sure there are tight regulations about having 'em just knocking round your bedroom."

"Why, what sort of skulls were they?" Eleanor asked.

"Oh babies... human babies."

"Pick up your car?" asked Laurence, as he pulled onto the Expressway. Eleanor was lost in her own thoughts and didn't seem to be listening.

"Look, I'm sorry. I was..." he began.

"Rude, intrusive, judgemental?" Eleanor offered, managing a tight smile.

"How about protective?" he countered.

"How about a polite truce, while you work out your last few weeks?' she added, softly. "I hear you've requested a transfer."

"Yes," he said, uncomfortably. "I thought..." his voice tapered as he pondered.

"I don't need an explanation," she said as gently as she could. "It's not too late. How about we visit Parminder Kaur and see if she can provide us with some info on Giselle?"

"How about I do that after I drop you off. You've been on for eleven hours and don't look great," he said firmly but with obvious relief.

"I look fabulous, you've just got to lower the bar a little."

He stared at her for a moment and then nodded, "Ok but last call. You got pain killers?"

"I'm good," she said emphatically. "You're heading for Rowton Drive, off Jervis."

There was very little daylight left by the time they reached Ms. Kaur's apartment complex. The streetlights were beginning to hum into life, drawing moths, beetles and opportunistic little brown bats, in a kaleidoscope of avoidance and detection. The buildings were uniformly red brick, and generally three-storey apartment lets. There were no well-kept front lawns to indicate the presence of families or elderly settled residents. Rather, a multitude of trash cans, each bearing an anti-raccoon device, ranging in sophistication from a house brick to an elaborate locking mechanism, clustered around the entrances. By the sound of the squeals and rummaging, not all of the devices could claim any degree of effectiveness.

Parminder Kaur peered at them suspiciously, for a moment or two, before letting them in.

"Apologies for the lateness of the hour but we have been following up an incident and were hoping you could help us with our enquiries," said Laurence, holding up his badge reassuringly.

"An incident?" said Parminder nervously. She was a slightly-built woman in her early twenties, dressed in an eclectic mixture of brightly coloured sari, draped languorously around her shoulders and waist, accompanied by a T-shirt and jogging pants. She smiled at Laurence's gaze.

"I'm trying it on for my aunty's wedding. I'll be wearing something more appropriate on the day." She giggled lightly and invited them into the kitchen, where a delicious sugary almond cloud was battling the deeper tones of cumin and ginger. Eleanor looked at Laurence's glazed expression, fully expecting him to start dribbling.

"Wow," said Laurence with heartfelt pleasure.

"Badam burfi and vegetable samosas," cooed Parminder, pushing laden plates towards them. "You must try them both for me."

"You're a student at the catering college?" asked Eleanor, beginning to succumb to the enticing aromas.

"Was," replied Parminder nudging a plate of samosas towards her. "I graduated this summer and work at the 'Orient Express' now."

Laurence nodded his approval. "That the one over towards Tommy Thompson park?"

"You know it?" she said.

"You reported a snake to Toronto Zoo last year, when your room-mate disappeared," said Eleanor.

Parminder nodded, making a little moue of disgust. "Giselle, my room-mate, just left it here and I wasn't going to feed it. So I called the zoo. A guy came and collected it."

"Did Giselle ever contact you, or come back to collect the snake?"

"No, she didn't," said Parminder frowning. "Oh my God! Is that why you're here? Is she ok?"

"We don't know," replied Eleanor. "Have you received any communication from Giselle's friends? Any correspondence?"

Parminder shook her head and sucked in her lips thoughtfully.

"Giselle would appear to me to be a rather odd choice of room-mate for you," said Eleanor slowly.

Parminder nodded and rolled her eyes expressively. "I come from a very traditional family and I was only allowed to live away from home if I could find a female room-mate, preferably someone from the same background. But I couldn't, so Giselle fit the bill nicely. My parents only ever visited on an evening when she was out working and all her stuff made it seem like I lived with a girl."

"Did she ever bring anyone back to the flat with her?" asked Eleanor.

Parminder shook her head vigorously, "No, never. I laid down rules about that and she stuck to them."

"When Giselle left what did you do with her belongings?"

"I got introduced to Angela a few weeks after Giselle disappeared. She needed to move out of her place and so I sub-let because I just couldn't manage the payments myself."

"Giselle's belongings?" repeated Eleanor.

"Well it wasn't my stuff, so I put it in boxes and took it down to the basement. The landlord lets us keep our bikes down there and it seemed like a good place but..." her voice trailed off. "I think the raccoons must have got in there because all the boxes were trashed. Everything was open and dumped all over the place. It was such a mess, so I just gathered together what was left, put it into some boxes and took it up to the loft." She looked uncomfortable.

"But you don't think it was raccoons do you?" asked Eleanor carefully.

Parminder shrugged. "Look I don't know. I must have left the door unlocked or open when I took my bike out."

"Go on," said Eleanor leaning towards her.

"There were some things that had been taken."

"What was missing?"

Parminder began to fidget. "I don't really know."

"Was it a pair of baby skulls?" asked Eleanor.

"Oh my God! How did you know?" she asked uncomfortably.

Eleanor was nibbling on a samosa and let the accompanying silence run.

"I wrapped them carefully and put them in one of the shoe boxes but they were gone. Raccoons tend not to take the box," she added. "So I guess they were stolen." Parminder leaned back, her arms spread on the table.

"May we see the rest of Giselle's belongings?" asked Eleanor.

Parminder looked relieved. "Of course." She carefully unwrapped the sari and folded it. "Don't want to get it messed up."

Laurence pushed the ceiling panel open and shone his torch around the loft space and noted three cardboard boxes shoved towards the eaves. There was little else of note in the cramped and dusty space. Piles of mummified scat surrounded the cold-water tank and torn out lagging material attested to its efficiency as both loft and nesting insulation. There was a broken lamp, several fans and some suitcases, all heavily covered in dust.

"The three boxes in the corner, that all of Giselle's stuff?" asked Laurence trying to work out the best way of removing them. He was balanced precariously on a pull-down loft ladder and didn't want to have to pass them down to Eleanor.

"Yes, can you reach them?" asked Parminder from the landing.

"Uh-huh," he replied hooking his fingers around one and dragging it towards him. He cautiously opened the flap to look at the contents. Clothing, shoes, female underwear and a shell collection in a small lacquered box, were placed neatly on the top layers. Not wanting to disturb the contents further, Laurence folded the boxes' flaps over and backed down the steps, holding the box above his head.

"That looks pretty heavy," said Eleanor reaching for it. She saw Laurence hesitate for a moment and turned to Parminder. "How did you manage to get this up in the loft on your own?" she asked.

"I had a friend help me," she answered.

Eleanor nodded. "I can't imagine you doing this on your own," she said, firmly grasping the corners of the box and taking the weight. "Have you any objections to us taking Giselle's belongings to the station?"

Parminder shook her head. "You haven't told me what the incident is yet?" she asked quietly.

Eleanor looked at her carefully for a moment or two before replying. "We've found a body."

The traffic had been unusually heavy on their way back to the station. A couple of streets had been closed for an open-air gig and street party and the detour was snarled with parked cars and over-large vehicles. Eleanor felt heavy and tired and wanted to have a long soak and think about the day. Laurence had lapsed into a brooding silence, which suited her perfectly. As she studied the excited revellers scurrying between cars, carrying cans and bottles, she pondered the reasons Parminder Kaur could have had for lying to them.

The department was virtually empty when Eleanor and Laurence finally manhandled the three boxes into their office.

"Now, or the morning?" he asked, reaching for a box of latex gloves.

"Tomorrow," she answered, waving him on. "I'm tired."

He nodded and left the room with a wave.

Eleanor flicked off the lamp, grabbed her keys and bag and had almost made it to the door when curiosity overwhelmed her. She made a firm decision not to stay for longer than half an hour, as she pulled on the gloves. The first two boxes yielded nothing more exciting than a rather gaudy collection of women's low cut tops and slim fit jeans, though a hairbrush and a bag of rollers held sufficient long auburn hair to promise DNA analysis. There was a well-plundered box of industrial strength condoms and a large make-up bag filled with both prescription and non-prescription drugs. Eleanor carefully bagged these without analysing the contents, which could wait. In fact all of this could wait. She was exhausted and desperately needed to drive home and sleep but that last box had to contain something interesting, something that would shed a little light on Giselle's life, preferences and contacts.

Opening a can of soda and washing down three painkillers she repacked the first two boxes, lifting them stiffly onto the trolley they'd borrowed from reception and dragged the third onto her desk. This box had a different smell to the others, which had a dusty aroma mixed with the damp earthy tones of mould setting in. She peeled back the cardboard flaps and inhaled the heavy, volatile notes of a patchouli-based perfume. An oil-stained towel had been folded over the contents and Eleanor peeled it back to reveal the source of the smell. A small turquoise scent bottle, with an expensive gilt stopper, had been leaking. Its contents had saturated the towel and left a large brown stain on a pack of photographs beneath. The photographs were not of a uniform size or paper type and were held tightly together by a pink ribbon and the oily perfume, which had seeped through them. By gently lifting the edges of the photographs she was able to make out the image of a strong-featured, attractive woman with friends. It wasn't clear whether the woman was Giselle but the pair of earrings and matching necklace she wore in the photograph were in the second box. Madame Angela had been right: if this was Giselle then Mackenzie's Polaroid neither confirmed, nor disproved they were the same person. Not wanting to lose any valuable images by trying to separate them further, Eleanor placed them in a paper evidence bag.

The wall clock was inching past midnight now and Eleanor had to stifle a yawn. There were only a couple of items left, a manila envelope containing seven birthday cards, a city museum guide from two years earlier outlining a special exhibition of 'Animals in Art', and wrapped in a fluffy balled up sock, was a wooden snake. With extreme care, Eleanor gently extracted it. The snake had been hand carved from a single length of bowed wood, every vertebra held in place by a small metal clasp. She'd owned a similar one herself as a child. When you held the snake by the tail, it would writhe and whip round in imitation of the real thing. This snake was considerably older than hers and by the detail on the carving she had no doubt that it was valuable both financially and culturally. With great care Eleanor placed the snake in an evidence bag and tidied up the last box.

CHAPTER FOUR

Toby approached the main gate of his house with the usual degree of trepidation. He was acutely aware that there was a fine line between security and invitation and had let the fascia take on the dilapidated appearance of the 'down at heel' over the past few years, in order to deter possible intrusion. The six-foot-high gate, that allowed access through the dense ring of privet, was barred with a small but effective titanium bolt. Before he unlocked the gate he took a quick look up and down the street, checking that no one was watching. Stepping onto the footpath that led up to the front door of 'Crowthorne', he gave a final visual sweep along both sides of the street and methodically re-secured the bolt.

The house was an early red-brick Edwardian detached, bearing a single magnificent gothic turret to the east wall. Built in the professorial belt in the Annex region of the city, it had been purchased by his family for sixteen hundred dollars in the late nineteen forties. Toby, an only child, had inherited the house, a collection of World War One memorabilia and the space to house his collection.

Despite the overwhelming heat of the city in high summer, the interior of the house was always cool and Toby sighed pleasurably as he placed his jacket on the coat stand by the front door and made his way towards the kitchen.

"Honey! I'm home," he trilled. The kitchen was unusually small, a six-seater oak dining table set for two, squatted heavily in the middle of the room. Toby placed his briefcase on the end of the table and rolled up the sleeves of his white day shirt, gratefully loosening his cravat. For a moment or two he stood completely still and let his surroundings calm him. His day had been filled with niggling irritations and frustrations and he'd have to spend several hours after supper going through the mountain of paperwork he'd received regarding the late Mr Forester's bequest to the museum. According to the solicitors who were handling the estate, the collection comprised, 'an eclectic mixture of East African artefacts acquired legitimately by the late Mr Forester, during his years there as cultural attaché'. There were over three hundred objects of varying significance and value, each one having been assigned a number, photograph and description by Mr Forester. It was this understandable enthusiasm for cataloguing, which would make the upcoming theft more challenging for Toby.

The delicious aroma of lamb hotpot snapped him out of his reverie and, slipping on oven gloves, he lifted the heavy iron casserole dish out of the oven and opened the lid.

"This smells delicious!" he called out. "Will you be joining me?" He paused for a moment or two, before taking a single plate out of the cupboard, scooping a generous portion onto it and settling down to eat. Olivia, he concluded, must be having one of her headaches.

The item that most intrigued Toby was an Ethiopian redwood headrest. It was, in his opinion, undervalued at three hundred dollars due to its exquisite hand carved ridges and brilliant conker shine. He could probably source a similar item on the internet or by trawling local dealers but he coveted this particular headrest and knew exactly how to utilise it in his collection. What he needed to decide was whether to just make the item and catalogue number disappear or to replace it with a similar but inferior piece. As he mulled this problem over, he realised that it was now close to midnight and he'd made no effort to check on his wife. Contrite, he quickly washed and dried his utensils and poured two glasses of single malt. Checking again that the kitchen door was locked, he made his way up the stairs to the master bedroom.

The bedroom was illuminated by a small, low wattage lamp, which had been left on so that he could enter the room without disturbing her. Olivia?" he whispered to the shape on the bed. "Livie, are you alright darling?" Slowly and gently Toby placed the two glasses on the bedside table and sat on the bed. The light illuminated her beautiful porcelain skin and highlighted her long auburn hair, which fanned across the silk pillowcase. For a moment he felt quite overcome with his good fortune at having met such a wonderful creature as Olivia. Quietly, he leaned back against the footrest and humming a tune from his youth, began his nightly ritual of massaging her feet.

Eleanor wasn't particularly surprised when she found herself pulling into an unlit street in the downtown area, rather than the allocated space below her apartment. The parking was moderately secure and a stone's throw from 'La Reine's', a private, unadvertised club for the discerning client. La reine herself was, Eleanor knew, a senior lecturer in demographic studies at one of the city universities, and had designed her dungeon as an indulgence, rather than an ongoing financial concern. Dressed in a black, patent leather cat suit and mask, la reine presided over her lair with dignity and flair. She understood her client's need for redemption, indulgence and privacy and charged accordingly. So, for Eleanor this was to be considered a rare, if necessary, treat.

The club entrance was, to the uninitiated, nothing more than a fire exit for what looked like the rear of a shop. There were no handles or obvious means of entrance but a small enamel button bearing a yin/yang symbol in the left hand corner of the door, rang a buzzer internally. It usually took about ten minutes for the door to be opened, thus giving the supplicant time to reconsider his or her commitment level.

The first minutes of these sessions were the most painful to Eleanor. Not in a physical sense, as not a finger had been lifted by the mistress. It was the transition from DI Raven back to herself, which caused the most distress. Letting go of status, power and physical dominance always caused her to balk. But her needs had taken on a physical urgency and as she removed her clothing and let la reine fasten her hands above her head and attach her to a chain she felt the accumulated fear and horror that had haunted her for the past few months begin to ebb away. As la reine tightened the leather fastening she whispered into Eleanor's ear, "What is your safe word?" The safe word was a bond between the mistress and her supplicant; a word that once uttered would stop all actions immediately. It was a fall back, for when the pain outweighed the pleasure or the climax was reached. Eleanor's safe word empowered and protected her and was treasured as such.

"Caleb," she whispered.

"The safe word?" la reine repeated.

"Ca-*leb* Eleanor said slowly, articulating the syllables carefully and with reverence.

La reine had taken time and pleasure in understanding each of her client's very specific needs and desires and quickly took in the numerous injuries Eleanor had sustained. She began slowly, allowing the leather tail, to expend its energy in sound, rather than impact. Eleanor's breathing was laboured and shallow; she was holding back, so la reine stopped and slowly twisted the lever that raised Eleanor onto the tips of her toes. She was given a moment or two to adjust her balance.

Eleanor needed to control her breathing. The shock of losing her balance and being unable to support her weight was focusing her mind. The flow of pain began at her fingertips, spread along her spine and ended in a knot between her legs. She wanted to lift her feet, let gravity purge her but la reine controlled the pace and began to flick at her calves and buttocks with a thin, tapered cane. The pain was razor sharp and contrasted with the lower tones spreading downwards from her wrists. She was close to orgasm and her breathing betrayed her. La reine stopped and waited, watching the slim, well muscled body shiver with emotion and lactic acid. Slowly and deliberately, la reine dug her tapered, immaculately polished and hardened fingernails into Eleanor's belly, tracing a ring around her waist, chest and breasts. The pain was loud and urgent, making her struggle. For a moment or two before her brain released its tide of hormones, the need to breathe, excuse or justify her desires vanished, leaving an exquisite peace.

Eleanor was barely aware of the woman gently lowering her to the ground, unfastening her and wrapping her in a blanket.

CHAPTER FIVE

"Ok, this is everything I could find on Richard Leslie Baker, aka Leanne, Tiffany and most recently, Giselle," said Sarah Wadesky, placing an ominously plump file on Eleanor's desk. She began to leaf through the numerous arrest sheets and summonses that characterised the life of a fairly low-rent street prostitute.

"Apparently, I arrested him six years ago when I worked vice," mused Wadesky, narrowing her eyes as she looked Eleanor up and down. "But I'm damned if I can remember. Anyway, how are –"

"How's baby Tessa?" Eleanor cut in quickly.

Wadesky smiled broadly and selected a couple of photographs on her cell phone. Eleanor stifled a laugh when she saw the baby.

"It's ok," giggled Wadesky. "Timms has this one printed out and stuck to his dashboard to cheer him up." Baby Tessa was as round as a football and sported a magnificent halo of soft, fluffy, dark hair, hazel-green eyes, skin the colour of Demerara sugar and a beaming smile. "I have to put in a written application to get a cuddle!" smiled Wadesky. "Joe won't put her down. Doubt she's ever gonna learn to walk."

"She's lovely," said Eleanor, a little surprised that she actually meant it.

"Anyway girl, just letting you know that Samuelson has asked me to 'evaluate' –" she drew air quotes and rolled her eyes "– whether this case is too big for you to handle, in your present delicate condition."

Before Eleanor could proffer an opinion on this Susan Cheung tapped lightly and peered round the door. "Good morning fellow workers. Hear you've got some boxes that need collecting and as I was in the vicinity... Those them?" She pointed to the trolley. "Say they're not full," she groaned.

"Sorry," replied Eleanor.

"Don't suppose there's a hair sample going is there?" asked Susan.

"Yes." said Eleanor, pointing to the third box.

"Well, I set some tissue samples processing overnight and got a reading for arsenic."

"High?"

"Non-lethal levels but something I wouldn't expect to find."

"You think the guy was poisoned?" asked Wadesky.

Susan wrinkled her brow. "I'm thinking arsenic was used as an embalming agent, not a method of murder. Which is why I'd like to analyse a hair sample for elimination."

"Why the hell would anyone use something as danger-ous as arsenic to embalm someone?" asked Wadesky. "Why not just use formaldehyde? Jeez, you can order it on Amazon for next day delivery."

Eleanor thought for a moment or two before answering. "Maybe because he has time, a taste for experimentation and lives by his own rules."

"I don't like what you just said," said Wadesky unhappily.

"Why?" asked Susan.

"'Cos Raven's just defined a serial killer," she replied. "I'm gonna tell Samuelson that you're all over this case and it's a slam dunk because me and Timms don't want none of this ugly shit coming our way."

The door flew open behind Wadesky and Timms strode in. "Morning all!" he boomed.

Wadesky let out a shriek of laughter. "Really... *Really*? You're gonna win over Joe's nasty babushka mama with a suit that maybe fitted you back in the nineties?"

"This suit fits like a goddamn glove," said her partner, unruffled.

Wadesky pulled open his jacket and poked his stomach. "You sit down and seams will pop!"

Timms snorted.

"Tell all why you are dressed up then," smirked Wadesky. Eleanor and Susan had never seen Timms in anything other than un-ironed shirts and baggy slacks held up by a set of braces.

"I am taking Joe Wadesky, my partner's husband and his *delightful* mother out to lunch today in the confident belief that I will be selected as little Tessa's godfather," said Timms, gingerly lowering his backside onto the corner of Whitefoot's desk.

"But you're already Aaron's godfather aren't you?" asked Eleanor.

"I am indeed," said Timms proudly. Aaron was Wadesky's eldest son. "I have, I believe, been an excellent example of a godparent and..."

Wadesky held up a finger. "No one is questioning that. It's the birthday present that initiated your de-selection process isn't it?" She poked Timms in the stomach once more. He chose to ignore her.

"What d'ya buy Timms?" asked Susan.

Timms pursed his lips and said nothing.

"For Aaron's tenth birthday you bought him a Glock 9mm, didn't you? And then proceeded to teach him how to load and shoot the damned thing," said Wadesky pointedly.

Timms threw his arms up into the air, "What the hell sort of godparent doesn't teach his kid to shoot?"

"I *warned* you not to do it! Joe said no guns and you just ploughed ahead like a bull in a china shop."

"*Maan,* why is everyone so touchy!" With that Timms flung himself upright, slid off the desk and stormed out of the room. Wadesky turned to follow him.

"I didn't know you were Catholic?" said Eleanor.

"I'm not but it's important to Joe to do things properly. Mainly, I think, it's because his mother terrifies him. She sure as hell does me." Wadesky was just closing the door behind her.

"Could I have a photo of Tessa?" asked Eleanor.

Wadesky's head peered back round the door, her eyes slightly narrowed. "Yeah," she said suspiciously. "You want a baby pic... You having some sort of hormonal crisis?"

"Have you one of her asleep?" asked Eleanor cautiously.

There was a slight pause, "Urm... Sure. I'll print one out for ya!"

Susan, smiling and shaking her head, turned to the boxes. "What have you got here?" she asked, pulling out a pair of latex gloves from her white coat pocket and approaching the first box.

"Giselle's flat-mate boxed up his/her possessions after the disappearance. There are a couple of interesting items. First, a pack of photographs," Eleanor reached into the box and brought out the solid mass of photographs. "Unfortunately, a bottle of perfume broke over them and glued them together."

Susan cast her eye over them, carefully peeling back a couple to test the amount of damage. "Hmm, this is going to challenge. Not sure how much of the images I can retrieve. However, Jan over in the documents department is a dab hand at photo restoration. He'll scan it in and reconstruct but I know he's got a backlog at the moment, so we might have to be judicious about what we send through. Leave it with me."

"And this," Eleanor handed Susan the wooden snake already sealed into a plastic evidence bag. "Looks like a kid's toy. It's old and I want to get it appraised but need it dusting first. Could you prioritise this one first and then the photos?"

"If you're willing to send up lunch I can have it done for one."

"You're a star," said Eleanor. "Still the usual?"

"You got it," she replied, securing the seal on the boxes and manoeuvring the trolley between the desks.

"Ooh, and one of those peanut things."

Eleanor nodded, "Roger that."

There were several arrest photographs covering a four-year period that showed Giselle in various stages of transformation, from androgynous teenager picked up for possession of narcotics and soliciting, to the latest taken two years ago. In this Giselle had grown her hair, adopted a more aggressive make-up regime and acquired a rather unconvincing cleavage. The older Giselle had a harder expression, duller eyes and exuded hopelessness from every pore. There were only two addresses associated with Giselle since 2007, one of which was presumably parental as it was listed as a hardware store on the outskirts of the city and the second was the apartment share with Parminder Kaur. Eleanor scowled and checked her notes. If the files were correct it appeared that Giselle had been a resident of the Rowton Drive apartment for some considerable time before Parminder started her college course. This intrigued Eleanor; she knew that Parminder had been deceitful but not why, or about which thing. She made a note to call the landlord and find out who sublet to whom but first she wanted to contact Giselle's parents. Running a quick check she established that both Mr and Mrs Baker still ran the store and dialled. It took nearly a minute for the phone to be answered. A man answered, his tone brusque, "Baker's hardware."

"Is that Mr Baker speaking?"

"Yes," answered the voice after a momentary pause.

"Are you the father of Richard Leslie Baker?" she asked.

A sigh accompanied, "I am. Who are you?"

"Detective Inspector Eleanor Raven. I wondered if it would be convenient for me drop by this morning and speak to both yourself and Richard's mother?" The silence was interestingly long. Eleanor let it run.

"What's he done?" snapped Mr Baker. Eleanor could detect a slight tremor in his voice.

"Would ten thirty be acceptable?" she asked. A grunt preceded the phone being disconnected. Sifting through the catalogue of Giselle's misdemeanours she noted that the last state sanction meted out had been a community service order for a land conservation project in the Annex area of the city. Perhaps the jails were full or an enlightened magistrate had calculated the lack of redemptive effect in any of the light custodial sentences that Richard Leslie Baker had received so far. She noted the name and contact details of the probation officer and began to dial. After several minutes of switchboard inactivity and redirection she tracked down Samson Orbrook, Giselle's probation officer.

"Jeez, yes I remember Giselle. "Hang on." Some faint keyboard hits and scrolling sounds were accompanied by a tuneless humming sound. "Richard Baker, liked to be called Giselle...Three short terms in The Don, each one earned an early release for good behaviour. Last sentence was a community service order, land clearing the new park in the Annex. Gotta say there are no missed appointments, he attended rehab when asked and seemed to have actually benefitted from his community service order, as there's no sign of him having offended again."

"That could be because he's dead Mr Orbrook, rather than some epiphany with a spade and bin liner."

There was a pause. "Shall I update my records then?"

"I'd wait. Who organised his community service?"

"Urm... In the office that would be me but on the ground it was Jacob Hareton. He's the city parks officer and organises the volunteers, and those less civically minded, to clean and plant areas that need it."

"Have you got contact details for Mr Hareton?"

"Should have. Uh-huh... Hang on..."

The door opened and Laurence walked in, accompanied by Monster. He had an armful of reports, two coffees and a large pastry balanced precariously on top of one of the cups. As he manoeuvred round the desk the pastry slid off the cup and onto the floor. There was a fraction of a second when the words, "Leave it!" were processed by the dog, before he leaned his huge head forward and deftly lifted and swallowed. "You complete bastard!" yelled Laurence. Monster gazed at him with incomprehension and then sauntered over to Eleanor, plonking his head on her lap.

"Did you see that!" said Laurence outraged.

"Thank you Mr Orbrook. Perhaps you could send that over to me?" She slipped her phone into her bag and stood up. "Can you pick up a DNA swab test kit?"

"Sure. You found a relative?" replied Laurence, scowling menacingly at Monster.

"Giselle's parents are still living off Dupont. Did you get any joy from the reconstruction?" she asked. While Laurence wrestled with the folder, Eleanor tentatively stroked Monster's head.

"Ok, what d'ya think?" said Laurence, placing a series of grey and white print-outs in front of her. The images formed a series of reconstructions from the initial morgue skull x-ray, through a standard block composite, to a rough software interpretation of the features. "I've asked Lucy to pop in today and see if she can give us a forensic sketch."

Eleanor nodded and repositioned the print out next to the series of departmental mug shots.

"I'd say we've identified our victim," he said taking a long swig of coffee.

"We've a meeting with Giselle's parents at ten thirty. Let's get a DNA sample for Susan."

"Ok, going to run this idiot down to k9. I'll pick you up out front in fifteen," replied Laurence.

The drive over to the north west of the city took considerably longer than Eleanor had anticipated due to a tremendous summer storm that was causing traffic mayhem. Black clouds boiled menacingly and the clatter of the rain made in-car conversation difficult.

"We got a cause of death yet?" asked Laurence, as he rubbed his hair vigorously with what Eleanor suspected was a dog towel off the back seat.

"Not yet," she replied. "Go right here and double round." Flinging the towel into the back, Laurence swung the car out of the gridlock and onto a residential street. To their right a row of shops, probably all established in the nineteen sixties, advertised wares of dubious quality and purpose. 'Baker's Hardware' was squeezed between a launderette and a grocery store. An array of metallic and plastic utensils, all linked by a chain, dripped water onto the cracked paving slabs. What struck Eleanor most was that not one single item, attached by its lifeline to the shop, had strayed even a millimeter onto the territory of its neighbour. Moving quickly out of the rain and into the shop, it took several moments for her eyes to adjust to the gloomy interior. Standing behind the Formica counter-top stood a man of indeterminate later years. His hair and face were grizzled and unkempt and his expression seemed sour and put upon. "I'm Detective Inspector Eleanor Raven and this is my partner Detective Laurence Whitefoot," she said, approaching him with her identity card held aloft. Mr Baker stared back at them, his lip twitching fractionally. "We need to talk to you about your son, Mr Baker."

For a moment the man seemed more alert, his features almost relaxing. "I have no son," he said slowly and carefully.

"We need to talk to your wife as well Mr Baker," she said calmly.

"She won't want to talk to you…"

"It's alright love," came a quietly spoken Welsh voice. "I'm Maura, Richard's mother. Is he in any trouble?" She was a small, dark-haired, worried looking woman. She wore an apron and was rubbing floury hands against it. "I've been baking," she held out her hand. "Has anything happened to Richard?" her voice was beginning to tremble slightly.

"When was the last time you saw your son?" Eleanor asked, noting that Mr Baker's body language became slightly more defensive.

"Three years ago!" he said too loudly.

"Have you had any contact with him since then?"

"No I haven't," he snapped. "Now what the bloody hell is this about?"

"He's dead isn't he?" said Maura quietly. "He never did anything bad enough to warrant attention from a Detective Inspector, so you're here to tell me that aren't you?"

There was a pause as Eleanor studied the woman in front of her. "Would you mind if we went somewhere a little more private?"

Maura Baker nodded jerkily and led them behind the counter and into a cramped but tidy kitchen. "I'll put the kettle on," she said mechanically. "You'd better say now."

Eleanor slowly pulled a photograph from her bag and held it up so they could both see it. "Is this your son Richard?" She'd selected an early police mug shot, which showed a less feminised image. She noted that Mr Baker turned his head away but Maura reached for it. She nodded. "That's him yes," she said, clearing her voice. With a quick nervous glance at her husband she added, "He doesn't really look like that now though." Her husband's face was growing crimson.

Eleanor caught her partner's gaze, giving an imperceptible nod.

"Mr Baker would you mind if I spoke to you in private for a moment or two?" Laurence said moving towards the man. Mr Baker's eyes narrowed suspiciously. Laurence moved closer, speaking discretely into his ear. "It's a rather delicate matter and I think it would be better for your wife if she was to hear things from you later, when we have gone."

Sighing, he led Laurence out of the kitchen and into the main area of the store.

Eleanor pulled one of the chairs out from the table and invited Maura to sit down. "It is our belief that a body found yesterday was that of your son Richard."

Maura swallowed hard and then nodded. "Was…Was he harmed by someone?" she said in a barely audible voice.

"Why would you think that Mrs Baker?"

Maura began to roll her apron between her hands, flattening the material and dusting off the flour. "He had made a rather… dangerous lifestyle choice."

Eleanor nodded but remained silent, letting her continue in her own time.

"He didn't like being a man," her voice trailed off. "But you'd know that by now, wouldn't you?" A tear rolled down her cheek. "He was unhappy. Always had been since he was a little boy. He used to put on my clothes and make up and swan around in 'em. Drove Harry insane it did. He called him a 'Nance', couldn't bear the thought that he was different. He'd not listen to anything I said. Pushed him out like a dog…" she paused and shuddered. "So he had to make his own way and no wonder he ran into trouble."

"When did *you* last see him?" Eleanor asked.

Maura spoke almost in a whisper. Eleanor found herself leaning closer in order to catch what she said. "About eighteen months ago. I used to meet him at a little café over on Queen Street West. It was nice there. The Liberty it was called… He wanted to be part of the family. But on his terms… as Giselle." She bowed her head.

"Your husband wouldn't have coped with that?"

Maura snorted.

"Why did you stop seeing your son?" Eleanor asked carefully.

Maura's head lifted. "I didn't. We used to meet sometimes on a Friday evening when Harry went to play pool. Then he stopped coming. I texted him lots of times. He never answered them or picked up the phone. I begged him to meet me but there was nothing. He'd met someone you see. I think it was an older man. Someone with money and he was going to go and live with him. He said the man wanted him as a... as a woman, you see. That's all he wanted really, to be part of a family." She shook her head and looked away.

"Did you find out who the man was?"

"I've no idea." She rubbed her cheek and forehead. "How did he die?"

"At the moment we don't know how he died or when."

Maura searched Eleanor's face, "I don't understand."

"Your son's body was discovered on a waste site yesterday. He appears to have been killed some time earlier."

"He was murdered?"

"It seems likely at this this stage of the investigation." Eleanor let Mrs Baker compose herself for a moment or two. "What did Richard say about this man?"

Maura sighed and shook her head. "I didn't really listen. I was uncomfortable I suppose. He did say he'd money and had given him presents. He had a big house somewhere but I don't know where."

"Did he mention a name or where he'd met him?"

Maura chewed on a fingernail and crinkled her brow. "I really can't remember anything more... Did he suffer?"

"Mrs Baker we need to take a DNA swab from you in order to establish..." Before she could finish the woman's cheek had transformed from an ashen pallor to a hot red.

"You don't need to have Harry's blood do you?" she whispered anxiously.

Eleanor looked at her for a moment and then shook her head. "No yours will be sufficient. Would you prefer to come down to the station on your own to give your sample?"

She looked at the floor, "Yes... Thank you."

Eleanor stood up and handed her card to Maura. "If you call me on this number I will arrange for someone to meet you and if there's anything you remember that might help us please don't hesitate to call me at any time."

Before she could reach the door, Mrs Baker stopped her with a light hand on her arm. "The park I think. He was working in a park or something and met him there."

"I'm not seeing a Liberty's anywhere," said Laurence, scanning the buildings as he drove slowly east on Queen. "You want to stop and ask?"

"There!" said Eleanor pointing to an orange and green shop front. The hand-painted words, The Libertine in curling font were barely visible between two heavily over-planted hanging baskets. The lunchtime crowds, which seemed to consist mainly of male customers, had spilled onto the narrow pavement. There were no seating arrangements but an ample bay frontage allowed diners to cram together, their backs to the window and balance plates of pasta and salad on their laps.

"What did Susan want?" shouted Laurence, as he slipped past the noisy diners.

The interior of the café was similarly crowded, all table spaces having been more than filled. Several harassed waitresses were moving efficiently between the tables dispensing food and drinks.

"Wanna order drinks? There should be a table free in ten if you wanna eat in. We do 'take-out' though," said a woman mechanically from behind the bar, as she poured wine into three glasses lined up in front of her.

"Take-out will do," said Eleanor as she grabbed two of the menus from a box next to the coffee maker, handing one to Laurence. The waitress scooped up the glasses and sped past to deliver them while they perused the options.

"What'll it be honey?" said the waitress, squeezing past an irritated looking colleague and smiling at them. She had a round, open face, her skin shiny with oil and sweat and a damp lock of hair was plastered over her forehead. "Sweet Jesus, I'm gonna die if it gets any hotter! Now, what d'ya both want?" She reached for her notepad, her eyes and smile never straying from Laurence's.

"This is excellent!" trilled Susan, folding in another mouthful of the Libertine's special mozzarella burger. "And this is?" she said, peering into one of the paper bags Eleanor had placed on her desk.

"It's pecan pie. Sorry, no peanut things," said Eleanor, scanning the information sheets that Susan had passed over to her.

"What did you have?" Susan asked wiping her hands and mouth on a napkin.

Eleanor shrugged and carried on examining the file. "Have we got a cause of death yet?"

"We'll be saying the same about you if you don't get some calories down you," worried Susan. "Eat the pie or I take my official lunch break." She raised her eyebrows.

Eleanor sighed, reached for a slice of pie and took a small bite. "Happy?"

"Delirious! Now do you want your snake?" Susan handed the wooden toy over, sealed into a marked evidence bag. "I've managed to extract fourteen whole prints and three partials. We ran the prints through Richard Baker's AFIS tag and got a positive on eleven wholes and one partial. The unidentified prints are being processed but time-wise it's anyone's guess. Even if the other prints are in the system it could still take days." She stood up and walked over to a fridge next to a row of filing cabinets that took up the rest of the room in her office. She selected a couple of opaque plastic bottles with loud writing on the front and handed them over to Eleanor. "What's the problem? I doubt it's psychological so what is it?"

Eleanor read the label, "Protein shake?"

"Four hundred calories a bottle and I'd say you need at least six a day in your current condition. Which you're just about to explain to me and me only."

Eleanor paused uncomfortably but Susan carried on staring with raised eyebrows. Eleanor sighed, "I find it hard to swallow."

"Why?"

"I don't know... some scar tissue, apparently."

"When Lee Hughes attacked you?" asked Susan, carefully.

"Uh-huh. It's nothing," she said quickly. "Just makes it difficult to swallow."

"It's going to get better?" asked Susan.

"Everything does... Eventually," smiled Eleanor. "This is great" she waggled the protein shake. "I'll have it later." She took in Susan's expression. "I'll have it now."

"I've been having a little play with those photos you gave me." Susan got up and opened the glass partition that separated her office from the lab. On a long bench next to a row of high tech equipment banks, punctuated by microscopes, was a tray covered in photographs. Each one had a small tab with a number on it. "I've managed to separate most of them and am putting digital copies into a work base for Jan. If you look –" she slipped on a latex glove and turned one over "– the oil lifted some of the ink and glued it to the back of the adjacent one, or in this case…" She pointed to one image that had a second snapshot partially imposed upon it. "We've just got to separate the two images."

Eleanor picked it up and scrutinised the chaotic swirls of colour, trying to pick out a recognisable face.

Susan handed her a heavy magnifying glass. "That'll help. I'm not sure what it is but I reckon that's a bandstand. Like the ones they have in parks."

CHAPTER SIX

Toby had been staring at the display cabinet for so long that he no longer truly knew what he was looking at or essentially why. He had slipped into a familiar reverie, that of his upcoming conversation with Olivia regarding their future family. He had pondered long and hard about how he would broach the subject to her but so far had failed to come up with an adequate scenario. Should he be direct about his desire or more circuitous? He couldn't really imagine walking up to his beloved Livie and demanding that they should be thinking of expanding their family to include a child. His wife was not a robust woman and the thought of seeming ungrateful or brutish in her eyes, was more than he could bear. But he was a man of complex needs and desires and to miss out on such a small window of opportunity might leave him feeling resentful. In fact he'd even seen the ideal child for them, a small boy who came regularly to the Saturday morning children's club. So far Toby hadn't managed to learn the child's name but he had estimated him to be about six years old, he had a mop of blond hair and round tortoiseshell glasses, which made him seem studious and considered.

"That was a big sigh Tob*ee*," came the nasal twang of Enda Miller, his assistant technician from somewhere behind him. Toby loathed everything about Enda, from his snide tone to his sanctimonious approach to the artefacts under their charge. Why he had endorsed his appointment three years ago was an endless source of disbelief to Toby. "You thinking of changing this display then?" Enda said tapping on the glass with his knuckle.

"There are so many beautiful items in the Forester collection, I thought it would be an idea to start thinking about making a little space for some of them," Toby replied, carefully.

"Hmm, well you can't go clearing out the Native People's cabinets. There'd be an uproar!"

"I seem to recall that you were vociferous in your condemnation of our Native People display in last month's meeting. You felt it was *colonialist* if I remember correctly," Toby hissed.

"Oh I do stick by what I said about that but you can't boot out our history to stick some other bugger's in can you?" replied Enda, a smug grin splitting his acned features.

"Well something's got to give," snapped Toby, turning abruptly and heading back to his office.

"I think it might be that nasty display of stuffed birds," Enda called after him. Toby recognised that he was being baited but couldn't rise above it.

"What do you mean?" he said, grittily.

"Those stuffed birds. No one wants them anymore. People come to see the dinosaurs, not some flea-bitten, badly stuffed penguins. I propose that we clear out those three cabinets… Maybe, leave the little one with the hummingbirds and then we can expand the Native People to include the Old World as well," said Enda, provocatively.

Toby took a deep breath. "Our bird collection is the greatest in Canada and rivals a great many of those across the continent."

"Mmm, no doubt. However, Isabel seemed extremely interested in the idea when I spoke to her earlier this morning."

Toby was more than a little perturbed by this knowledge. Isabel Drake was the Head Curator of Mankind at the Museum and generally her ideas held sway.

"By the way!" called Enda. "Some woman's been trying to get in touch with you. She called twice. I wrote her name and number down and put it on your desk."

Toby let the door slam behind him. As he walked briskly towards his office he contemplated whether there could be any truth in what Enda had just said. Surely Isabel wouldn't have considered moving the birds? They were, he knew, the highlight of many a school visit. Children were astonished as they walked under the giant wingspan of the Wandering Albatross and saw the huge central display of birds that varied in size, ferocity and colour. He idly picked up the note that Enda had scrawled and propped against his telephone. It took several seconds for the name to fully register with his consciousness but considerably less for the feeling of nausea to spread throughout his body.

"Thanks for your help sir. If there's anything else you can think of please don't hesitate to reach me on that number... You too." Mo put down the phone, stretched and rubbed his right ear energetically. "I'm still pressing the phone too hard to my goddamn ear."

Eleanor raised an eyebrow. "Why not use the headset?"

"Doesn't feel right. Anyway, here's the latest on the preservation front. No one is claiming to having embalmed Richard Baker slash Giselle and no one is admitting that they may have mislaid a body. Apparently after the Tri-State Crematorium incident in Georgia, the authorities have tightened up on funeral homes and their ilk. It's almost possible, that your body was embalmed and then stolen but the chances are infinitesimally small. I also spoke to the EPA at city hall and they said they're all over these guys. Every body that goes through the system has to be accounted for."

Eleanor tapped her pen against her teeth and considered.

Mo leaned back in his seat and stared with interest at the coffee maker. "No one uses arsenic in embalming processes either. It's way too dangerous. Seems like the sort of practice that took place last century. Apparently, they used to use it on taxidermy specimens, brushed against fur or feathers it stopped mite and bugs attacking."

"Coffee?" Eleanor asked, standing up. "So, if I wanted to embalm Giselle, what would I need?"

"Decaff." Mo swivelled his seat around. "I'd say you'd have to have a gurney of some description."

"Why not just a table?" asked Eleanor replacing the filter paper.

The door opened and Laurence walked in. Mo nodded at him. "Because there's blood. You pump in embalming fluid and the displaced fluid has to run out. That's messy. You need sides to a table and preferably one that can be hosed down easily."

"Want a coffee?" asked Eleanor. "We're just discussing what our perp would need to embalm Giselle. Mo suggests a gurney."

Laurence shrugged. "They managed okay before we had stainless steel."

Mo nodded, "True. Some sort of tubing set-up so he can get the embalming fluid in. Maybe a pump?"

"Gravity works, you don't need anything too complicated," responded Laurence, wiping out his mug and handing it to Eleanor. "Privacy. This isn't something you can do if other people live with you... I'm assuming."

"Knowledge. He needs knowledge of how to find and mix the chemicals, the proportions. How to position the body so that it remains rigid in that pose? I think we are looking for someone with an intimate knowledge of the embalming process. Maybe he's worked in that industry before," said Eleanor watching the steady trickle of coffee.

"So, we've got a guy who knows something of the industry, lives alone and has resources," said Mo taking his coffee. "Happy to do some more calls this afternoon. What's your plan?"

"I'm going to get another snake identified," she replied.

"Where'd you get it?" asked the heavily spectacled owner of Past Present, on King Street East. She turned the snake carefully over and peered between the vertebrae. "Very nice," she purred. "Do you have a price in mind?" she looked at Laurence.

"Can you tell us a little bit about what we've got?" asked Eleanor.

The woman sighed, as if resigned to it being unobtainable. "I'm not an expert on Victorian toys but I suspect it's mid-nineteenth century and most likely British. There's been a recent interest in wooden toys but mostly the mechanised ones and as it's a limited supply market they tend to go quickly. This is simple but really nicely constructed... looks as if it's made of walnut, which would have been expensive even then." She turned the snake back again and examined the metallic clasps that held the joints together. "These are brass and I'm not seeing much wear on them. I don't think this was ever played with. If it was, it wasn't for long and there's nothing to indicate it was thrown into a toy box. This was looked after."

"What's it worth?" asked Laurence.

At this the woman smiled. "I'd give you a hundred dollars for it."

"Do you know of anyone who specialises in these sorts of toys?" asked Eleanor.

"They won't offer any more than I did."

"I'm not selling," replied Eleanor bluntly. "I'd like to know more about these toys."

"Well, you could ask Lester Byers four doors down. He's a bit of a collector," she answered tartly.

"Thank you for your time," Eleanor replied.

Lester Byers was slightly more generous in his offer of one hundred and twenty dollars but provided little more in the way of historical information. What he did say that piqued Eleanor's interest was that the Head Curator at the city museum, was known to specialise in everything to do with childhood.

"Shall I head for the museum?" asked Laurence, as he slid the car into the traffic.

"No, Winston Street off the Expressway," she replied, as she finished reading the text message from Mo. "We are going to visit a Mr Marcus Baxton, who was forced to close his business premises when a series of unpleasant and criminal activities were discovered."

"Ok and what business was this?"

"Baxton's Funeral Home," she replied.

"Ah."

Winston Street looked as if it had been created by a set designer, as a backdrop for a movie depicting life 'on the edge'. Half of the houses were derelict and boarded up and the rest had the starved quality that was the stamp of social deprivation. Eleanor could only assume that the city no longer provided trash collection, due to the mountains of garbage that were strewn across the overgrown yards and cracked walkways. Only the truly desperate or afflicted took lets in this neighbourhood. Eleanor took out her badge and walked up to the front door and rapped. A curtain twitched in the downstairs front window. She waited for thirty seconds before knocking again, "Mr Baxton this is DI Raven and DC Whitefoot, we'd be grateful if you'd open the door voluntarily." Laurence shot her a questioning look, to which Eleanor shrugged one shoulder.

"He's not here," came a voice from behind the door.

"Then we'll come in and wait for him," Eleanor replied. There was a heavy sigh from behind the door.

"He's not done anything wrong," said the voice, rising in pitch.

"Perhaps your neighbours might know where your son is Mr Baxton?" she said. A shuffling sound preceded the sound of a chain being drawn through a channel and a lock being twisted open. An elderly man held the door open with one hand and rested his weight on a hospital-issue walking stick. He was heavy and grey, with stooped shoulders and a startled expression. "Come in," he hissed, taking a quick glance at the house opposite.

Despite the humidity, the interior of the house was relatively cool and dark. Eleanor breathed in slowly through her nose. Mr Baxton led them down a corridor narrowed by precariously stacked towers of tins, toilet rolls, catering sized tubs of coffee and powdered milk. A bicycle was squeezed between the stairwell and the supplies. They stepped into a small room containing two leather-backed armchairs, a glass coffee table and a couple of bookcases, over-stuffed with books and magazines. Like Mr Baxton the room seemed uniformly grey, the only colour provided by a stuffed macaw, its blue and red feathers dulled by years of accumulated dust. He lowered himself painfully into one of the chairs. "Is your son here?" asked Eleanor firmly, looking around the room.

The man looked as if he was considering his reply but nodded. "He's in his room."

"We need to speak to him," said Eleanor.

"He's done nothing wrong. *That* can't happen any-more," he whispered. A sudden movement from behind Eleanor caused them both to spin round. A curtain between two bookcases was pulled back and Tyler Baxton stepped into the room. He was mid height, with an oddly elongated skull, pale skin and eyes, and a noticeable overbite.

"We are investigating a case at the moment, which you may be able to help us with," said Eleanor calmly.

"He can't!" blurted Mr Baxton, "I sold the business thirteen years ago and he hardly ever leaves his room!"

"An embalmed body has been discovered and it appears to have been sexually abused," Eleanor said bluntly.

Tyler began to shake his head wildly. "No! I'm not allowed anywhere near them. Am I dad?"

"Them?" asked Laurence.

Tyler's eyes flicked from Eleanor's to Laurence's, a line of sweat appearing on his upper lip. "The dead. I'm not allowed near the dead."

"Mr Baxton do you have a cellar here?" she asked.

"No!" he yelped, struggling to his feet. "You're not looking round this house without a search warrant. I know our rights and you're fishing!"

Eleanor looked at him calmly. "I can get a search warrant Mr Baxton and be back with marked vehicles and a CSI van. All of which will be of interest to your neighbours, I imagine."

Laurence watched the little colour in his cheeks disappear and noted his sudden change of breathing. As a former doctor, he registered with growing alarm the physical changes that could indicate a potential heart attack. He leaned across and put a supporting hand on Mr Baxton's elbow. It was as if the man had been electrocuted.

"I don't need your help!" he hissed, gasping for breath. "I need you to leave us *alone.*"

"I'm sorry sir," said Eleanor in a quieter voice, "but Tyler lost the right to privacy when he invaded that of the bodies that had been placed in your care." There was a long silence punctuated by Mr Baxton's laboured breathing. Slowly he sank back into his chair.

"If your son is unconnected to this case then you have nothing to fear," said Eleanor more softly.

"I swear, I ain't been near a dead body since I got out," said Tyler desperately. "I swear!"

"Then let us take a look round, with you and your son's permission, and we can register your co-operation and begin the process of elimination."

"No!" spat Mr Baxton, his chest heaving. "You get your warrant and bring the cars with lights and horns blaring. You can block off the whole street, for all I care. You're not doing this to us again!" His energy spent he sank back into his chair and clamped his jaw tightly shut. Tyler looked away from them, focusing his gaze on a corner of the room.

Eleanor sighed, "I am truly sorry that you wish to take this particular path to proving your son's innocence." She nodded to Tyler and handed him a card. "If you would like to contact either myself or my partner, please don't hesitate to call on this number." She made a step towards the door

and stopped, studying the macaw. "What a beautiful specimen. Is this your work?" she asked neither man in particular. It was greeted with silence. Suddenly, Eleanor ran her
left hand slowly over the bird's head and down its back. "He
could be alive."

Nothing further was said, so Eleanor and Laurence
made their way out of the house. As they stepped into the
brilliant sunshine, closing the front door behind them,
Laurence noted that her left hand was balled up.

"Have you got a ballistics test kit in the trunk?" she asked
quickly.

"Should have, why?"

"Drive round the corner and then swab my hand," she
said, as she stepped into the car.

"Not sure I'm getting this," said Laurence, pulling away
from the kerb and turning into a small cul-de-sac.

Slipping on latex gloves, Laurence broke the seal on the
sample tubes and, using a swab, swiped it thoroughly over
her palm and fingers. "We think the parrot was shot?" he
quipped.

"Well he may have been but I'm running this through
as an arsenic test."

Laurence looked at her with interest.

"Susan picked up high levels of realgar and orpiment,
which are –"

"– Arsenic compounds," he interrupted. "You're thinking that Tyler used arsenic as a preservative, when he
embalmed Giselle?"

Eleanor shook her head and wiped her hands thoroughly
with a sterile wipe. "I'm not thinking anything that certain.
If there's arsenic on that bird it makes Tyler more interesting but nothing about his personality indicated *organised*.
From what Mo said, he was convicted of having intercourse

with at least twelve female cadavers prior to their burial but after their embalming."

"Classy," replied Laurence starting the engine.

"Tyler denied having carnal knowledge throughout the trial, two appeals and his subsequent seven-year sentence, even though there was ample DNA evidence to contradict that."

"Seven years? Seems a little steep for a quick bonk with the dead," replied Laurence, pulling onto the Expressway.

Eleanor raised her eyebrows and looked at him. "Apparently he got very attached to one of his victims – the twenty-five-year-old victim of a drug overdose – and kept her in one of their cold rooms."

"For how long?" said Laurence incredulously.

"Two months."

"And no-one noticed?"

"I don't have all the details but it appeared that when the coffin was exhumed it was found to contain weighted sand bags."

"He sounds like our number one suspect," said Laurence confidently.

"Mmm,"

"You don't sound convinced."

"I'm not. Let's get a little more information on him. I'd like to find a reason to bring him in for questioning but first I'm going to get Ruby Delaware to draw us up some profiling points."

"Have you got any open cuts on your hand?" asked Laurence. Eleanor took a quick look. "Not that I'm aware of."

"Good, don't want you as Exhibit B do we?"

"This is absolutely divine!" Isabel Drake beamed as she ran her fingertips along the wooden snake's spine. "Wherever did you find it?" She twisted a lock of titanium white hair behind her ear and readjusted her glasses. "I'd put this chap at round about 1870 or so. It's in tremendous condition, hardly a scratch on it. British and…" She stopped for a moment and contemplated. Eleanor waited.

"Funnily enough the museum bought up a toy collection from an independent gallery about two years ago." She gently placed the snake on her desk, walked over to a large bookcase, ran a finger along the spines and selected a catalogue. Flicking through the pages she stopped and after a moment or two passed the booklet over to Eleanor and Laurence. "See, very similar aren't they?" Eleanor looked at the columns of thumbnail photographs and saw what Isabel meant. There were at least six wooden animal toys, all in similar condition, all made of the same dark wood. A crocodile and lizard had the identical brass clasps that articulated the toy. "I'd say that your snake may possibly have been created by the same individual or company. Would you leave it with me for a few days?"

"I'm sorry, that's not possible but I've got some photographs I can leave with you," said Eleanor. "If this toy is part of the same collection or by the same toymaker, what would that mean?"

"It would mean that you have a very unique item on your hands."

"Which might make it easier to trace?" Eleanor inquired. Isabel nodded. "It might."

"Is it possible that this item could have been taken from the museum?" asked Eleanor.

"Goodness, I can't say no for certain but I'm sure to about ninety-nine percent. The museum has on display about thirty to forty percent of its artefacts at any one time. The rest are in one of four places, either on loan to other museums or the education department, all of which is highly traceable. Generally there's a paper trail that could circle the earth!" she said lightly. "The rest is either in the workshop being conserved or studied or in the vaults."

"How safe are these vaults?" asked Laurence.

"We're not Fort Knox but only qualified personnel has access, due to the value of much of the items held there. Most of it is irreplaceable rather than of monetary value though."

"The snake didn't appear in the catalogue," said Eleanor pointing. "Does that mean it couldn't have been part of your collection or just part of the display?"

"I'm not sure yet. I'll check the inventories and talk to my colleagues and get back to you over the next couple of days.

"Does the museum have, to your knowledge, a collection of human skulls?" asked Eleanor as an afterthought.

"Hmm, we were willed a small private collection of medical curiosities, comprising mainly of skeletal abnormalities. They'd been used as teaching aids by the Ontario Medical Examiner in the fifties and sixties." Isabel said as she searched her bookshelf. "Here you are. You're welcome to keep both of those catalogues as I seem to have a couple of spares." She handed Eleanor a small dun-coloured booklet. "Off-hand I couldn't place where the majority of the specimens are but it shouldn't be difficult to locate them if you need me to." She looked at Eleanor with a polite but time-aware smile.

"Thank you for your time Dr Drake, it's much appreciated."

"Is there anything else I can help you with?" she asked, ushering them towards the door.

"Would you happen to know if your restaurant serves iced tea?" said Laurence pointedly.

"I do believe that to be true," Isabel replied warmly.

While Laurence wolfed down an impressive mound of restaurant fare Eleanor studied the catalogues. Tapping a finger against a page, she turned the booklet round so he could see it. A small black-and-white image of two tiny con-joined foetal skulls, was displayed below that of a twisted vertebra and a pocked and eroded syphilitic jawbone.

"I think I'm going to run this past Parminder and Dieter. Neither mentioned that they were conjoined though…"

"Yeah but that's a temporal join, if they were placed on a table you wouldn't know," Laurence replied.

Eleanor checked Parminder's number and called. After several rings it jumped to her message box. "That's the third time she's not picked up. Wonder why not." As she lowered the phone it began to vibrate.

"Why the fuck do you *never* pick up your cell?" bellowed Marty. "I've left you at least ten messages –"

"Three sir to be exact," butted in Eleanor.

"I *said*, if this proved to be more than just a dead hobo it was to handled by Timms and Wadesky. I want you on bike crime and missing cats! Am I making myself clear to you? I've had several calls from your counsellor and she says, if you don't attend this meeting she won't endorse your bond. And no bond, means no detective!"

"I am in the middle –"

"I don't give a flying fuck what you're in the middle of. Get yourself to this session or hand in your badge. Have you taken this on board?"

"It's on board… sir."

Toby stood silently, to the left of the small bridge and watched with fascination as a small, lithe mink flitted in between the gaps in the stone bridge support. She had spotted him several minutes earlier but having determined he posed little threat, had continued with her task of dragging the carp she had caught, to a higher level. The fish was, he believed, a bighead carp: one of the numerous invasive species that were systematically crowding out their native fauna. He was jolted from his reverie and the mink her catch by the noisy arrival of Parminder Kaur, on a bicycle.

Toby considered what her plan was going to be, or even if she had one, other than the desire to extract money or favours from him. Why else would she contact him now, after all this time? From where he stood, he could see in both directions for at least five hundred yards, which meant that they would have privacy for this meeting. He had imagined, naively as it now appeared, that she would have been content with the generous payment he'd made for the two unique and exquisite skulls he'd retrieved from the apartment and felt saddened that what had been a loving act, had been sullied by this greedy, intrusive woman.

Toby had been completely smitten by the beautiful and exotic Giselle, to the point of offering her a fine home, security and his undying love. When she'd left him, he was distraught. He had tried absolutely everything in his powers to prevent her from having to go but sometimes, he mused, there were events beyond even his abilities to control. He missed her terribly and had recently taken to roaming her old haunts trying to rekindle those happy feelings. It was on one of these trips that he'd met someone who he felt sure was about to turn his life around and fill the void Giselle had left. When he had first taken a mistress, he'd spent many a long night battling with his conscience. He adored his wife but due to her constant ill health and delicate constitution, he seldom imposed his sexual needs on her. But that hadn't prevented or dampened those desires. It was not in his nature to contemplate paying for sexual favours, that was a degrading act for both himself and the lady in question; rather he had sought a mistress that he could lavish gifts, love and security onto. It was this penchant for gift lavishing that had instigated the thefts of the skulls and the toy snake, a fact not lost on Parminder Kaur.

Toby hadn't really considered the effect on Parminder of his approach from under the bridge. She let out a shriek and clutched at her chest, as if she was having some sort of seizure. This level of theatricality irritated Toby beyond measure but he stood his ground, gritted his teeth and asked her calmly what she wanted.

"I *know* what you've done," she spat.

Toby lowered his head; he felt a pulse of anger that cancelled out any perception of her as another human being. He saw her waving her arms around and pointing a finger at him in an ugly, accusatory manner. A wash of angry sound came out of her face and there was only one action that could restore peace. Instantly, the hideous sounds were reduced to grunts and pants. The piano wire, linked by two pieces of dowel, was remarkably efficient. He had been a little disappointed that she'd managed to trap two of her fingers behind the wire and this was prolonging what should have been a simple and efficient exercise. With several intended and then involuntary kicks, Parminder Kaur quietened and slumped to her knees. Using the garrotte much like a handle, Toby dragged the body to the edge of the bridge and lifted it over, letting it splash into the shallow water below. He suspected that it would only be a matter of hours before she began to emerge on the surface, so picking up a large rock from those strewn around the pathway, dropped it onto the body.

Toby was about to enjoy the short walk back to his car, when he realised that Parminder had left her bike for him. He couldn't remember the last time he'd ridden a bicycle and it was with some degree of trepidation that he lowered himself onto the frame and then pushed off. There were several moments of uncoordinated lurching and rebalancing but, noted Toby happily, once a skill is acquired it is seldom lost.

CHAPTER SEVEN

Eleanor sank back into the leather armchair and waited impatiently. She'd attended at least fifty per cent of the sessions so far and felt aggrieved that this bullshit was considered by the department to be both necessary and important enough to take her off a homicide. She sighed and waited for Doctor Lehmann to appear wearing her customary tight-fitting black trouser suit and patent court shoes that pinched her toes and swelled her ankles. A loud and frothy shirt always contradicted the ensemble, as if to remind the patient that despite her professional appearance there was a warm, humorous and unconventional woman waiting to burst out. Eleanor believed this to be a knowingly manufactured affectation.

The door opened and an unfamiliar voice chirped, "Detective Inspector Eleanor Raven?" A tall, clean-shaven twenty-something, wearing linen trousers, a T-shirt and a noisy collection of bracelets, thrust his hand towards her. "I'm Doctor Seb Blackmore and I'm going to be conducting this session.

Eleanor raised an eyebrow, to which he smiled and raised his index finger. "And that's why!" He dragged a chair towards her and sat on the edge, leaning towards Eleanor. His eyes locked onto hers, his face beaming with bonhomie.

"It's because you refused to talk to Doctor Lehmann that I am replacing her as your counsellor."

"I didn't *speak* to Doctor Lehmann because she didn't ask me a single question in four sessions," exclaimed Eleanor.

Seb Blackmore nodded sympathetically. "It's a well-documented technique that does work with a great many patients. People need to fill in the gaps and they do it despite themselves. Before they know it they've opened up and are well on the way to being mended." He looked intently at Eleanor. "But you're not one of those people, are you detective?"

"You tell me, doctor," she said, slowly.

He smiled and put his hand on the lip of the seat, about to drag it even closer to Eleanor's but catching her expression he leaned further back. He opened his mouth and then snapped it closed again, as if he'd changed his mind. Eleanor turned her face away and gazed out of the window.

"You know why you're here don't you?" he said quietly.

Eleanor turned to look at him. "Because all serving officers that suffer an attack by a member of the public, are obliged to receive some sort of psychological evaluation before they can be trusted by the authorities."

Seb nodded and held her gaze. "You are here Eleanor because a member of the public murdered you."

Eleanor felt a tightening sensation in her throat and a quickening of her heart rate. "Is that some sort of metaphorical statement?"

Seb Blackmore leaned towards her. "Lee Hughes suffocated you and when he realised that he'd killed you prematurely, he injected you with adrenaline and restarted your heart."

"How do you know that? Hughes is dead and I haven't suggested that to anyone!" Eleanor was suddenly aware that she was being too loud. She took a deep breath and concentrated on slowing down her heart rate.

Seb pulled a large folder from the briefcase, unwrapped the elastic band and flipped open to a page bearing a small coloured tab. He looked at her. "These are the notes taken by the registrar who admitted you after the assault. It reads, 'Fractures to sternum and ribs…'"

"Hughes hit me several times," Eleanor cut in. Her chest was beginning to ache and she was aware that her hand was pressed protectively against her left breast. She wilfully lowered it to her lap and focused on Seb Blackmore, as he dismissed this with a wave of his hand. His eyes barely moved across the page, as if the words had already been memorised. "ST-T changes indicate that at some point your heart stopped beating. An EKG showed areas of possible infarction and there was some evidence of central nerve damage, due to increased levels of CO_2." He dropped the report casually onto the floor, his voice hard and triumphant. "You were killed in that warehouse Detective Inspector Raven. Lee Hughes murdered you."

Eleanor felt a surge of anger that threatened to launch her out of the chair and into the personal space inhabited by Seb Blackmore. It took a gigantic effort of will to calm herself sufficiently to speak. She leaned closer to him, swallowing hard. "This *new* approach to my rehabilitation is going to have a similar effect to the last one. It's going to fuck me off!"

Seb Blackmore nodded sagely. "I don't doubt it but you don't require rehabilitation, detective."

"So what the fuck am here for then?" she hissed.

"Because at some point you're going to have a breakdown and we want to make sure that we know when it's coming and how to treat it."

Eleanor smiled and relaxed. "And this is something you're sure about?"

Seb's expression was one of absolute conviction. "It's a definite," he said, glancing curiously at her wrists.

Eleanor stormed out of the therapy room, nearly knocking over a coffee table piled with magazines and a potted peace lily. Dimly aware that a female voice was calling her name, she barged through the reception swing door and headed for the exit, her face burning. It was only when she had jumped into the car and locked the door that she was able to collect her thoughts and calm herself. Her phone buzzed loudly and for a moment or two she allowed the urgent tones of normality to soothe her. She started the car and pulled out of the parking bay as Laurence's voice threaded its way through the Bluetooth.

"You free?" he asked quickly, ignoring her dry laugh. "Wadesky says they're pulling an Asian female out of the lake at TTP. I've just got here."

Her irritation evaporated instantly. "Keep me posted I'm heading there now."

Tommy Thompson Park was bathed in rich, dusty sunlight as Laurence waited for an overdressed and sweaty patrol cop to raise the barrier for him. The spit had begun its creation in the fifties and was now brimming with bird and insect life. If you could ignore the huge, rubble-bearing trucks that thundered past and zone out the steady stream of wheeled and lycra-clad Torontans, you could almost imagine your-self in conservation paradise.

"Follow the road straight for about a half mile and then you'll see them on the left. You'll be directed from there." said the officer, swatting a persistent black fly away from his face. "Is your dog a serving officer?" he asked suspiciously, gazing at Monster seated in the back. "Because this is a conservation area and no dogs are allowed."

Laurence sighed, "Absolutely."

The officer stared at Monster unconvinced. "Uh-huh."

"He'll be kept on a lead officer," Laurence replied quickly, pulling away.

Timms and Wadesky were deep in raised conversation with two men, who were variously squeezing themselves into wet suits and carrying out technical checks on their tanks. Wadesky waved a hand and nodded, as she saw Laurence approaching the bridge.

"Look, the vic *is* submerged but only in three feet of water. Not even I'd drown in that!" bellowed Timms, wafting his coffee around in an agitated manner. The two diving officers looked non-plussed by Timms' outrage and carried on with their preparations.

"What the fuck! There's a goddamn fish eating her now!" despaired Timms, "Look!"

Laurence peered over the railings and looked at the face staring back at him through the water. Parminder Kaur's long dark plait had become tangled in the wire mesh that was used to prevent non-native fish entering the protected wetlands from the lake and gave the bizarre effect of her head nodding from side to side in the water's ebb, one hand tucked firmly under her chin.

"Mo told us you were interviewing an Asian woman of about the same age in connection with your case. Kinda made sense that we ran it past you before we started the ID," said Wadesky hurrying over. "That her?"

Laurence noted she was wearing chef pants and T-shirt and nodded. "Pretty sure it's her but wait till she's out."

A sudden surge from somewhere further out in the lake twisted Parminder's body into the bankside, revealing the twisted wooden handles of a garrotte, tightly tucked below her hairline.

"Well, that's just made it first degree," noted Wadesky.

"Is the ME here yet?" Laurence asked, nodding to the divers as they slid into the water.

"Over by the vans. They arrived from the other side of the bridge." As if on cue they could see Dr Hounslow, Susan Cheung and half a dozen white-clad crime scene officers making their way towards the bridge, all laden with boxes of equipment and a portable gurney.

"Have you any witnesses?" he asked.

Wadesky shook her head. "If there were, we haven't found them yet.." Timms turned from the bridge and waved to Wadesky. "Hang on," she said moving away. Laurence looked around him and wondered what was relevant to the murderer about this place. "I'm going to have a little walk around, that ok?" he shouted to her.

Monster had been tied to the tow bar by his lead and was passing the time by barking enthusiastically at a muskrat, which was rummaging about on the shoreline. Laurence unhooked him and watched for a moment as the body was lifted out of the water. Leaving the path he walked along the lakeside, unsure of what he was looking for. Monster punctuated the trip by swallowing all the muskrat scat he could nose out. As he turned to climb up the bank, Monster pulled him back, reluctant to leave a couple of empty liquor bottles. The label on one was too perfect to have been exposed to the elements for long. Bending down, his face uncomfortably near Monster's, he inhaled the whiskey vapours.

It took him less than ten minutes to find the boat. It had been dragged onto drier ground and was partially concealed by low-level shrubs and thicket. A damp and mangy sleeping bag was pushed into a corner along with a few empty cans. Laurence concluded that the absent tenant survived on a mostly liquid diet.

The track down to the lakeside would have been unapproachable by a vehicle but that was probably as well because 'Muntjack', as he was known to his ex-army buddies and the park officials, would have fled. According to Helga, who was responsible for that particular quadrant of the park, Muntjack was regularly turfed out in the summer but some leeway was granted when the colder months came and the nesting birds had all migrated. If he wasn't lurking around the boat, he was generally to be found in a small derelict hut by the lakeside.

The track began to widen onto a sloping, stony incline as it reached the shore. Suddenly, Monster began to bark hysterically and lunged towards the deep grass surrounding the path. Laurence, taken off guard, barely managed to cling onto the leash. The barks changed to a yelp, as a stone clipped Monster on the shoulder. "What the fuck!" yelled Laurence. A second stone flew out from the deep grass and bounced off the top of the dog's head. Monster shook his head viciously in an attempt to free himself from collar and leash, his curled back lips left little doubt as to his next planned move.

"Those are police officers, so put down the rock!" said Eleanor firmly to the figure crouching in the grass.

"Fuck you!" screamed the figure and hurled the stone held tightly in his hand with alarming speed and accuracy, hitting Laurence on the cheek with a palpable crack. Eleanor grabbed the man's hand, twisted it behind him, pushed her right knee into the small of his back, slammed him face down onto the ground and cuffed him. Muntjack kept up a steady stream of muffled monosyllabic abuse while Eleanor examined Laurence and Monster's injuries. "You ok?" she asked Laurence, who was searching for a handkerchief.

"Guess so," he replied, embarrassed. "Didn't hear you and didn't see him!"

"There were signs," she said quietly. "Just got to get tuned into them a little more."

Hoisting Muntjack into a sitting position, Eleanor spoke calmly into his ear. "We're here to talk to you about what happened last night and if you want to wake up to the sunrise, rather than a cell wall, you'd better co-operate and fast. Guessing compulsory rehab and psych evaluation doesn't hold much appeal to an outdoors man like yourself, does it?"

There were several moments as Muntjack processed the information. His greasy, heavily furrowed skin was now coated in a thick layer of dust. He squinted at them, curling his lip to reveal a few blackened stumps that stood in for teeth. He spat a heavy bolus of phlegm in the direction of Monster, who snarled menacingly. "I hate po-*lice*," he spluttered wetly. "Fuckin' hate 'em!"

"That's as maybe. But we need to know what you heard and saw last night."

"Nuffin!" Munjack growled, preparing another bolus.

"Ok, that's enough," said Eleanor grabbing him by his collar and arm yanking him to his feet. "We'll talk when you've had a chance to benefit from a couple of nights without a bottle."

A steady shriek began to emanate from the hunched grey figure, accompanied by the acrid smell of urine and sweat. "I don't know nuffin about that!"

"About what?" said Eleanor, leaning closer to the frightened man. "You definitely heard them but did you see them?"

Muntjack sucked his lips in, collapsing his face. He struggled with a thought and then shook his head. "You let me go if I tell you?" he whispered to her.

"Let's see how truthful you are," she replied.

"I heard 'em arguing. I couldn't see 'em 'cos I was in the boat. They were really pissy with each other. Then it went quiet and I heard a splash and then they must have went."

"Uh-huh. You're lying. Let's go," she said flatly, shoving him in the direction of the path.

"I ain't... I ain't lying!!" he screamed, staggering alongside her. Laurence and Monster followed behind. "I told you the truth!"

At that, Eleanor span him round and shook him. "You told me what you heard, not what you saw and you *saw* something and that makes you an accessory to the fact. You're looking at three to six for that." She span him back round and continued walking.

"I didn't see 'em. I didn't!" he shrieked.

Eleanor carried on pulling him along the track. "See those cars Muntjack," She nodded to the first flash of sunlight bouncing off a prowler's windscreen.

"I'll tell ya!" he sobbed. "*He* got there first."

Eleanor stopped walking and turned to face him. "No lies now."

"What did he look like?"

"Too dark then and I can't see well. I only knew she was a girl 'cos of 'er long hair and the smell," he mused. "He walked up 'cos there weren't no car sounds." Muntjack began to suck his lips noisily, his attention beginning to waver.

"Hey!" Eleanor shook him but Muntjack was confused. Monster, several feet behind him was snarling aggressively, the wound on his head bleeding profusely now, despite Laurence stopping and applying a handkerchief to it.

"I hate dogs!" shrieked Muntjack, regaining some of the plot.

"I'm guessing it's mutual," Eleanor replied, pulling him towards the bridge where Timms was in mid rant to someone on his cell phone. "See that officer?" she pushed her chin in Timms direction. "He's in charge of this case and he loves the dog you just stoned." Muntjack peered balefully at Timms. "Want to tell him or me?" There was a pause as he mulled over his options.

"You," he said with finality.

"Good. So you saw the woman, whose body's in the water under the bridge and…?"

His lips curled and eyes narrowed, as if trying to express what he'd witnessed. "She was pissy… Kinda demanding. Like she wanted some'at."

"What do you think she wanted?"

"I dunno," he answered mystified. "Guess what we all want," he smirked.

"Can you describe the man at all? Fat, thin, young…?"

"Heavy. He had a cap on, that's all I can think of. I couldn't hear what they said it was too far away. I need one of them things that goes in your ears…"

"Focus!" she hissed, poking him sharply in the chest with her fingers.

"Je-sus… I heard a splash. When I looked no one was there. I waited and then I saw him drop some'at big into the water. Then he went."

"How? On foot?"

He shook his head. "Bike. He was on a bike."

"Did he arrive on the bike or was it hers?"

Muntjack shrugged and lapsed into silence.

"Anything else?" she asked.

"Yeah, you takin' these cuffs off 'cos I've…"

"What happened to the puppy?" snarled Timms, barging past and wrapping his hands round Monster's head. "Did you do this?" he turned slowly to face Muntjack. Suddenly, the smell of urine became intoxicatingly strong.

Toby was going to be late for work. This was unusual and he knew it was likely to draw attention from Isabel and unwanted comment from Enda but he had been so busy that the hours had just slid past without him noticing, or eating for that matter. He grabbed his linen jacket off the hook on the door and swung it over his shoulders, casting a final satisfied glance around his workroom. He'd been absolutely right about the headrest. Despite the attendant risks of appropriating it, it gave the room a sense of cultural heritage.

The antique table had been acquired by his father in the early nineteen fifties and he had gone to considerable lengths to have it shipped over from Italy, where it had been dragged from the bombed out rubble of a university. Toby had made various adjustments to it; covering the wooden top with a metal plate, to stop blood and fluids accumulating and creating a hole at the end, complete with a metal overflow tube to allow for drainage. The table could be tipped either to the head or foot end, with the aid of a cogged metal rod on a ratchet. At some point in its history someone had replaced a broken lever with a cast iron death's head, much to Toby's continuing delight. Up to today he had been forced to use a standard metal headrest, the type purchased easily on medical supply websites and it had always been a source of friction. Its hygienic galvanized surface and ergonomic design, sat at odds with the hand crafted *memento mori* that was his dissecting table.

He gave the room a final visual sweep and smiled to himself. It was spotlessly clean, despite the fact that Monty, his Irish setter had been spending a great deal of time down there recently, due to Toby's continued allergic reaction to the animal. The carboys had been carefully positioned below the sink in the corner and the necessary tubes, trocar and buckets had been cleaned and arranged in order of usage. As he flipped the light switch, he became dimly aware of the hammering sound coming from the soundproofed room at the other end of the corridor. He held his breath anxiously, wondering if the sound would permeate the building and draw attention but it hadn't on any other occasion, so why should now be different? He felt a little frisson of pleasure as he thought about the events of the last few days and his plans for the evening.

Eleanor sat in the car and felt a bead of sweat break from her hairline and trickle down her back. All the windows had been opened but the car felt like the inside of an oven, slowly cooking her from the top down. She wondered why she didn't seal herself in and start the air con but no good reason came to her. "Whoa, you trying to kill us?" asked Wadesky, jumping into the passenger seat. Eleanor started the engine and pulled into the traffic. "Ok, as of now, Parminder Kaur's father has just confirmed her ID and Timms is wrapping up at the morgue. He's going to city hall to get permission for phone and bank account access and should be back in a couple of hours. How about we go to…" Wadesky consulted her notepad, "… The Orient Express and then check out her apartment?"

"Sounds like a plan," replied Eleanor, thoughtfully.

"What you thinking?"

"I can't see the connection between Giselle and Parminder."

"They lived together, maybe she knew who the killer was?" suggested Wadesky.

Eleanor nodded. "But Giselle was murdered about eighteen months ago and she didn't call the disappearance in. She packed up her stuff, put it neatly in the attic and got another room-mate moved in."

"Uh-huh. But she was murdered twenty-four hours after you and Whitefoot spoke to her. That's not a coincidence."

"She lied about something," mused Eleanor. Wadesky glanced at her, waiting for her thoughts to clarify. "It was something to do with a couple of skulls I think. She said that Giselle had a pair of babies' skulls that she'd secured in a box soon after Giselle's disappearance and left in the basement. The boxes were rummaged through, and the skulls taken."

"She make any suggestions as to who took 'em?" asked Wadesky curiously.

"She said raccoons but then countered that saying that, 'raccoons don't take the boxes'."

"She was implying that someone had stolen them?"

Eleanor nodded and thought for a moment or two. "Because she knew who took them and why and I think that's what got her killed."

"What was so important about the skulls, apart from them being in bad taste?"

"They could identify who gave them to Giselle and who murdered her."

"So why'd this all blow up now?" asked Wadesky.

"Because Parminder Kaur saw an opportunity to make a little bit of extra cash. She hadn't known Giselle had been murdered until we came round the other day and started asking questions. The skulls were either stolen or, more likely, she gave them or sold them back to the guy and when she realised that he'd murdered Giselle, she contacted him to meet her by the bridge in Tommy Thompson Park."

"To blackmail him?"

Eleanor nodded. "I imagine so."

Wadesky raised her eyebrows and thought for a moment or two. "Then Parminder would have had to contact him in some way wouldn't she?"

"So, you're saying that she met up with a guy and got herself murdered?" said Amrit Chandry, his eyes wide with a mixture of disbelief, outrage and a whiff of theatrics, thought Eleanor, as she explained the facts to Parminder's boss. "I cannot believe that!" he said, slapping a hand to his forehead.

"Mr Chandry, perhaps you'd like to explain exactly what happened yesterday with Ms Kaur," asked Eleanor.

"Well… she came to work at about ten in the morning. Prepared the vegetables for the evening staff, set off a couple of dishes that needed a long cook and then left at about six, when the chef and the evening team arrived."

"Were you aware of anything being different about her yesterday? Did she leave for any reason or receive any calls or visitors perhaps?" Eleanor watched as he scratched his head and then pinched the top of his nose.

"I don't remember but I spend most of the day in my office, not in the kitchen. Maybe Jaden can help. Please come with me."

Eleanor and Wadesky followed Amrit Chandry past the set tables in the main restaurant, through a swing door, along a heavily-scented corridor and into the kitchen. The back door had been propped open, due to the intense steamy heat generated by several hobs. Two white-clad kitchen staff were in the midst of frying, chopping and stirring. Both were heavily sweat stained and appeared to be in less than affable moods.

"Jaden, these are police officers and they need to know about Parminder yesterday."

Jaden scowled but nodded his head as he stirred a huge pot of spiced chicken. "What d'ya wanna know?" He killed the flame and wiped his hands on a tea cloth. "She was here yesterday but didn't show today. There a problem?"

"She's dead. Murdered," said Eleanor bluntly.

"Shit. Big problem then," replied Jaden, his scowl softening. "You know who did it?"

"Not yet, hence the importance of getting all of the facts straight."

Jaden nodded. "I got here about ten minutes before Parminder yesterday. She worked a single shift but I stayed on for the double. So, she left about sixish, I guess. Can't be more accurate I'm afraid."

"When did your shift end?"

"Round about midnight I think."

"Can you remember whether Parminder was on foot or bike?"

Jaden shook his head. "She usually biked here but I can't say for certain if she did yesterday, as I can't see the bike rack from here." He made a step towards the door and gestured round the doorway. "There's a bike rack round the corner."

"Can you show me?" asked Eleanor moving towards him. "Sure."

The bike rack was a rusted metal support consisting of eight ports, which currently supported three bikes, each secured with various locking mechanisms.

"Is Parminder's bike here?" Wadesky asked Jaden, who was lighting a cigarette. "No, she had a black and silver racer." He waved his hand along the bikes. "Dunno whose these are but that one's mine." He pointed and inhaled deeply, holding onto the fix for several moments before letting the smoke creep slowly out from his nostrils.

"There's an extra bike lock there." Eleanor pointed to a plastic sleeved chain and lock wrapped twice around the metal and secured with a small brass padlock. "This hers?"

Jaden looked at it and shook his head. "Dunno. Might be."

"Did she use her phone here or speak about meeting someone?" Wadesky continued, wafting away the smoke from her face. Picking up the cue, Jaden turned his head away and blew the remaining lungful away from them. "Sorry... I really didn't pick up on anything like that. No one came to the kitchen, apart from the girl who delivers the veg. I didn't see Parminder go and don't think I really said anything of any interest to her." He shrugged, took a final drag before crushing the cigarette against the wall and putting the remains into a nearby trashcan. He started back to the kitchen. "One thing's for sure she won't have called anyone from her cell 'cos we're in a dead spot. Never any effing signal here. Middle of the city and all... go figure!"

Eleanor pulled her cell phone from her pocket and checked her signal strength. There was none.

"You're not far from TTP here. Did Parminder ever go there? Maybe during her break?"

"When the weather's good we all pop over with our lunch."

CHAPTER EIGHT

Sergeant Andy Harrison stood behind the desk that served as a barrier between those trespassed upon; those who trespassed on others, and himself. He sighed deeply. "Have you called Child Services?" he ventured cautiously, to the woman glaring at him.

"You're trying to fob me off!" the woman shrieked, jiggling a bemused toddler violently in her arms. Andy Harrison watched sympathetically as the child's head bounced around and a large bubble of snot appeared below his red nose. "She said one night that's all! One frikken night and that was three nights ago! How the hell am I supposed to go to work with a sodding kid in tow?"

Andy Harrison rubbed his dyspeptic abdomen and stifled a burp. "Has she done this before? Disappeared and left you with...?"

"Justin." She turned and looked at the boy, tutted, and using the grimy bib looped over his head she attacked the runny nose enthusiastically, causing little Justin to screw up his face miserably. "Don't you start!" This seemed to have a less than salutary effect and within seconds Justin was roaring fit to wake the dead.

"Holy mother of God!" bellowed a drunk handcuffed to a bench several feet away from the desk. "Shut him up!"

"*You* shut the fuck up!" screamed the woman.

Andy Harrison reached below the desk for a couple of antacids and a lollipop. He smiled at Justin as he handed the sweet to him, who turned off the misery as if it were controlled by a tap. "Now, let me get this right," he said carefully. "Your friend Tara; a working girl like yourself..." he added wearily. The woman scowled at him. "Left Justin with you on Sunday night. She informed you that she was going to 'work' for a couple of hours and then she'd be back to collect him. Is that correct?"

The woman rolled her eyes and nodded, "That's what I *said.*"

"But she didn't return, didn't call you and has been missing from her workplace..." Andy consulted the sheet of notes in front of him, "... the Costco car park off Dundas. And none of her friends or colleagues have seen her either. Can you give me a description of Tara?"

"Look her up under Mother of the Year Awards," proffered the drunk.

"Why don't you go fuck yourself!" screamed the woman, shaking a fist menacingly.

"Tara...? What's her surname?" Andy raised his voice over the chaos.

"Huh?" said the woman still glaring at the drunk.

"Tara what?" barked Andy, irritated and indigested.

"Don't get fucking snippy with me!" she snapped back. "She's in your files. Tara Rocks."

"Rocks? That her real name?" asked Andy.

"That's what she *said.*"

He typed 'Tara Rocks' into the computer on his desk and smiled as 'Tara Roques' was offered as a possible match. He turned the screen round so the woman could look at the mug shot. "Yeah! That's her." Andy pressed the print icon and reached over to retrieve the sheet.

"So, what are *you* gonna do to find her?" snarled the woman, leaning across the barrier and poking a finger in Andy's direction.

"I'm going to send this up to the detectives on the second floor and stress the importance of finding Justin's mom."

"The fuck he will!" snorted the drunk. "Yeah... DEFCON one, for you and Mizz Rocks."

"You shit for brains!" screamed the woman, dumping Justin on the floor, as she prepared for battle.

"Look!" bellowed Andy. "Here is Detective Inspector Raven and I am handing her the papers, as we speak.

Eleanor had adopted a low profile, as she headed past reception to the stairs, but apparently not low enough. Reluctant to get involved with the saga, she grabbed the print out and report sheet from Andy Harrison. "I shall give this my full consideration," she said firmly and put on a spurt towards the stairs. She could hear Andy Harrison's mollifying tones fade below her, as she sped up the stairs. Making her way along the second floor corridor towards her office, she glanced at the papers in her hand and stopped dead.

"What you got there?" asked Laurence as he stepped out of their office, his cheek conspicuously bandaged. Eleanor turned the sheet containing the mug shot of Tara Roques around and held it up to him. "Who'd you see?" she asked.

"It's Giselle..." began Laurence but Eleanor was already half-way down the stairs. "Isn't it?"

Lula-Bell Martin lolled in the chair and exhaled two giant funnels of smoke, whilst keeping the cigarette firmly clamped between her bronze coloured teeth. "I told him downstairs it was fucking important!" she raised her tattooed eyebrows and snorted.

"Did Tara say that she was going to meet anyone in particular?" asked Eleanor.

Lula-Bell shrugged, "I dunno. I don't remember her sayin'."

"Did she have any regular customers?"

"Well who don't?" responded Lula-Bell, with a coy smile. "Some clients get very attached." She winked knowingly but then her face turned stony. "But most are just douchebags!"

"Is it possible that Tara could have decided to move on. Leave Justin behind?"

"No, that's one thing she wouldn't of done. She wouldn't of asked me to look after him but there was no-one else," she shrugged. "I ain't no good with kids. Not that I'd hurt 'em or nothing. I just ain't the motherly type." Laurence struggled to keep his eyebrows from lifting judgmentally. The effort wasn't lost on Lula-Bell, who curled her lip contemptuously. "We ain't all Mother fucking Teresa!" she snarled.

"Did Tara have a boyfriend?" said Eleanor quickly.

"I never saw him but there was one guy who was interested in her."

"Interested how?" asked Eleanor curiously.

"Well he gave her presents and stuff. Weird shit mostly."

"Like what?" asked Eleanor, trying to keep the excitement out of her voice.

Lula-Bell sucked her teeth noisily as she thought. "Old shit. A comb and some hair stuff." She was getting bored and began to pick at a red, crusted patch on her cheek. Laurence winced.

"What?" she snapped.

"That sore," He pointed at her face. "Have you got them anywhere else?"

"What the fuck's it to do with you?" she asked, outraged.

"You have non-bullous impetigo and it's highly contagious." His voice trailed off as he saw Eleanor's face cloud with irritation.

"It's what?" asked Lula-Bell, studying her fingers for evidence of contamination.

"Impetigo. You need some antibiotics."

"What are you, a fucking doctor?" she spat.

"Yes, I am… I was," he replied cautiously.

"*Detective* Whitefoot *was* a doctor and is *now* a police officer," said Eleanor, by way of an explanation..

Lula-Bell leaned towards Eleanor, confusion squeezing her features. "So, you're a doctor too?"

"No, just Detective Whitefoot. He's special," she added.

"So you're gonna write a prescription for me then?" she asked Laurence..

"Urm no, I can't do that as I don't practise anymore," he replied, uncomfortably.

"Huh? I don't get that. You're a doctor but you don't do prescriptions? What the fuck!" with that she flung herself back into the chair, her arms raised in disbelief.

"Detective Whitefoot will get you a prescription when we've finished the interview." Eleanor ignored the look on Laurence's face. "Now tell me about the comb and the hair stuff."

"It was big and white. I didn't like it much and there were some hair clips but they were crap. Never stayed in your hair. I think she binned them."

"Were they heavy?"

"Listen can I go now?" said Lula-Bell, her urgent need to locate Tara considerably diminished now that Justin had been scooped up by child services.

"Could you describe the comb and the hair clips to an artist so she can draw them?"

"You're shitting me!"

Eleanor raised an eyebrow to convey the unlikeliness of that.

"How long is this gonna take?" she groaned.

"Do you know who this is?" Eleanor pushed the mug shot of Giselle across the table. Lula-Bell snorted. "Yeah it's..." She stared at the photograph. " Jeez, they could be twins!"

"How the hell am I supposed to get Lula a prescription," bleated Laurence, as he followed Eleanor along the corridor and past the interview rooms.

"You're a detective and a medical practitioner now, so it shouldn't be a problem," she said, stopping and staring at several metres of biohazard tape zigzagged across the entrance to Interview One. "What happened here?" she asked.

"Timms was interrogating Muntjack and saw some small louse-like creature run across his forehead. So he dragged him off for a shower and a dose of DDT," said Laurence smiling.

"Who's in Two?"

"Mo is talking to Tyler Baxton about his whereabouts last night."

Eleanor nodded.

"Wanna watch?" he asked.

She glanced at her watch and nodded.

Tyler Baxton's strangely elongated head lolled despondently in his hands, as he listened to Mo's questions. There were a couple of empty paper coffee cups littering the table, the one in front of Tyler had been systematically shredded and spread open in front of him like a flower. But all attempts at therapeutic artistry were long gone and he was now sinking into silence.

"How long have they been in there?" asked Eleanor, as she looked through the two-way mirror that allowed observations to take place without disturbing the process.

Laurence glanced at his watch. "About an hour. Any chance he did it?"

She shook her head. "Tyler isn't a killer, he's a sex offender. We're looking for someone organised."

"Keeping a body in cold storage for a couple of months and filling a coffin with sand bags requires organisation, surely?"

"No, it requires opportunity. I imagine Tyler has a fairly low IQ. He wouldn't be able to deal with or understand the intricacies of avoidance, planning, and execution. He watched the women's bodies being prepared and handled them with his father. A corpse would be non-judgmental of his appearance and therefore a source of comfort. He wouldn't want to be parted from them. As to his father, I imagine that he knew or at least suspected what his son was doing."

Suddenly Mo stood up and left the room. Eleanor went round to meet him.

"He's confessed," said Mo irritably. "The second he sat down, out it all came but none of it's matching what we've got. I pleaded with him to have legal rep but he wouldn't. I was hoping we could exonerate him quickly and get him back home but now I've got to get a psych evaluation set up and do the paperwork." He sighed heavily. "What do you want me to do with him?"

"Give the duty solicitors a quick call and see if they've got someone sympathetic who'll have a talk with him," suggested Eleanor. "And I'm sure psych owe us a couple of favours."

"Yeah, no problem," said Mo.

"In the meantime we've no choice but to keep him downstairs."

CHAPTER NINE

Toby had made an exception to the rules today and drove to and from work in his father's ancient but beautifully maintained Oldsmobile Super 88 Deluxe. It drew considerable attention from both colleagues and pedestrians. Attention was not something Toby wanted but just sitting behind the wheel and listening to the engine's heavy cardiac beat, made him feel like a man of considered taste. As he pulled the garage doors to and secured them with the double lock, he took a deep inhalation of breath. It was time.

The basement had been ready for weeks. Toby was extremely cautious when it came to purchasing chemicals and equipment. Never buy in bulk, as that drew suspicion. Never buy from the same outlet, and always stockpile. You never knew when an opportunity would arise to further the collection; neither could you anticipate when artefacts would need emergency conservation. He gritted his teeth at that thought and shook his head. He still couldn't account for the persistent mould that had covered Giselle's face and torso. There was nothing wrong or lax about his technique, which had been perfected over the past fifteen years. Admittedly, he had only just started experimenting with plastination as a preserving medium but it had produced some exceptional results. Whereas before he'd been content with the 'sleep-ers', now he had the means to create his family in life-like poses. Giselle had been a touch of genius. She had been given a room in the east end of the building, far away from his wife's. It would have been intolerable to have housed his mistress so close to his beloved Olivia. Never let it be said that Toby Adams was tactless.

Giselle's room had been a homage to fifties bordello chic. He had painted the room a deep purple-red and covered the bed with silk sheets and a thick burgundy bed-spread. The lighting had been dimmed almost to nothing and the dressing table was littered with authentic cosmetics and some extremely titillating night attire. His original idea had been to arrange her in a provocative pose across the bed but this new technique had allowed him to have her seated on the edge, in an attitude he described as 'come hither', mixed with 'not tonight!'.

As a youngster, Toby had stayed with a distant aunt on her farm in Vancouver. Nothing about the place had particularly caught his eye, apart from the cattle crush. A cow requiring either medication or artificial insemination was driven into the steel cage and then a lever was thrown and the box immediately concertinaed, clamping the cow into a vice-like grip. What had astonished Toby was that the animal, once clamped, didn't fight the process, rather it became strangely subdued and still. When he'd asked one of the farm hands why this should be the case, they'd replied that it calmed them, just like being swaddled calmed a baby. It was with this in mind that he had designed and constructed his own cattle crush out of domestic scaffolding and pipe insulation.

Tara had been placed inside it several days ago. Persuading her to get in hadn't been as easy as it was with

Giselle. He thought he'd have to resort to aggression but after explaining that it was just a 'little game' that would excite both of them, she had ventured in nervously. After chatting to her for several minutes, he had turned off the lights and left her there. She could, of course, move around because he hadn't applied the crush mechanism. Twice a day he'd cleaned up her mess, provided her with water and engaged in non-confrontational conversation. After the first few embalmings, Toby had decided that a couple of days' fasting would purge the subject's system and make his work easier and less unpleasant. However, experience had taught him that by denying water, the skin became less hydrated and more vulnerable to post mortem damage. Neither did he want any premature deaths. The art of preservation depended on precisely calculated chemical procedures and any short cuts or aberrations could lead to disaster.

Toby had already filled the 50 ml syringe with a saturated solution of potassium chloride and had placed it in a small kidney shaped bowl, covered with a hand towel. When he first applied the crush she fought like a cat and, somewhat surprised by this, he hurried the mechanism, only to find that she'd snapped her wrist as the arm-lock swept into position. He could hardly bring himself to look at her hand, which was twisted unpleasantly to the left, a little shard of bone having poked through the skin. There was a moment's silence before Tara began to howl. Big, lung-splitting animal howls. In a panic he lost his grip on the bowl and let the syringe skitter across the floor to within inches of her feet. She had instantly understood that a momentary hope was to prevent him from getting this and thrust her foot through the bars, stamping it onto the syringe and, allowing the needle to dig in, she scraped it back towards her. Fascinated, Toby stared at her face, which displayed nothing of the serenity to come. Her blood-shot enraged eyes were made more feral by the streaks of dirt and make-up. "You fucking bastard!" she screamed. He felt flecks of saliva spatter his face. "Let me out!" He waited; this was usually the preliminary stance to complete subservience. The rest of his collection had all begged and bartered for the release that would never come. Perhaps she was different to them, feisty, more unpredictable?

"I've got a baby! Please let me go! I ain't gonna tell anyone..." her voice trailed off as she saw Toby's expression harden. He was tiring of this stage of the proceedings now. The noise was intolerable and the longer he dithered around in here, the later he would have to work this evening. He lowered himself to the level of her feet. She was whimpering miserably, shaking her head at the injustice or the finality, he wasn't sure which. He squeezed her foot, lifted it and extracted the syringe tip from the soft pad of skin at the top of her arch. Her howls began to thrum his eardrums once more. He could have reassured her that he had calculated the necessary dose of potassium chloride by gauging her weight, calculating the LD50 dose and adding twenty per cent for good measure. He had dissolved the dose in 50 grams of warm water, ensuring that even if the solution cooled there was still sufficient water to stop any premature re-crystallisation of the compound. He knew that injecting such a large amount of salt solution wouldn't be distressing; that her heart would stop within minutes and that she would drift away peacefully like all of the others but he suspected she wouldn't listen, so he didn't bother.

Her pulse rate had fallen within ten seconds to a sluggish irregular throb. He held her undamaged hand as she struggled to maintain consciousness but one pupil was already beginning to dilate and her skin had taken on the all too familiar clammy sensation. Toby understood that the last sense to depart would be her hearing, so as he loosened the mechanism and gently extricated her from the apparatus, he spoke slowly and reassuringly to her of how loved and valued she would be as part of his collection. He placed his hand on her chest and waited as her breathing became low and sporadic. In several specimens there had been some spasm, so wary of this he lowered her onto the mattress in the corner of the room and waited, as patiently as he could, for the end.

There was always the temptation to hurry matters by multitasking but Toby had really clamped down on that aspect of his personality recently. He had noticed that, whereas previously, the technique had been the most exciting part, he was now becoming more enthusiastic about the post preparation period, where the new artefact could be arranged, displayed and enjoyed. Perhaps, he mused, it was indicative of his growing maturity and sense of responsibility. So, he focused his energies on the embalming process, not allowing the lure of cosmetic enhancement to detract him.

Tara lay naked on the dissecting table. The two studio lights positioned at the head and foot of the table made her appear more delicate than he'd expected. It had taken her heart nearly twenty minutes before it finally gave out, her brain, he supposed, had ceased to function within the first ten or so. Toby always shaved and sterilised first, as the stiffening caused by formaldehyde could result in unseemly razor burn. He used an electric shaver to take off the bulk of Tara's shoulder length, chemically overloaded hair, switching to his father's 'cut throat' ivory handled blade, which had to be handled with extreme care and a great deal of foam lubrication, if he was to avoid cutting the skin. Her face was a little too small and misshapen to accommodate the four-inch blade and, if he was honest, he only used the 'cut throat' for its historic value, so he switched to a disposable razor on her face, legs and underarms. The cut hair, foam and sloughed skin were rinsed away with a large bucket of warm water and not wanting to wade through organic mess as he tackled the embalming stage, he methodically sluiced it into the drainage grid positioned below the table. The house had originally been serviced by a large septic tank buried in the garden and although the plumbing in the upper floors was now all connected to the main water and sewage supply, the basement still filtered into it.

The only aspect of preparation that Toby disliked was the removal of the specimen's eyes. Not because he was particularly squeamish but because it required such a dexterous touch. He would have loved to have left them in but experience had taught him that they didn't respond well to the chemical processes and tended to dehydrate, sink and cloud over. So, having withdrawn most of the vitreous humour, to reduce the dimensions of the eye, he inserted a small metal evisceration scoop and carefully removed both, dropping them into a small glass jar filled with alcohol. Everything else was easy. Her eye sockets were plugged with appropriate plastic cups, to ensure that the glass ones would fit when the time came. Toby checked his watch, it had been three hours since her time of death and he knew that post mortem changes had already begun, despite the coolness of the basement there was already a slight stiffening of her jaw. With a practiced hand Toby carefully incised the carotid artery and inserted a threaded arterial tube, which he attached to his rather dated fluid pump. He then placed the drainage tube into the vein and capped it. Having performed at least twenty-five embalmings, he'd learned that a careful build up of the arterial pressure lead to better saturation. He'd give the pump a few minutes and then open the valve to let the blood drain. He'd recently adopted a formaldehyde product with a deep pink dye; this had the advantage of making the skin seem more vibrant and alive later on. Some of his earlier efforts had a rather cadaverous look and these less favoured specimens tended to receive less interest from him. He sighed and straightened his back, admitting that he was feeling rather tired now. As he stood vigil over the transformation he allowed himself a small glass of single malt, appreciating its warmth as it flowed through his veins.

It was well past eleven pm when Mo knocked quietly on her office door and stuck his head round.

"You're not supposed to be here," Eleanor replied, getting up from her chair and limping stiffly towards the door. Mo stood in the corridor; a large envelope tucked under one arm and two mugs of coffee balanced on top of a Tupperware lunch box in his hands.

"Yeah, says who?" he smiled and walked past her, placing the food on the desk and drawing up his chair.

"Minnie for one!" Eleanor closed the door and turned on the main light.

"I've been home, got yelled at and then sent out with supper for you," he said, carefully peeling open the plastic cover from the lunchbox. "From Minnie and she says she'll know if you ate it or me," he said shaking his head. "Though I'm fucked if I know how."

Eleanor smiled and looked at the chicken salad. "It's kind of her."

Mo shrugged and handed her a fork. "Eat!" She began to pick at the chicken. "Here!" Mo selected a sheet of paper from his file, placed it next to her and tapped it with his index finger. "While you fanny around with your food, read it."

Eleanor glanced at the heading, her eyes immediately picking out her handwritten name next to the typed heading, 'Patient'. It was a photocopied sheet and dated from the previous November.

"Sue Cheung says you're having difficulty swallowing…" ventured Mo cautiously.

"So much for 'just between her and me'," she snipped.

"I *am* 'just between her and you!" he said in an outraged tone. "You don't get to be treated as an individual when you have a partner. We are one. As soon as you agree to take a bullet for one another, you're closer than a marriage.

"But you're not my partner any more are you?" she said quietly.

"I will always be that. Always. We didn't get divorced, I just got old and fat."

Eleanor felt her throat tightening again; a thick band of leather cutting into her skin and rationing her air supply. Mo stabbed his finger on the paper again. "Read it." She skimmed through the mundane observations on urine output, ECG readings and temperature charts to the 'observations' at the bottom of the page. She read it through twice, struggling with the slanting script as much as the information it revealed. "Do you understand what it's saying?" Mo said quietly pushing the untouched supper closer to her.

"Where did you get this? I don't understand how you got this?"

Mo sighed, "Dr Blackmore gave it to me."

"And you read it?" she asked in disbelief.

"He *asked* me to read it and then make sure that *you* understood the implications," he said slowly. "Do you understand?"

Eleanor shook her head silently.

"Then read it again," he said firmly. "It says that…"

"I know what it says!" she could hear her voice bang against the walls of the small office. "It just doesn't make any sense. They didn't understand…"

"They did and they do," Mo said carefully. "It's you Ellie."

The silence between them hung for a minute before Eleanor spoke. "There's no damage to my throat."

Mo looked at her and shook his head. "There's no scar tissue. Nothing." She stared at the food in front of her, a pain radiating from the back of her neck around the crown and pulsing steadily between her eyes. Mo cleared his throat and turned the sheet of paper around. He pulled his glasses out of his breast pocket and slipped them onto the end of his nose. "'Eleanor complains consistently about a tightening of her throat, which is making swallowing extremely difficult for her. Both CT and MRI scans have indicated that there is some slight residual swelling but no evidence of any pathology. Nasal Endoscopy and Laryngoscopy show no trauma to area. Results forwarded to Psych.'" He waited.

"It's in my head."

"They think so," he replied.

"Do you?" She studied Mo's face carefully.

He sighed deeply. "Based on this and the conversation I had with Dr Blackmore… Yes. I think it's in your head but that doesn't diminish any of the symptoms. You're in pain and you're making it a physical one and that's why it won't get better. You're starving yourself to death because you can't or won't start your healing process. But" He pointed his finger at her. "You don't have to do this on your own."

Eleanor turned away and let her eyes defocus. "I'm tired," she said flatly.

Mo slid his hand over hers. "You need to get yourself home. Start eating, so you have the strength to do this job."

There was a pause as Eleanor shifted uncomfortably in her seat. "I need a bath."

Mo smiled. "Well you have to go home to get one. After you've eaten." Eleanor took a bite of the salad and grimaced. "You've gotta eat it all *and* in front of me so we can both suffer!" he snarled. "See how I share the misery!" Mo flung himself back into his seat. "I didn't get chicken salad for dinner. I had tofu! Fucking tofu!" They sat in silence for a moment or two while she slowly ate.

"You have paperwork," she nodded at the stack of paper hidden from view by a manila wrap.

"I do."

"It's not my entire hospital records from birth is it?" she said drily.

"It is not. It's interesting information from Sue Cheung. But…" he slammed his hand on top of the file. "You don't get it till I see you drive off in the direction of home." Eleanor smiled and nodded, polishing off the food as Mo watched her with approval.

As he saw her into her car, Mo handed her the file. "Minnie asked if you'd come and stay for a while." Before Eleanor could answer, he put up his hand. "I know what you're going to say but we're here and there's a room for you. Think about it."

She nodded. "Thank you." She started the engine. "By the way why did Blackmore give you my file? Isn't he liable under patient confidentiality?"

"You named me as next of kin when you were admitted," he replied quietly.

CHAPTER TEN

"Have you seen Toby yet?" asked Isabel Drake, poking her head round the door of his office.

Enda made a show of looking round the ten by ten foot room speculatively, much to Isabel's irritation. "Nooo," he drawled slowly and ominously.

"When he arrives would you ask him to page me please?" She withdrew quickly but Enda had managed to launch himself like a torpedo at the door giving her insufficient time to disappear from sight.

"Is there a problem Isabel?"

She could hear his feet paddling the floorboards as he hovered expectantly. "Just ask him to page me please. That's all," she replied without slowing down or turning around.

The museum wouldn't open for another hour and although she was grateful to every single patron who walked through the doors, she loved the echoing silence of the empty building before and after closing. Her heels clacked on the stone stairway as she made her way down from Admin on the third floor to the basement where Storage and Restoration were based. Below ground level and the temperature fell dramatically to somewhere between seven and twelve degrees Celsius, which necessitated the fleece that she'd flung over her shoulders. "Hello Jack," she smiled as Jacqui Harper, Head of Conservation jumped at her arrival.

KAREN LONG

"Good grief! I can't even accuse you of sneaking," she giggled, taking off her glasses and waving her hand in the direction of the chair on the other side of her neatly organised desk. "Social or business?"

"Mainly business," Isabel answered sitting down and placing a large canvas shopping bag on the desk between them.

"Shoot!"

Isabel sighed, "I think we may be mislaying some of our artefacts."

"Qualify 'mislaying'?"

Isabel carefully lifted out and opened a catalogue at a tabbed page and rotated it so that Jacqui could see. "Okay, why do you think this is missing?" Jacqui queried, placing her finger on a black and white thumbnail image of a piece of Mayan pottery.

"I'm not sure that it is, which is why I'm running this past you unofficially first. Look at this." Isabel extracted and opened a levered file filled with several hundred sheets of paper, each one covered in lists of catalogued items, accompanied by numerical identifiers. She located the corresponding tag line and presented it to her colleague. "What don't you see?"

Jacqui checked again and flipped through several other pages.

"Try this one!" Using her index finger she slid it under the next tagged page of the catalogue and turned to it. Memorising the numerical ID and item description, Jacqui turned to the corresponding file and searched.

"They're not listed," she said blankly and looked at the pile of catalogues that Isabel had brought. "How many?"

Isabel opened her hands and sat further back in the chair. "Of these catalogues, which span the last two years, I've located thirty-four anomalies."

"Thirty-four? That's impossible... surely?"

"It's not a calculating error for sure. I'd expect three, maybe five, at most but thirty-four items that were recorded and then disappeared from the computer log doesn't make any sense to me. Unless..." she raised her eyebrows.

"I'm going to need several days to check all of these," said Jacqui heavily. "Can I recruit help?"

Isabel slowly shook her head. "I'd rather you didn't, just yet."

Jacqui widened her eyes and then nodded. "Is it just the one member of staff?" she asked quietly. Isabel nodded. "All of these were the responsibility of one person to catalogue."

"Who?" Her voice was scarcely above a whisper.

"Enda Miller."

Eleanor arrived just as the paramedics were wheeling the gurney through the double doors of the main entrance. She spotted Andy Harrison encouraging members of the public to move back and clear some space and headed over. "What's going on?" she asked him.

"Marcus Baxton. He arrived about an hour ago, wanting to speak to either you or Whitefoot. He'd got himself pretty riled up. Next thing he was on the floor having a cardiac event. This is the result," he replied in an exhausted tone.

Eleanor headed over to the ambulance, just as the gurney was being prepared for transit. "Mr Baxton? It's DI Raven," she said to the grey, sunken face covered by an oxygen mask. Marcus Baxton's eyes, which had been closed, opened and focused on hers. "It's going to be alright. Tyler is going to be taken care of."

"Ma'am we're leaving," said a paramedic, lifting the gurney onto the vehicle.

She watched his eyes as they clouded with a mixture of hatred and fear. The doors were secured and the engine started.

"A day that starts with a crisis don't get any better in my experience," stated Andy darkly, as he retreated back into Police Headquarters.

Johnson was clearing the murder board with his usual degree of methodical enthusiasm when Eleanor walked into Homicide. Timms and Wadesky were arranging photographs and maps on a desk, ready to visualise the current case.

"You and Whitefoot need to brief in the next hour, ok?" said Timms, with barely concealed irritation. As he pushed photographs and papers around he managed to knock a pile onto the floor.

"What the fuck!" he bellowed.

"Right! Get yourself a coffee and pancakes in the canteen before I'm forced to shoot you for the good of mankind!" said Wadesky her hands firmly planted on her hips. Timms opened his mouth in protest. "I'm reaching," she hissed. Throwing his hands up in a gesture of surrender, Timms backed away from the table. "You are outta my sight for twenty! Got that?"

"Yes Ma'am," he replied, contritely.

"You come back fatter and happier!"

"What's happening?" asked Eleanor, helping retrieve the papers.

"Joe's hideous mother has told him he can't be Tess' godfather," said Wadesky, angrily.

"Was it the gun or the suit?"

Wadesky smiled. "Timms tries so hard it breaks my heart. You know he's set up a college fund for the two boys?"

Eleanor shook her head, surprised. Wadesky nodded. "He adores the boys. Takes them to ice hockey every other Friday, even goes to their school plays, which is more than I do."

"What does Joe say?"

"Joe doesn't want to disagree with the old witch."

"But you could…"

Wadesky nodded. "I *could* make a stand and tell Joe what to do but have you any idea how much shit Joe takes from me?"

Eleanor tried unsuccessfully to conceal her mystification at that concept.

"Exactly! He doesn't make a decision without running it past me first. I suspect he married someone like his Mama but don't quote me on that," she mused, re-organising the papers. "Just about the only goddamned decision I leave entirely up to Joe, is that he chooses who is godparent to the kids. Hell, he raises 'em. I just show up for the birth! So, if I bully him into choosing Timms against his Mama's wishes, I leave him without a shred of autonomy," she scowled.

"Who does Joe want to be godfather to Tess?" asked Eleanor.

"I think he's too scared to offer an opinion," chuckled Wadesky. "You wanna take the left?" she nodded to the board, pinning two photographs of Parminder Kaur in the middle, one ante the other post mortem.

"Look who shared my pancakes!" said a noticeably more relaxed Timms as he walked in, Monster and Whitefoot at his side. The dog sported a plastic collar the size and shape of a giant lampshade and had a large swathe of missing fur over his eye.

"I'm assuming Monster, rather than Whitefoot," quipped Wadesky.

"You bet your ass the puppy!" chirped Timms, rubbing Monster's back vigorously. "Ok what have we got?" he said running his eyes over the board, which was now busy with photographs of Giselle and Parminder both in life and death, a mug shot of Tara, a map with highlighted locations and a tentative timeline linking the three events.

"We're sure we are dealing with one perp?" asked Timms skeptically.

Eleanor nodded. "I think so. Giselle and Parminder were roommates. When Whitefoot and I approached Ms. Kaur on Monday evening she seemed genuinely not to have known about the murder. She went to work on Wednesday and was murdered in Tommy Thompson Park later on that evening. So far we've got no sightings or information from her workplace or apartment that she was meeting up with anyone. What we haven't got is her missing bike, which *may* have been used by her killer to leave the park and what we need to find out is whether she contacted her killer or vice versa."

Timms shook his head. "Nothing on her cell phone records that was out of the ordinary. Calls to and from mom, work, her room-mate and aunt over the past week and to her dentist, which we are looking into. Still checking the workplace landline but patrol have covered about sixty per cent, which all appear genuine so far. Mainly suppliers and people making reservations."

"Any reservations not kept?" asked Whitefoot.

"Yup and being checked out but seems genuine. So what is the thinking?" Timms said leaning back into his chair and looking pointedly at Eleanor. "How many perps we got here?"

Eleanor paused. "There's just the one." There was a palpable groan from everyone around the board. "I've got Ruby Delaware coming in any minute to take notes." All eyes turned to Timms, whose vocal opinions on the art and competence of profiling were well known to anyone who'd had the misfortune to sit in on a meeting attended by a member of the psych team and him.

"What?" he said. "Let it not be said that I will not listen and inwardly digest all of the bullshit put out by profilers. In fact, I feel that now we've got the likes of Doctor Delaware on board, the case is in the bag."

"Well I'm glad to hear that," said Ruby Delaware primly, as she sat herself down at the table and began to arrange her stationery.

"All ears," said Timms affably. "What are your thoughts doctor?"

"Well, firstly can I say how lovely it is to be working with you all again," her eyes frostily planted on Timms' face.

"Uh-huh! Great for us too doc," said Timms.

Wadesky had also focused her glare onto Timms.

"These are only my preliminary ideas and I will need more information if I am to proceed with any degree of accuracy. Firstly, I agree with Detective Inspector Raven that the killer of Richard Leslie Baker, also known as Giselle, is likely to have murdered before and is likely to kill again in the foreseeable future. The murder and subsequent preservation of the corpse is not unknown to forensic science but it's certainly unknown to me. This is a very unusual crime and requires intelligence, meticulous planning and strength of character. The murderer is a white male, probably of age range thirty-five to fifty-five, who lives alone and has done for some considerable time. He will most likely be a single child of older parents and have an above average IQ." Ruby paused and consulted her notes.

Timms opened his mouth but Wadesky shot him a ferocious look and it snapped closed again. A gesture not lost on Ruby Delaware, who lifted one eyebrow and pursed her lips.

"He is a *collector...*"

"What do you mean?" asked Eleanor, intrigued.

"He will place a great deal of value on possessions, particularly objects that are considered so by other people."

"An antiques collector maybe?" suggested Whitefoot.

"Possibly but I doubt he leaves much of a trail behind him. He will buy things for cash or steal things but not in an adventurous manner."

"So, it's unlikely that he's been picked up for burglary then?" asked Wadesky.

"Very unlikely. He's private, psychopathic, but most likely functioning within some form of social setting. I doubt it will be manual work though."

There was a pause. "I'm afraid until you have uncovered more evidence there's not a lot more I can add, apart from my belief – perhaps that's not the right word – my *suspicion* that he will look slightly out of place. His clothing and demeanour will be unfashionable. He will consider himself to be cultivated and sophisticated, which will be at odds with his appearance. I think it very unlikely that he surrounds himself with modernity or the trappings of. He won't have a mobile phone or a television but will be computer literate."

"Do you think it likely that he murdered Parminder Kaur?" asked Eleanor.

"Oh, I have no idea. That's one for you to link. It's certainly feasible but I'm a little surprised that he threw away the body. If he kills he will want to have the victims nearby. Possibly within his home."

"What sort of house would he live in?" asked Wadesky making notes as she spoke.

Big, probably inherited from his parents. He's very likely to have an obsession with security. No one will have access to this house, so it may need some work doing to it. He's likely to have rerouted his post to a mailing box," she added confidently.

"Perhaps," said Timms, pushing forward a sheet of blank paper. "You could jot down the address for us."

Ruby Delaware's lips pursed with irritation. "Of course," she said, pulling the piece of paper towards her and smiling. She wrote a couple of words and folded it in two. "I'm going to get my thoughts written up and sent to you as soon as possible. Thank you for photocopying the material and I shall be available whenever you need me. Tapping her finger on the paper and staring at Timms, she collected her belongings and made for the exit. Timms reached for it and slid it towards him, smirking. He unfolded it, read it and let out a bellow of laughter.

"You know I'm beginning to like the doc much more than I thought I would," he said pinning the paper with the words, 'Fuck You' written in Dr Delaware's delicate handwriting, onto the murder board.

Samuelson stared at the board. His eyes flicked from Giselle to Tara and then to Parminder. "What the fuck have we got here?" he said quietly. "You see a connection between these three vics?"

"Yes sir," replied Eleanor, getting to her feet and moving towards the photographs. "Richard Baker lived as a transsexual prostitute known as Giselle and disappeared approximately eighteen months ago. He was believed to have had a wealthy boyfriend, who was willing to set up home with him as his female partner. Parminder Kaur was his roommate and after learning from us that his burnt remains were found on the Westex Landfill, was found murdered in Tommy Thompson Park."

Samuelson screwed up his forehead and sighed. "Where does Tara Roques come into this?"

"Tara Roques disappeared three nights ago, leaving her toddler with a fellow prostitute," she replied. "It's my belief that the same killer, after disposing of Giselle probably due to escalating decomposition, replaced her with Tara."

Samuelson rubbed his forehead vigorously. "Based on what?"

"She could be Giselle's twin and appeared to solicit in the same area," she offered, with more confidence than Samuelson's expression merited.

"That's tenuous on a good day," he said shaking his head. "What about Tyler Baxton? I've heard he's a shoo-in for perp."

"I don't believe it to be him."

"Why the fuck not?" snapped Samuelson, irritated. "He carried out the exact same crime and was at large during the time period. You think we have a whole team of embalmers on the loose in the city, just waiting for that special someone to get the formaldehyde pumping?"

"No sir. Tyler Baxton was an opportunistic sex offender. He didn't murder anyone, neither was he responsible for the preservation of the women's copses he abused. The murderer of Giselle, Tara Roques and Parminder Kaur was a very different man."

"You don't even know that Tara is dead. She could have gone on a bender for a week! If we start finding links where there are none, we're going to be chasing our tails and not solving crime."

There was a long pause, as Eleanor held Samuelson's gaze.

"What do you think?" he said, turning to Timms.

Timms gave the board a final sweep. "I see what Raven is saying and think she's on to something."

"On to something? What the fuck sort of non-statement is that?"

Timms shrugged. "Best I can do."

Samuelson grimaced. "None of this is making me happy and I've just heard that Tyler Baxton's father had a coronary, while waiting for you –" he pointed an accusatory finger at Eleanor "– to turn up this morning. If he's not a contender, why is he sitting in a cell?"

"He was brought in for questioning and so far hasn't managed to convince either us or himself that he's innocent," said Timms.

"What does that mean? Is he going to confess to something he didn't do?" snarled Samuelson.

"Yes sir. He confessed," said Eleanor, carefully.

Samuelson threw his arms up in despair.

"However, Ms. Turner has just arrived to represent him," smoothed Eleanor. "She should be able to help clarify Tyler's statement for us."

"I want regular updates on this clusterfuck is that clear?"

Timms nodded sagely. "Roger that!"

"Yes sir," said Eleanor. With a final shake of his head, Samuelson left.

"Ok, what have we got to link these events, now that I've hitched my fortunes to it?" asked Timms stretching himself out and looking pointedly at Eleanor. She spread out a series of photographs and reports from the medical examiner's office.

"Ok, it's not a great deal and so far it's all circumstantial but the tox screen makes for interesting reading."

Laurence picked up a page and began to peruse.

"Giselle's tissues revealed large amounts of formaldehyde, eucalyptus oil and various synthetic dyes," said Eleanor.

"Regular embalming products then," said Laurence.

She nodded. "But there were also high levels of acetone and..." she checked her notes, "...tetraethoxysilane."

"That's a hardener isn't it? Used in plastination," offered Whitefoot, tentatively.

"What the fuck is that?" asked Timms.

"It's a method of preserving and hardening tissues, for the purposes of anatomical display," replied Eleanor.

"But that's incredibly specialist stuff. It takes anything up to a year to preserve one of these specimens. Von Hagens had an exhibition called Bodyworks, didn't he?" said Laurence tapping his pen against his teeth.

"Body*worlds*," Eleanor corrected. "There was a showing at the Ontario Science Centre in 2005 and 10."

"Anyone seen it?" asked Timms. Everyone shook his or her head. "Ok, so what do they look like?"

Eleanor pushed forward some colour prints of partially anatomised bodies. Some were freestanding, others were held in position by thin, supporting wires. One human form sat on horseback, its brain held in its right skeletonised hand, neither animal clothed in skin.

"What the hell are those? People spend money to go and see that?" said Timms. "Really?"

"Gives people an opportunity to see what they're made of. I think they're beautiful," said Laurence.

"Yeah well, that apart, how does this happen? How'd you make your own?"

"You embalm the body and then soak it in a bath of acetone. Then vacuum the acetone out and position the body. Then you seal it into a plastic cover and pump the hardener in and that sets it rigid. Have I got that right?" Eleanor said and turned to Laurence.

"I'm no expert but it sounds about right," said Laurence.

Eleanor turned her attention to Laurence. "Could *you* do this in the confines of your home?"

Laurence opened his mouth and then paused as he realised the importance of what he was about to say. "Not in an apartment but in a house, maybe."

"Could I? Someone without your medical knowledge or skills?" asked Eleanor.

There was a pause. "You'd have to have some awareness of chemicals and how to use them, so you weren't hurt. And be physically strong enough to manoeuvre a body around." He shrugged and glanced at the ME's toxicology report. "You'd have to have a basic technological grasp of how to rig up a vacuum chamber. But there's nothing here that I couldn't put together using high-street bought equipment."

"How long do these things last?" said Timms.

Laurence shrugged, "I guess if they're done well years, maybe tens of years upwards. The ones set in plastic could be centuries but I think you'd need to talk to someone who does the procedure, whether one that has the skin on is as good."

"Hmm, we know how Giselle died?" asked Timms.

"No indicators apparently."

"So *you* think that Tara has been or is in the process of being..." Wadesky drew air quotes, "plasticised?"

There was a silence, eyes on Eleanor. "I'd say so, yes."

"How we going to find her?"

"Ok, yes the link's come through now," said Laurence, after glancing at his phone's screen. "Can I contact you on this

number later? Fantastic, you've been incredibly helpful...
You too."

Eleanor lifted her eyes from the traffic and glanced at
him.

"Leda Schmidt, one of the techs at the University of
Michigan. They've been plasticising specimens for ten years
now, for the anatomy and med students. She sent me a link
and password to their teaching video, so I can take a look."

"It's round here," said Eleanor slowing the car to a crawl.

"There!" said Laurence pointing towards a break in the
houses and a newly painted length of railings. "Where you
meeting him?"

"There," she replied, pulling the Taurus over to the
right and squeezing between a portable hot dog seller and
a line of new cars, the majority of which sported 'Baby
on Board' and 'Mom's Taxi' stickers on the rear window.
Ahead of them, leaning against the entrance was a bearded
man, wearing a khaki uniform and official cap. He peered
at them and then made an acknowledging wave.

The blinding heat of the early afternoon, hit them hard
and both Eleanor and Laurence reached for their sun-
glasses before shaking hands with Jacob Hareton. "Gonna
be thirty-three degrees this afternoon. Let's grab a soda and
I can show you the files on Giselle."

A red-tarmacked pathway led them out of the sun into
leafy cool, its access clearly delineated into pedestrian and
cyclists by a solid white line. The area of grass beyond the
trees was heaving with pre-schoolers and mothers. Eleanor
noted that most toddlers were equipped with small cycles
and over-large helmets, in pre-anti-gender labelling pinks
and blues. Prams were invariably the three-wheeled, ergonomic models favoured by young, wealthy Torontans. She

doubted whether any of these families had to survive on less than a robust, six-figure salary.

"You get any social issues here?" she asked Jacob.

"Annex kids seem to consume as much sex and drugs as the less socially placed. But the graffiti tends to be grammatically better."

A timbered shed, tucked under two large oaks, served as Jacob's office. It was cool and cluttered and had an uninterrupted view onto a small lake. "Okay, this is all the info I've got on Giselle," he said, passing Laurence some paper-clipped sheets. "I remember her better than most due to the God-awful fuss she made."

"What annoyed her in particular?" Eleanor asked.

Jacob sighed. "We'd allocated a fairly large percentage of the year's grant to developing local park areas. I'm in charge of four other newly rehabilitated areas in the GTA. As a way to cut further costs and gain a little charitable funding, we teamed up with the Probationary Service and offered Community Service programs to low risk offenders. I had six parolees that season and most of them preferred to dig and clear weeds. Not Giselle. Never did a stroke of work and spent most of her time loafing around."

Eleanor passed him a photograph of Giselle. He nodded. "That's her."

"It says she worked over on the north side of the park for three weeks?" noted Laurence.

"That's right, the only job I managed to get her focused on was painting picnic benches over by the play area."

"Can we take a look?"

"At the benches?" asked Jacob puzzled.

"The area she worked in."

The play area was easily located by the cacophony emanating from the swinging, sliding, dangling children that played with the ferocity of gladiatorial combat. Jacob made a looping gesture as he indicated where the park benches were situated. "It was pretty different two years ago, as it was closed to the public."

"How often did you come over to check on her?" asked Eleanor. "And when you did was there ever anyone here? Someone not on the program?"

"Sorry I really can't remember. I didn't check that often because we were in the process of clearing the pond and it was pretty intense work."

Eleanor handed him a photograph. "Could that have been taken here?" she asked as Jacob peered at the partial image.

"That looks like the old bandstand." He pointed over to the left of their visual field. It was beyond repair, so we had it removed about eighteen months ago." He brought the photograph closer to his face. "You're gonna ask but I don't know who that is. Maybe if there was a little more of his face..." He handed it back to her.

"You've been very helpful. Thank you."

"Glad to help."

Laurence and Eleanor studied the street view that lay beyond the railings. The houses were detached two- and three-storey builds. Each was buffered from the traffic with a lawn area and either privet hedging, or a wall. "Didn't Ruby Delaware say that our killer would live in a big house, probably inherited?"

CHAPTER ELEVEN

Eleanor lay in bath water that was far too hot and felt the scar tissue on her leg shrink and tighten unpleasantly. Shifting her position she decided to ignore the discomfort and focused her eyes on the two photographs pinned to the mirror at the bottom of the bath. She wasn't, nor doubted she ever would be, a mother, and to her both photographs – one of Tessa Wadesky and the other, Rosalia Lombardo – looked like sleeping children, though she doubted whether Joe or Sarah Wadesky would agree. Perhaps to The Collector, as she was beginning to refer to him, it was difficult to differentiate between the living and the carefully-preserved dead. Or, maybe because the dead were more pliable and less judgmental than the living, they had greater appeal to a man who didn't fit into society with any degree of ease? He had inserted a cylinder that enabled him to have sexual intercourse of some flavour with Giselle and, by the look of the body from Mackenzie Webber's photograph, he had taken considerable effort in the dressing and presentation. Giselle would have to be seated and then manhandled into a more accommodating position, if penetration was to be achieved. She frowned and thought about Lola Andrews' hand. It had been firm to the touch, cold and irredeemably dead. So, what about that appealed to the Collector? Jeffrey Dahmer had wanted to keep his victims in a state of compliance, so killed them and kept their body parts. He'd kept some pieces in the fridge but his killing spree had all the elements of wanting to preserve the moment, not necessarily to create an aesthetically pleasing and useable sex object. The Collector was eluding her mentally. Killers, particularly those that murdered strategically, could be understood, anticipated and thereby captured but so far she had nothing.

She glanced at the bowl of uneaten rice she'd meant to consume but had left on the chair next to the bath and then at her shrinking frame. Her legs and arms were losing muscle tone and density and it was only a matter of time, she suspected, before she was deemed unfit for work. Growling, she sat up, ignoring the water that sloshed onto the wooden floor and the sudden tightening of her throat and began to spoon rice in mechanically.

Toby was frustrated with the pump, rather than concerned. It had been notoriously temperamental during its last usage, and time and storage had not improved its reliability. He wouldn't need it for another couple of days but anticipating further trouble he'd taken it to pieces, in order to ascertain exactly what the problem was. He suspected that his rather 'Heath Robinson' designs were probably the source. The system had been cobbled together using a combination of a vacuum pump, a homemade filtration system and various cooling and condensing sections that would clean and recycle the acetone. He rubbed his tired, sore eyes and treated himself to another glance at the wonderful creature that was metamorphosing in the tank.

The original 'tank' had been an old galvanised container, covered in a heavy perspex sheet. It had proved rather unwieldy, as the hole he'd managed to drill through to insert the tube wasn't a snug fit and on several occasions the tube had slid down into the liquid and flooded the pump. In order to seal the 'lid' he had applied a silicon medium, which had to be sliced away in its entirety for later stages of the procedure. This was time consuming and tended to make further sealing operations less effective. His second attempt had involved a chest freezer, which had seemed perfect, as its ability to lower the temperature of the acetone speeded up the process of saturation. Unfortunately, its size had meant that the body had been squeezed into an unnatural position, which shouldn't have mattered, but sections of the specimen had not been adequately suffused with either acetone or later the polymer and like Giselle, that body had begun to flatten, discolour and eventually decompose.

Tara had been suspended in two hundred and fifty litres of seventy-per-cent acetone. All the scientific papers recommended that the acetone be completely replaced at least twice before the polymerisation process began but the tank's construction and weight made drainage almost impossible, which was why he had designed the filtration and recycling mechanism; the very thing that now wasn't working. He sighed and put his hand on Monty's head, casually stroking him. He'd fix it, as he had all of the other problems, including the tricky subject of his future family planning. He'd plucked up the courage to present his thoughts and desires to Olivia and had been rewarded by her complete acquiescence. She loved the idea of having a child and the young lad he'd described to her filled her with maternal longing. He'd been absolutely right in his choice of Olivia as his wife. It was true that she was a little young for him but compared to all the others he'd been wedded to over the years, she'd proved to be the most enduring and desirable. He didn't want to bore her with all of the complications surrounding the acquisition of a child; that was his task as husband and provider. It was enough that she was willing to accept another's child as her own.

Eleanor turned off Dundas and tucked her car into a discrete temporary parking lot, next to a condemned building awaiting demolition. The area was dark and only a couple of hundred meters away from the Good Times. She wore a man's tailed suit with a white shirt, platinum shoulder-length wig and heavy eyeliner to make her natural features less discernable and her clothing more appropriate to the evening's theme. The street was alive with glitz, glamour and the falsetto shrieks of the partygoers. Sliding between the smokers, Eleanor made her way to the entrance, which was being patrolled ineffectually by an overweight bouncer dressed as Spartacus, whose attention was focused less on the crowds and more on easing the chaffing from his leather pant arrangement. A noisy queue had formed on the stairs leading up to the bar and dance floor, the hold-up seeming to be due to excessive red tape at the ticket booth. Eleanor allowed herself to be squeezed between two middle-aged men, dressed convincingly as Bette Davies and Joan Crawford in 'Whatever Happened to Baby Jane?' mode. A ripple of movement and momentary increase in the music caused everyone to take another halting step upwards. She relaxed and let her mind drift into neutral, allowing the snatches of conversation around her to swim in and out of her consciousness. Suddenly, "Daaarlinng... I knew you'd come!" and a pair of strong arms thrust through the collective sequins and grabbed her. "Come with me," whispered Madame Angela, as she was extricated and led through the crowds, past the ticket booth and into the bar.

It was filled to maximum capacity, if not beyond. The clientele were a mixture of opportunistic middle-aged men, un-costumed apart from shorts and T-shirts, mixed gender prostitutes, transvestites, whose costumes had been scrupulously selected and arranged, and transsexuals, a large proportion of whom seemed to be of Thai origin. Eleanor was ushered towards a table tucked strategically between the exit to the washrooms, the stairwell that led to the 'meet and make-out' rooms and which presented a panoramic view of the stage, dance floor and bar. Several chairs were tucked underneath the top, which had a large 'Reserved' notice propped against a bottle of chilling 'Grey Goose' vodka.

"I call this The Bridge," he giggled. "Keep my eye on everything and steer us out of trouble if necessary. How's the investigation going?" he asked, as he helped her to a seat and poured two glasses of vodka. "I've not seen anything about Giselle in the papers yet. However...." He leaned towards her conspiratorially, "...I did see that a young lady named as a Ms Parminder Kaur had been found drowned in TT park. Would that be?" he raised his eyes questioningly.

"The connection is being investigated," replied Eleanor conspiratorially.

Madame Angela nodded sagely. "Now, I've been doing a little bit of nosing around myself and have someone you might like to meet. Hang on... You good on your own for a few tiny mo's?"

"I am," Eleanor replied sipping the drink.

She watched as he sashayed through the crowds, tapping guests on the shoulder, smiling and air kissing his way across the bar floor, the pink beehive acting as a beacon. She sat back and absorbed the ambience, looking for anything that might tick a box in her head. A man, probably in his early forties leaning languidly against the bar, stared intently at her. He wore a simple dark suit and looked as if he'd just stepped out of a board meeting. He was surrounded by a determined gaggle of garishly dressed transvestites but so far hadn't given them more than a cursory glance. Eleanor wasn't entirely comfortable with this level of scrutiny and, after holding his gaze for several seconds, slowly turned her attention back to the crowds.

"Here she is!" declared Madame Angela, helping a clearly intoxicated 'Madonna' onto one of the chairs. The 'Madonna' spent a few moments trying to fix her focus on Eleanor but failing that let her gaze drift into neutral. "This is Chantelle and she was a personal friend of Giselle's. She's got a teeny bit of information that might help you." Madame Angela looked at the catatonic Chantelle and dug a couple of fingers into her ribs. "Tell Detective Whitefoot what you saw," hissed Madame Angela.

"When?" said Chantelle, unnerved.

"Remember, we were talking about *Giselle* the other day?"

"Giselle?" Chantelle looked mystified.

"The car!" said Madame Angela flinging her arms open in frustration. "You saw Giselle with her new boyfriend in a fancy car just before she disappeared."

There was silence as Chantelle worked her jaw, in an effort to clear her thinking. "It was an old car," she said with finality.

Madame Angela curled her lip in despair. "Sweetie, can you remember what sort of old car? You told me it was a fancy one. A classic."

Chantelle nodded helpfully. "It was an old car."

"Did you see the driver, Chantelle?" asked Eleanor.

"Old guy. He musta had money 'cos Giselle looked happy," she noted.

"Did they stop the car and speak to you?"

"Nah, Giselle just waved."

"Where did you see them?" asked Eleanor.

"They drove past."

Madame Angela sighed and leaned over to Eleanor. "She told me that they drove past her on Moss Park. That's Chantelle's special night patrol spot."

"I see. What were they doing Chantelle?" asked Eleanor.

"Jus drivin' I guess."

"Would you recognise the man Giselle was with?"

Chantelle looked at her with surprise.

"Ok, so was that the last time you saw Giselle?'

Chantelle shrugged. "Guess so."

"I need to find out more about the man who was driving the car."

"I said what I know."

"Could you identify the car in more detail?" she asked hopefully.

"I *told* you. It was an old car."

"Can you remember the colour or the make maybe?" Eleanor asked.

Chantelle pondered this. "It wasn't really coloured. More like grey or something."

"So it was dark."

Cantelle nodded carefully. "Yeah...Maybe."

"Was it a big car? Like an SUV or something smaller?"

"Look, them old cars look all the same don't they?" she replied, letting her eyes begin to stray to the bar.

Eleanor changed tack. "Did Giselle talk to you about her new boyfriend before she disappeared?"

Chantelle pondered this, "I don't remember. She might have but it was so long."

Having shooed Chantelle unsteadily on her way, Madame Angela beamed at Eleanor. "Well that just might help," he said optimistically. Eleanor raised an eyebrow unconvinced. Madame Angela smiled and shrugged. "Maybe Chantelle will sober up and remember a little more…But I doubt it."

"Is there anyone else here that knew Giselle?" asked Eleanor, her gaze slipping to the figure at the bar, whose eye was no longer on her but roaming across the sea of availability.

Madame Angela sighed and topped up her glass, Eleanor declined. "Well I'm not sure… Everyone tends to appear to be very chummy with everyone else but it's not like real friends, if you get what I mean."

"Perhaps I'll go mingle," said Eleanor, standing up. "Thank you for your hospitality."

"It was my pleasure."

As she made her way through the crowds, a hand grabbed her. Chantelle, a colourful cocktail precariously tilted in her right hand, used the other to anchor herself to Eleanor. "I remember something," she hissed into her ear. "Giselle said his eyes made her feel sick."

"Why?" replied Eleanor, ignoring the cold liquid that splashed onto her leg.

"Dunno. But she said it was disgusting."

"Can you remember *anything* else?" asked Eleanor after several seconds of swaying had passed. Chantelle slowly shook her head. "I'll give you my card." Eleanor slid her hand into her pocket and selected a card.

"No, I have one for *you*," she smirked. Letting go of Eleanor's arm, Chantelle handed her the drink, while she extracted a business card from amongst an eclectic and optimistically large collection of condoms in her small purse. "From him," she turned to look at the man in the suit, who leaned against the bar. He tilted his glass at Eleanor and then turned his back slowly to them. Puzzled, Eleanor turned over the card. There was no name just a cell phone number below a black and white yin/yang symbol.

It was three am when Eleanor opened the door to her apartment, letting it slam shut behind her. She felt a momentary twinge of conscience as she heard her next door neighbour's elderly pug yap in surprise. Stripping off her clothes she balled and flung them into the wash basket, extracting the card from her pocket, before quietly closing the door to the laundry room. Grabbing a box of make-up wipes, she began to vigorously work at the heavy eyeliner, watching as it bled across her cheeks. Turning on the shower, she stepped in before it had had a chance to run warm.

Eleanor woke a little after seven am, bathed in sweat and feeling nauseous. She flipped on the air conditioning unit and wondered why she'd turned it off the night before. She had just turned on the coffee maker when her cell rang. "Is that Detective Raven?

"Speaking."

"This is Larry Beatman from Westex Landfill."

CHAPTER TWELVE

Whitefoot loosened his collar and glanced critically at the acid blue sky and then sceptically at Larry Beatman. "So, you're saying that you knew absolutely *nothing* about this?"

Larry shook his head vigorously from side to side. "Bolt outta the blue!"

Laurence narrowed his eyes and watched as the cars, vans and mobile forensic units kicked up clouds of dust as they rolled towards the security gates of the landfill site. He could see Eleanor standing outside Mackenzie Webber's hut leaning into him, listening intently. Mackenzie appeared to be crying. Laurence sighed. "You think he's lying?"

Larry shook his head. "He's scared and doesn't want to get into any trouble."

Laurence snorted. "Bit late for that!" The silence grew for a moment or two. "So how many did he say he'd found?"

"Dunno. He don't seem to think like that. Things don't seem to link together as they do for other folks." Larry made a complex gesture with his hands, as if trying to illustrate Mackenzie's elliptical thought processes.

Laurence gave him a hard stare.

"He seemed to think that there might have been a few... Maybe two or three," said Larry, cautiously.

"*Jesus.* Have you any idea of the implication of this? And he never mentioned this once?" asked Laurence.

"If he'd told me that he'd seen three or four bodies, don't you think I'd have called you?" said Larry desperately.

Laurence pursed his lips and watched Eleanor going through the motions with Mackenzie of trying to pinpoint an area on a map that might reveal more bodies.

Eleanor was making her way over now, a miserable looking Mackenzie lagging behind.

"We need to start about here," she said to Laurence pointing to an area of the site at least half a mile away from the entrance.

Timms stood on a peak of the undulating landfill and sighed deeply. He looked at the sullen faces of the CSI teams, the police department and the cadaver dogs with their handlers and waved his hand in a gesture of defeat. "Okaaay, this is a thousand acre site, which has been constantly tamping down Toronto's unwanted shit since nineteen eighty-six. According to Mr Webber over there –" he jabbed a finger towards Mackenzie, who was leaning unhappily against a spade he'd brought along to show willing, "– there could be between two and four bodies that have been preserved in much the same way as Richard Leslie Baker was. Mr Webber *didn't* report this..." He raised his voice a few decibels. "Because he's a fucking moron! So, we will now have the pleasure of digging in thirty-four Celsius heat until we find these bodies! According to Mr Webber, the bodies were all wrapped in black plastic bags and had been placed in this area. *However*, his memory appears to be a little vague on these matters." Timms scowled at Mackenzie and then at the assembled agencies. "Any findings should be reported to any of the detectives on the first four numbers of the call sheet."

Timms made his way over to Eleanor and Laurence. "He give up anything else?"

Eleanor shook her head,

"Do you believe there are more bodies here?" asked Timms.

Eleanor gave herself a second or two to rethink and then nodded. "They're here."

Timms snarled and leaned closer to Mackenzie's terrified face. "If you don't start trying to remember where and when you saw those bodies, I'm gonna get the psych department to stick some electrodes to whichever part of your anatomy does the thinking and zap some recall into you. Are we on the same wavelength?"

Mackenzie nodded furiously but unconvincingly.

Tommy Banks was, thought Toby, one of the most beautiful children he had ever seen. His hair was ash blonde and delicate; the fringe a little too long over his eyes and there was a bloom of coloured ink at the corner of his mouth, where he had sucked on his pen. Tommy was drawing a barn owl and every now and then he'd lay down his pen and surreptitiously stroke the feathers of the beautifully mounted specimen that Toby had provided for him. Most of the children, grateful that their parents had dumped them and departed, were racing around noisily, manhandling the irreplaceable fossils, minerals and bugs, much to Toby's irritation but Tommy sat quietly and drew.

Tommy always elected to sit next to a disabled girl, who's name Toby didn't care to discover. She had a tendency to dribble and her hands would frequently shoot out uncontrollably and knock artefacts over. It warmed Toby's heart that his child would pick items back up and make sure that she could reach them and access the crayons and paper. This seemed like a pointless exercise to him, as the girl was incapable of rational thought or movement and tended to put the crayons in her mouth, rather than try to create a picture. However, the desire to do good by his fellow child was a pleasing social grace in Toby's mind and attested to the boy's good manners.

Tommy was fidgety, squirming in his seat and letting his hand slip between his legs, while he painstakingly drew the feathers. Toby leaned forwards and spoke quietly to him. "Do you need to use the bathroom?" Tommy's eyes met his. They were large blue eyes with a watery, crystal quality that sent a spasm of affection through Toby's heart. He loved this boy already and felt his throat catch with emotion as he looked at him.

Tommy considered and then shook his head.

"It would be embarrassing for you if you wet yourself, wouldn't it?" said Toby carefully.

"I know where it is," Tommy replied, standing up and pushing his chair under the table.

"Your mother, Rosheen said that you weren't allowed to use the toilet on your own. You need someone to come with you," said Toby, authoritatively. He had never spoken to Tommy's mother and had little desire to but knowledge was power and he had already acquired the child's address and information on his likes and dislikes from the class register.

The boy was now crossing his legs uncomfortably but seemed reluctant to commit.

"I'll take you," said Toby pleasantly.

Clutching at his crotch, Tommy nodded and headed for the door nearest to the washrooms but Toby had other plans. "Let's use the ones near my office," he coaxed. "They're nearer."

Tommy glanced at the door and then followed Toby. A female colleague looked at him questioningly but Toby ignored her and carried on.

The corridor that ran behind the 'Touch and Learn' room was long and un-windowed. Toby noted with pleasure that the boy, who had kept an arm's length from him up to this point, was now creeping closer as they walked into the darkness.

"You're not frightened of the dark are you Tommy?" he whispered.

Tommy clamped his mouth tightly shut and shook his head.

"Good, because only weak children are afraid of the dark," said Toby quietly. He listened to the change in the boy's breathing. It was becoming shallower, less relaxed.

"I don't think this is the way," said Tommy, nervously looking behind him.

"Nearly there," replied Toby brightly. "Here we are." He unhooked a heavy loop of keys from his trouser belt and slowly selected the correct key.

Tommy hopped from foot to foot.

"Here it is, " said Toby, showing him a key with an orange plastic loop surrounding the head. He smiled at Tommy's face, which was pale and screwed up with discomfort. "I told you it wasn't far." With deliberate care, he slowly unlocked the door and held it open for the child. Tommy dashed in and headed for a cubicle, fumbling with his shorts he was too preoccupied to close the door behind him. Toby leaned against the sink and watched him silently. With a final pull, the boy loosened the button, dropped his shorts and pants around his ankles and, rising on his tiptoes, began to pee.

Toby relished the little sigh of pleasure from the child as he emptied his bladder.

He took in the child's slender body and pale skin as he bent to retrieve his shorts and savoured the elation that came when a new member of his family was finally selected and accepted by him.

Tommy turned round, startled to see Toby smiling and scrutinising him.

"Don't forget to wash your hands Tommy. Toilets are very dirty places," said Toby holding out a paper towel.

The row started about twenty minutes before the day was called. Monster, who had spent most of it in a state of terminal decline, draped across a tarpaulin stowed near to the mobile coffee wagon, had suddenly galvanized himself into action when a german shepherd bitch had arrived as part of the cadaver location team. He had managed to finally rid himself of the huge collar, together with most of the stiches, and was traipsing happily behind the bitch and her less than happy handler Police Constable Margie Beech, bleeding profusely from the now gaping head wound. PC Beech had sent several requests to have Monster removed but so far no action had been taken. Irritated and in need of an iced coffee, PC Beech put a lead on her own dog, Chance, and began to make her way back to base, Monster following purposefully behind. They were within shouting distance of the base when Monster began to dig. Allowing Chance to go and investigate, PC Beech was rewarded by the steady barking that indicated a find.

"What the hell sort of person lets a dog bleed to death in front of them?" bellowed Timms as he applied a towel to Monster's head.

"What sort of dog owner allows their dog to wander around a potential scene of crime when it's neither trained nor adequately protected!" hissed PC Beech, her gloved fist balled with exasperation.

"This dog holds a distinguished conduct medal!"

There was a pause as PC Beech assimilated this information with some difficulty. "I called Detective Whitefoot several times…"

"Yeah?" snapped Timms into his radio, holding up his hand.

"They've found one," said Eleanor's voice.

"Are you sure you are looking at a *human body*," asked Samuelson, emphasising every word in case she hadn't worked out the media consequences of the Toronto PD being caught tenderly zipping a lump of plastic into a body bag and carting it off to the ME. The Westex Landfill site had effectively been under siege for the last four hours. As news had seeped out that the police had closed off over half of the tipping area because bodies were being dragged out, the press had arrived in force. Satellite dishes, tripods, cameras and sound equipment barricaded the main entrance to both north and south access, accompanied by irritated journalists and news presenters, all eager to stake a claim in whatever information seeped out.

Eleanor stared at the body. It was female and although it had integrity, it was obviously beginning to decompose. The skin on its face was rigid and had a peculiar plastic sheen. The head was completely bald and one of the glass eyes had been fractured and was missing the iris. Even Timms had had to admit that if you were into single figures on the IQ scale and weren't expecting to find a body, you could be tricked into thinking this might be a mannequin of some flavour.

Laurence, wearing a paper bio-suit stood in the sea of crushed tins, used disposable nappies, discarded tins and plastic bottles and under the watchful gaze of a crime scene officer, examined the body. Finally he turned to Eleanor and nodded.

"I can assure you that the remains we have located are those of a human being that has been subject to some form of preservation," said Eleanor, nodding back.

Samuelson groaned. "I want it moving without fanfare or comment to the morgue. Is Hounslow attending?"

"She's agreed to meet us there."

"Keep me informed," he hissed, before disconnecting.

Toby sat quietly on the bus shelter bench opposite the boy's apartment building and pretended to study a newspaper. He had been sitting there patiently for the best part of an hour and knew that any time now he would get a glimpse of the child he was so desperate to call his own. He'd made a quick recce of the site earlier, making sure that he never strayed too far from the public right of way. The Banks' apartment appeared to consist of a living area off a shared hallway and a small shuttered bathroom window to its left. The building was long and counting the doorways indicated that it probably consisted of twenty apartments, ten along the ground floor. Cutting between the buildings was a short alleyway, which opened onto a small car park, festooned with 'Private! Residents only!' signs.

Pulling a set of keys out of his pocket, so he'd appear to any nosy soul as though he belonged, he wandered over to the back of the Banks' apartment. He had been pleased to see that there were no air conditioning vents attached to the rooms, which indicated that bedroom windows would have to be opened during the evening. Giving himself less than a minute to examine the layout, Toby peered into the first room, which obviously belonged to a young woman. He scanned to make sure there wasn't an adjoining door to the second bedroom and then slid over to the second room. He felt a frisson of relief when he saw the train set, child's bed with a Buzz Lightyear duvet cover and neatly folded shorts and T-shirts on the small pine chest of drawers. Of the grandmother's room there was no sign and he surmised that it must be located somewhere between the living area and her daughter's bedroom. A quick glance at the base of the sash window revealed a homemade security lock, consisting of a wooden jam that was pushed into one side of the frame to prevent the window being opened higher but strong fingers and a stretch would release it in a moment.

'Little Tommy', as Toby was beginning to think of him, looked exhausted and tearful as he kept up with the woman. He'd seen them both alight from the tram, Rosheen carrying a heavy plastic bag full of groceries. Little Tommy was reluctant to hold her hand and he'd smiled as the boy folded his arms petulantly across his chest and twisted his mouth down in a comic gesture of unhappiness. Rosheen had tried reasoning with him for several moments before grabbing one of his wrists and dragging him in the direction of her apartment. As they scurried across the road, Toby understood that all his searching for the perfect family was about to come to fruition. He had never doubted that his Olivia would make the perfect mother and now that marriage was to be consummated with a son. A son who would never grow old; never argue with his parents or cause them concern for his well-being.

Toby felt elated

I wanted to do some initial checks before identifying this lady," said Dr Hounslow.

"Identifying?" butted in Eleanor.

She was rewarded with a scowl and pursed lips from Dr Hounslow. "Perhaps I could speak first detective, before you bombard me?

She pulled back the green morgue sheet and invited everyone to move a little closer. "Now, there are clues here. What do you see?"

"She's abnormally tall and her limbs are slightly elongated," ventured Laurence. "She has a genetic disorder... A syndrome of some description, which is why you believe you can identify her."

Dr Hounslow smiled. "Care to take a stab at which syndrome?"

"Marfan?" he replied.

"Excellent. You are correct on all counts. Marfan, for those amongst us not fully conversant with the condition, is a genetic disorder that affects fibrillin production, ultimately leading to the excessive growth in limbs that you can see here..." She pointed to the hands and feet of the victim. "And can cause heart defects and lens dislocation. As the eyes have already been removed this is not something that we can check. However a scan may reveal any damage to the aorta and, if it is Marfan, then I have reason to believe that this *may* be a young lady who disappeared approximately three years ago called Michelle Brown."

"How'd you know this?" asked Eleanor, ignoring her expression.

"First, Marfan is unusual, affecting one birth in every five thousand and second because I autopsied her mother, who committed suicide following her daughter's disappearance and presumed murder. She was a Marfan sufferer but in a mild form. Now, I imagine you detectives have a great deal of work to do investigating this and as this autopsy is going to be unusual if not…"

"How did you know her name?" asked Laurence.

"Because her mother worked here as an office cleaner for ten years."

Detective Smith was not in a particularly positive state of mind. Up until this morning he had been enjoying life as the primary on a case involving stolen vehicles, schedule three and four drugs and a gang of criminals who, much to his pleasure, always resisted arrest. In fact, Smith was just preparing to attack the mountain of paperwork this sort of case generated, when he was dragged back into the Michelle Brown saga by Eleanor Raven. Smith had worked the Brown case for six months, off and on, finally having to place it in the 'cold case' files when every single lead went cold. Periodically he'd open the file and make a couple of phone calls, or check on a 'Jane Doe' that appeared in some distant morgue but he knew that nice girls like Michelle Brown didn't just walk away from their lives on a whim, particularly not for three years. He had tried, unsuccessfully as it turned out, to keep a little flame of hope alive in her mother Liza for no other reason that it did no-one any harm to live optimistically but the woman hadn't clung to that; instead she'd celebrated Michelle's twenty-first birthday with a pack of diazepam. Having only a peripheral knowledge of Raven's latest case, he found it difficult to grasp the information as presented to him by Matt Gains, the mortuary assistant. He shifted the phone from one ear to the other and tried to formulate a sentence. "So, you're saying what exactly?" he managed.

Matt began again, this time a little slower. "Doc Hounslow seems to think that this might be the daughter of Liza Brown. She's scanning the body due to its condition, so there shouldn't be a problem with the father identifying whether it's Michelle or not."

Smith took a moment or so. "So, when does the doc think she was killed?"

"Could've been a few years ago I guess. Maybe you should see the body yourself," suggested Matt, helpfully.

Smith sat in the car and rubbed the back of his head vigorously. He had formulated several opening gambits but he couldn't see how any of them would take the insanity out of the situation for Bob Brown. Turning off the engine and steeling himself, he walked up the narrow steps to the small house and tentatively knocked. He could hear Bob's halting tread as he hesitated over whether or not to open the door. Smith allowed him the few seconds before his world was turned upside once again and straightened his tie.

"It's Detective Smith here Mr Brown. I called you earlier."

Bob Brown raised his eyes and looked at Smith with a mixture of ferocity and hopelessness. "You've found her then?" he lifted his chin and squeezed his lips together, as if afraid some inappropriate remark would escape.

"This isn't the place Bob. I need you to let me in so we can talk."

Smith followed Bob along the corridor and into the small kitchen, which he'd remembered as being filled with photographs of Michelle at various stages of her short life. The fridge had been stripped of these memories and now stood starkly functional next to a small, uncluttered worktop. Sighing heavily Smith pulled a chair out for Bob Brown and encouraged him to sit. "We've found her Bob," said Smith quietly.

Bob nodded slowly. "Where?"

Smith sighed and launched himself into the story. "Michelle's body was buried in the Westex Landfill site…"

Bob made a small involuntary yelp and then tightened his hands onto the sides of the chair in an effort to maintain some sort of anchorage. "When was…"

Smith was determined to present the information in one large dose. "At the moment Doctor Hounslow isn't sure but it's likely that she had been dead for some considerable time. Possibly around the time she went missing." He let this small glimmer of hope give Bob the strength for the next stage. "It seems that the person who murdered Michelle also… preserved her body in some way."

"What? How do you mean?"

"She was embalmed."

"Like at a funeral? I don't understand what you're saying."

"We think that whoever murdered her embalmed her and kept her in his house for a while before disposing of her remains."

"What the fuck for?" yelled Bob launching himself to his feet, his hands shaking uncontrollably. Smith wiped his brow and neck with his handkerchief. "We don't know yet. There's no obvious sign of how she was killed."

Bob slowly sat back onto the chair. His shoulders sank and his arms moved protectively round his chest. His breaths were irregular and caught in his throat.

"Bob you have to do one more thing for Michelle… You have to identify her for us."

"Is she… viewable?" Bob asked carefully.

Smith nodded. "Doc Hounslow and me will be with you."

CHAPTER THIRTEEN

Eleanor stood on the highest point overlooking the excavation site and watched as the cadaver dogs swarmed over the mountains of tamped down waste, followed less enthusiastically by their overheated handlers. A private company was setting up a grid for the ground penetrating radar team and a group of police cadets were being instructed and equipped by a uniformed officer. The initial premise that Michelle Brown's body had been put into a dumpster and then transported, along with other waste to the site, had been dismissed by crime scene, who had analysed the disturbance to each layer and found evidence of later digging and re-covering of the trash. That implied that the murderer had brought the body to the landfill site and personally disposed of it there. That, Eleanor thought, was taking quite a risk.

Laurence was picking his way up the hill to meet her. She held out her bottle of water for him, noting with interest that he didn't bother to wipe the neck as he drank down to the last inch. She indicated he finish it. "Thanks. " He caught his breath.

"Who's winning?" she asked.

"My money's on Samuelson. City authorities have now cited health and safety and world health organisation guidelines as their argument for not closing the site in its entirety. The boss is going to put his views on the matter to the mayor, who's siding with his buddies, particularly as not collecting trash in summer is a major vote loser. So, I'm guessing there'll be a compromise and the west quadrant will be re-opened this afternoon and we'll have access to others for at least two to three days."

"It's not enough time," said Eleanor, shaking her head.

Laurence shrugged. "Unless they get wind of another body in the next forty-eight, we'll be restricted to this spot only."

Eleanor chewed her lip. "Maybe, this is all the space we need."

"You think they're all here, in this stretch?" asked Laurence.

"We are pretty certain that the body we're calling Michelle Brown, was not brought in by an unknowing third person."

"So the perp brought the body in and buried it," stated Laurence.

"If he brought in one body, then why not more?"

"But how'd he get them in here?"

"Has Johnson looked through the tapes?" she asked.

"He's doing it now but they only get stored for ten days before erasure, so unless we find a newly buried one, that can be linked to a car arrival, they're not going to help."

"Ok, but assuming he got one in by himself, let's find out how," she said, handing him a map of the site.

Laurence and Eleanor made their way down towards the concrete-pillared, steel-meshed security fence that separated the landfill site from the link road and its surrounding industrial units and fields. It was at least a quarter of a mile from Michelle Brown's grave to the fence. Eleanor looked at the map of the site, which had the definite body find marked in red and a larger green circle that indicated where

Mackenzie thought he'd found Giselle, which conveniently overlapped. She looked at the length of ten-foot-high panelling that ran for half a mile to their left and connected to the official entrance and at least two miles to their right. Picking her way through the increasingly dense foliage, she put her hands on the mesh and shook it. It was solid and didn't budge an inch. "He can't have gotten through here," she said. "But that's not to say that they're all like that."

"I'll go left," said Laurence, shielding his eyes and gazing at the overhead helicopters.

"Call me if you make a find. Press will be listening to the radio channels."

He nodded, checked his signal and headed off.

Eleanor had examined nine sections before she hit pay dirt. The panel was identical in every way from the others, apart from a slight yielding when she applied pressure to the sides. Whereas the others had no give as they had been welded to the steel uprights, this panel made a clanking sound when it was shaken. As she examined the panel she could see that there were a number of flat-headed bolts. She pushed her fingers through the links and felt along the bar. Every half metre or so she could feel but not really see, even with her cheek pressed against the wire, a small bolt standing proud of the post. She reached for her phone but waited while a helicopter's drone overhead diminished. "I think I've got it!"

She took a step backwards and assessed the panel. The mesh was too narrow to get a booted foot into but if she braced herself with her feet and knees she could pull herself up to the top and slide between the panel and the wire lip that lapped the fence. She zipped up her jacket and slipped on a pair of leather gloves. Pulling herself to the top, she was forced to pause and wait for a surge of energy to propel her over. As she flung her right leg laterally, she felt a sharp tug on her waistband and then felt two strong hands grip her leg.

"Come down. I'll do it," Laurence said, in a manner just shy of condescending.

Eleanor felt a sudden overwhelming surge of anger "I am not a fucking invalid. This is my job!" For a moment she felt like laughing at her over reaction then took a measured breath. "I'm fine," she managed, in a more controlled tone.

Laurence sighed and loosened his grip on her leg. "At least let me help you."

Eleanor needed to move, her leg was burning and her hands beginning to throb as they took her weight. "I'm fine, just make sure I don't snag on the wire."

"With three irritatingly confident bounds, Laurence pulled himself up to the top of the panel and pushed the wire as high as it would go, enabling Eleanor to slide between it and the panel. As she lowered herself through she felt his hand run along her back, smoothing her jacket down. She glanced at his face, which betrayed nothing more than sibling concern. "Thanks," she snapped, easing herself over and letting her shaking legs brace her as she established her grip with both hands. Lowering herself to the ground, clamping her jaw tightly closed so as not to betray the discomfort she felt, Eleanor began to study the edges of the panel. "The others have all been welded to the uprights. It looks as if someone's angle-grinded the join open and then drilled –" she counted the bolts "– five holes on either side and used nuts and bolts to fix it to the upright. She patted her pockets but Laurence, anticipating her need, pushed his Leatherman through the mesh; he'd already opened the pliers for her. Removing the nut, she wiped the glove against its edge and sniffed. "Smells like a mechanical grease."

"Ok, let's get Crime Scene down here and see if there are any..." A car speeding along the link road applied its brakes and mounted the grassy divide, heading straight for Eleanor. The SUV shuddered to a halt and Claddis McAvoy, the *Toronto Times* journalist, eased himself out of the passenger seat and made his way over to them. "*De*-tectives, what a pleasure," drawled Claddis, beckoning his photographer to get into position behind them. "Is there a problem with your phone detective?"

"Not that I'm aware of," she snarled.

"Because I've been leaving you messages regarding a deal we made last year and here you are top cat on a new front pager and me not getting first dibs on the coverage!" He sighed dramatically to emphasise his disappointment. "I put my neck on the line to help you and repayment included an exclusive interview."

"You broke the law McAvoy and the only reason you have a job to put your neck on the line for, is because we didn't press charges," said Laurence, angrily.

Claddis waved a hand dismissing the relevance of this. "No-one gave a shit about that but lying to the press has consequences." He raised his eyebrows and wagged a finger in Eleanor's direction. "So when am I getting face time with you?"

Eleanor felt her pulse rate escalating. "There is no interview."

"You took hell of a beating at the hands of Lee Hughes didn't you? Off work for six months and *still* under the regular care of psychiatric services, I'm surprised that you're allowed to be the primary on such a case. How many now? Two bodies found here and by the looks of the images they were all buried recently!" He slipped his hand into his satchel and brought out a pile of aerial photographs documenting the morning's efforts. "That helicopter's a godsend. Nothing escapes it... certainly not you Detective Raven!"

Eleanor was becoming aware that her breathing had changed and that both her fists were balled tightly. In an effort to regain control she drew in air through her nostrils and let it out slowly through her mouth. Claddis turned to his photographer who was fiddling with a camera setting. "Make sure all of this is documented will ya? Perhaps some engaging pics of Detective Raven here looking battle torn but ready to take on the bad guys for the City once more." With improbable alacrity, the photographer positioned the camera to his face, focused the lens onto Eleanor and began to gather images mechanically. Claddis leaned towards her, bombarding her senses with coffee fumes and body odour. "Maybe," he whispered theatrically, "unburdening yourself to our readership might have a cathartic effect. 'What I Suffered at the Hands of a Psychopath'," he suggested, blocking out the headline with his right hand and nodding vigorously at the concept. Eleanor felt her stranglehold on impulsive behaviour beginning to slip away and in an effort to regain control she turned her back on Claddis and the camera lens and focused her attention on Laurence whose red cheeks, stiff jaw and flared nostrils mirrored her own inner turmoil.

"I know!" said Claddis untroubled by the gesture. "Here's a better one," he said, slamming his hand onto her shoulder. "'How I Escaped Murder at the Hands of...'" Eleanor looked through the steel mesh at Laurence's expression. Curiously he no longer looked angry but a look of fear seemed to widen his eyes and dilate his pupils. She was still puzzling over this change of expression, as she turned to face Claddis McAvoy. She didn't need to slow down her subsequent actions by processing them through her frontal cortex because she'd practiced them many times in both the Academy and in the line of duty. Using her left hand she unhooked McAvoy's hand from her right shoulder and twisted it ninety degrees. Before he could vocalise his dismay or pain, Eleanor had spun him onto the ground and delivered a solid finger punch to his throat. This cut off air intake and expression for Claddis, who was flailing desperately in an attempt to unblock his windpipe. Barely registering the shouting from Laurence and the rattle of the fencing as he hauled himself over, Eleanor delivered what were intended to be a series of well-positioned blows to Claddis' face, designed to render him more accommodating and, most importantly, less talkative.

However, what spoiled the ensuing silence was the unremitting, mechanical click of the camera.

"Run that shit past me one more time will you? Because I swear the first time it sounded to me like no one really got hit and the photographs that are sitting on the DA's desk and on mine are not incriminating at all!" bellowed Marty Samuelson, snatching up a photograph from the large collection spread across his desk and flapping it in Laurence's face. "This looks like your partner, soon to be *ex*-partner, thumping the living shit out of a journalist." He turned the photograph around and drew it up to his face, pausing as he took in the image. "No, it doesn't matter how many times I look at it, it still says the same thing to me. Suspension pending further investigation!"

Laurence sighed and shifted his position in the chair. "Mr McAvoy, grabbed DI Raven's shoulder and her reaction was purely instinctive..."

"...*Instinctive* is when a bear eats you and a raccoon shits on your barbeque! There was nothing about that encounter that should have triggered an instinctive response. She could have warned him, or arrested him, or posed for a photograph. What she did was apply deadly force to an overweight journalist nagging her for an interview – one that she *had* promised him I hasten to add, at an undesirable time. Is that an accurate summation?"

Laurence thought for a moment and then shook his head. "Her back was to him and she interpreted his actions…"

"The fuck she did! Eleanor Raven is trained to assert deadly force and withhold it if the circumstances are not appropriate, as they *weren't* in this case!"

Laurence opened his mouth to speak but Marty cut him off with a fist thump to the table. "And you! In an effort to ameliorate the situation, arrested Mr McAvoy when what you should have been doing was calling for an ambulance."

"In my defence…"

"Fuck your defence. You are indefensible!" Marty pointed a meaty finger at Laurence, his face red and pinched with rage. "There will be no limit to the amount of front page coverage on this debacle. Full cover spreads of Toronto's finest beating a journalist into a near coma and then cuffing him. It spells IA and some serious personnel relocations to me!"

"Sir…" began Laurence but was cut off by a knock on the door. Samuelson held up a finger, "Enter."

Mo came in quietly and pulled a seat up to Samuelson's desk and flopped down.

"Well?" asked Samuelson.

"He's ok and is willing to withdraw all charges provided that Raven gives him the interview she promised."

Samuelson let the news sink in and then snorted. "What's the catch?"

"That's the catch! He wants a blow by blow account of what happened to her when she was taken prisoner by Lee Hughes."

"That's it?"

Mo nodded but neither Laurence nor Mo looked in any way relieved.

"What am I missing?" asked Samuelson scowling. "She gets a free pass and you two are lemon sucking?"

"She can't do it," said Mo simply.

"Can't or won't?" snarled Samuelson.

"She can't," said Mo.

Chapter Fourteen

"I need to get back to work," said Eleanor pointedly.

Seb Blackmore smiled and nodded. The silence grew. "What's that?" he asked, pointing to the front of her shirt. Eleanor didn't look. "It's blood isn't it?" he said leaning towards her and examining the stain. "Is it yours?" he asked with the same degree of concern.

"No. It isn't." Eleanor replied. "But you know that don't you."

"I don't know anything until you tell me," he replied simply.

"It belonged to Claddis McAvoy."

Seb Blackmore nodded sagely and leaned further back in his chair. "That was several hours ago; didn't you have the time to change into a clean shirt?"

She looked at him with irritation. "I was sent straight here by my commanding officer and was not encouraged to go home, shower and make myself more presentable."

"Why do you think you were sent here?"

"Because my actions were considered... excessive, I imagine."

"You imagine or know?" he asked.

"For fuck's sake! I was irritated by McAvoy's intrusive approach and... over-reacted. Is that enough?"

"Enough for what?"

Eleanor steadied her breathing and stabilised the rising tide of anger and discomfort. "Enough to get me out of this office and back into my own."

Seb Blackmore studied her for a moment or two before answering slowly. "No. It's not I'm afraid. I said categorically last session that you were on a knife-edge and sooner or later you would find yourself unable to control your anger. You are unravelling Eleanor Raven and my job is to pick up the stiches and knit you back together."

"And how do you propose to do that?" she snarled.

"I need to gain some trust and then take you through the healing process."

"Trust? How the hell am I supposed to trust a man who broke the patient's right to confidentiality and talked to her partner? You even gave him my hospital notes!"

"You can't and won't trust me at the moment, maybe never but you clearly indicated the one person you do trust and I reached for him. He knows nothing more than the fact that you had problems swallowing in hospital and that there's nothing physically wrong with you. I don't think I broke your patient confidentiality rights but, like you, I don't follow the rules to the letter. I see them as more of a guide. That's right isn't it Eleanor. That's how you and I solve our cases by careful and thorough research and betting on our own judgment."

She stared at him for a moment. "So what's the procedure now?"

Seb looked at her carefully. "We talk."

"Until I say the right thing and you call Samuelson and tell him I'm cured?"

Seb smiled. "Ah, that it were that simple. No, we talk until you don't need to talk anymore."

"And how will we know when I'm done with the talking?"

He smiled enigmatically.

She looked at him with scepticism. "Ok let's start." She looked at her watch pointedly.

Seb smiled at her for a moment and then his face hardened. "We're going to start with Caleb."

For a moment Eleanor couldn't believe that she'd heard him correctly. She tried to articulate but her mouth felt heavy; anaesthetised. "...What did you say?"

"We're going to start with Caleb. Caleb Tattenhall was your friend and you found his body when you were thirteen. That's correct isn't it?"

Eleanor shook her head. "I don't understand how you have that information."

"There was a police investigation and court hearing. You were a witness and as one of the investigating officers' daughter, you were mentioned in the national papers. It was an easy research and my position allows me access to sensitive archived materials."

Eleanor stared at him in shock.

Seb allowed her a moment or two before launching into his speech. "We have to start at the beginning and the beginning was Caleb. His stepfather had been sexually abusing him since he was eight and strangled him during one of these rapes. There was no evidence that he intended to kill him; it was a sex session that went too far. He didn't really try to cover it up did he? He just dumped the body by the trash cans. It was almost as if he were making a point about how little he valued his stepson's life." Seb saw the steady paling of Eleanor's skin and gave her a moment to recover before he ploughed on. "You went to find out what had happened to your friend because he hadn't been in school. You took your dog, tied it up to the railings when it wouldn't stop barking and then walked up to the front door." He didn't blink or move his focus from hers. "But you didn't knock did you?" His voice was slowing imperceptibly. "Something told you not to knock but to go and look at the basement steps. That's where his naked body was, underneath the trash cans and the rubbish. That's where you found his body."

Eleanor felt her body jolt with the exertion of pushing into the seat back. She swallowed hard and tried to get a handle of the rising nausea. "I really don't want to talk about this," she managed.

"What I want to know is why you didn't knock?"

Eleanor had had enough; she grabbed her phone and bag and headed for the door.

"If you walk away from this session I will have no choice but to call Samuelson and inform him that this department cannot endorse you as a serving officer. You will be suspended pending further evaluation."

Eleanor's hand was on the door handle. A wave of coldness swept across her, tightening her chest and throat. She concentrated on her hand, hoping it would make the decision for her but it neither activated nor loosened its grip on the door. Slowly she lowered her forehead against the door, feeling the pressure against her temple. "I don't know why. An instinct, a sense of foreboding maybe." She rolled her head and felt the pounding of her temple against the wood. "There was a sign."

"What was the sign?"

She closed her eyes and stopped fighting the image that had visited her so often over the last two decades. "I don't know."

Minutes passed.

"What was the sign Eleanor?"

She lifted her head. "He wanted me to listen."

He nodded expectantly.

"He wanted to tell me something." Her throat was so tight she could hardly speak or breathe. "I could have stopped it happening. Told someone... Got him out of there."

Seb shook his head. "No, you *couldn't* have Eleanor. Detective Inspector Raven could have stopped it. She'd remove Caleb from the household, piece together the evidence, and make sure there was a leak-proof case. Eleanor the child *couldn't* have understood because Caleb wouldn't have given you enough of the story for you to understand. He may have hinted at what was happening. He may have told you that his stepfather hit him but what he *couldn't* have told you was that he was being sexually abused. Do you understand what I'm saying to you?"

"You're wrong. There were signs and I ignored them."

"Eleanor, there were signs but they weren't for you."

The bath held no relief for Eleanor that evening. She looked at the two photographs tacked to the mirror and could only see two dead children. She turned away and tried to let her mind free associate but all it did was search amongst the trash cans for a lost face. Inertia and depression were settling on her like an anvil. For a brief moment she contemplated slipping below the water line and letting her lungs fill with water but even in the unlit place she'd retreated to Eleanor knew she still possessed the will to fight. It was with this in mind that she pulled a T-shirt over her wet skin and pulled down the loft ladder. The loft space for her apartment was only marginally higher than a crawl space and had been used mainly to store unloved gifts, several boxes of passed down memorabilia and to hide the photocopied file notes of cases she'd worked on. At the bottom of the first plastic tub was a dated folder, its corners thumbed and scored. Unlike the others this was an original file, designated for incineration when the City converted pre-1995 solved files to digital data only. She didn't like handling the paper; it had an aura of despair and hopelessness about it. Neither did she didn't want to read it. There was nothing more to be gleaned from the pages; she just needed to see him.

It was a school photograph and although the face was immediately recognisable she couldn't have pulled it up from her memory, it had long ago been replaced by the bloat of decomposed flesh. Caleb wore the same uniform that she had, shared the same classes and, possibly, aspirations but that's where the similarities with his life ended. On the occasions that Eleanor had forced herself to look at him she'd taste again the cascade of emotions that both defied and defiled her. Caleb was her 'safe word', the boy who had experienced all of the world's horror so she wouldn't have to.

Her hands steadier, she slid the remains back into the folder and piled her life back on top of it.

It was well past midnight when Toby slid the Oldsmobile into the residents' car park. He'd checked on his initial visit that there was no CCTV but still made every effort to tuck the car into the least visible corner. The sash had been lifted and there was sufficient room for him to slide his arm inside and unplug the wedge. When his eyes had finally acclimatised to the darkness of the room, he could see Tommy lying sprawled on the bed, clad only in pyjama shorts and vest top, the duvet flung to the floor. Climbing through the window was not as easy as he had imagined and his graceless landing made Tommy's eyes flicker momentarily before he turned himself onto his side and tucked his knees into his stomach. Toby waited, slowing his breathing down and calming himself before tiptoeing slowly towards the door and listening carefully. He held his breath… nothing. Both women must be asleep. He reached into his pocket for the small bottle of chloroform and the lint packed tea strainer and took a step towards the sleeping child. A sudden metallic crunch stopped him dead. Extracting the object from beneath his foot he saw that he'd stepped on a length of train track. The tin engines had been scattered haphazardly around the base of Tommy's bed and when Toby looked closely he saw that this was no ordinary child's toy but one of the very early Hornby models. Delighted, he scooped up the engines and placed them carefully into his pocket. How natural that his son would have been attracted to the same quality of artefact that he was.

It was with some degree of trepidation that he uncapped the bottle and measured out what he believed to be an amount sufficient to anaesthetise the boy but not kill him. Holding it at arm's length, so as not to inadvertently dose himself, he tipped a couple of drops of the pungent liquid onto the lint and with only a slight hesitation held the strainer close to Tommy's face so that it funnelled the fumes into his nose and mouth. For several moments nothing happened and just as Toby was beginning to question his ability to read labels the child shuddered and opened unseeing eyes. Toby stared into the blue eyes and noted with dispassionate interest that one pupil was beginning to dilate, making his appearance strangely off-set. For a touching moment Tommy's hands reached for his face and tried to swat at the strainer. Gently, Toby untangled the hands and reached for the carotid pulse, which after an initial panicked rise was beginning to slow to a steady thump. Tentatively he pulled away the strainer and leaned over the child. He was breathing, a little erratically but he was alive. With infinite care, Toby slid his arms underneath the small hot body and scooped him into his arms.

Little Tommy was coming home.

CHAPTER FIFTEEN

The call came in at six thirty am and within twenty seconds Emergency Services had been deployed. It took a further thirteen minutes for the two patrol officers to battle morning traffic and confirm the possibility of an abduction, before Timms and Wadesky were called to assess the situation. Rosheen Banks was in a state of hysteria when the patrol officers arrived and paramedics were summoned to chemically alleviate the situation to enable the officers to get some information out of her.

"What we got?" asked Timms, as he slid into the passenger seat. "Say that's mine!" he said pointing to a coffee.

"It's yours buddy," Wadesky confirmed, as she flipped on lights and siren. "Seven-year-old boy missing from his bed; window deliberately opened. Called in at six thirty by grandma, a Siobhan Banks."

Timms reached for the call sheet. "Patrol searching the streets?"

"Apparently. No signs of him yet."

"Eta?"

"Six to eight," she replied.

Timms dialled. "Johnson? You got the Thomas Banks call sheet? Yeah, on our way now. Run the names through the system will ya and call me back? Especially Dad...Thanks."

Rosheen Banks was considerably calmer when Timms and Wadesky arrived, the sedative having taken the edge off the turmoil. "Mrs Banks?" asked Wadesky.

"Rosheen Banks, yes," she replied. "I went in to get him up for school but his bed was empty. I asked mom if she'd... you are looking for him?" her eyes darted unhappily from Siobhan, to Wadesky, to the female patrol officer.

"We have patrol officers on the streets but the more information you can give us the faster we can target the search. Do you understand?"

Rosheen nodded her head jerkily, a fresh brew of tears working their way out noisily.

"You're putting out an Amber alert?" said Siobhan Banks.

"I need to make sure that an Amber alert is appropriate in this case Ma'am."

"What do you mean appropriate?" screamed Siobhan. "Tommy's been taken by god knows who and you're debating whether to let the media know?"

"You're not going to do anything?" shrieked Rosheen.

Wadesky spoke calmly but firmly. "I cannot call an Amber alert unless I have a strong belief that Tommy's life in in danger *or* that there is information that might help to locate either Tommy, a suspect or a suspect's vehicle. So far you've given me nothing. I need you both to work with me and trust that the *only* thing I'm going to be focused on is bringing Tommy home safely." She reached forward and took hold of Rosheen's hand. "I need you to answer my questions. Do you understand what I'm saying?"

Rosheen nodded.

Timms stood in the child's bedroom and took in the scene as he slipped on latex gloves. He noted that the window sash had been drawn up and that a small piece of wood had been wedged tightly in the groove, preventing it from sliding down. He applied a small amount of pressure to the wedge but it remained solidly in position. Sticking his head out of the window he noted that a patrol officer, showing some initiative, had placed police tape around the area in order to preserve any footprint evidence.

"What do you think has happened to your son?" asked Wadesky carefully.

Rosheen began to look wildly around the room.

"What are you afraid of?" Wadesky said more firmly.

"That someone came through the window and took him," she whispered, as if naming the fear somehow made it a certainty.

Wadesky nodded. "Why do you think that?"

"Because he'd never have climbed out of the window on his own. He wasn't that sort of a boy."

Wadesky turned to look questioningly at the older woman who sighed and shook her head.

"Ok, who do you think could have taken him?"

"I don't know. A paed..." The rest of the word was choked back. "I don't know."

"What about Tommy's father."

Rosheen looked frightened. "Ethan? I don't..."

"That no good piece of shit couldn't organise the putting of his trousers on, never mind kidnap his own child," spat Siobhan Banks.

"How well do you know Ethan, Mrs Banks?"

"Like the back of me own hand," she hissed. "He's my son."

Wadesky looked at the two women in surprise. "I'm sorry. I'd assumed you were mother and daughter."

KAREN LONG

"Rosheen's my daughter-in-law." Siobhan paused, as if unsure whether to continue. "Ethan took a hand to her and I threw him out. I never let his father use his hand and I'd not tolerate it from my own son."

"Ethan was violent towards you?" Wadesky asked Rosheen.

"Once," said Rosheen quietly. "Mom threw him out and we haven't seen him since Tommy was three." At the mention of her son's name, Rosheen burst into tears again. Siobhan put an arm around her shoulder and spoke quietly to her. "You have to help the detective. Clear your head girl so we can get our boy back.

Timms looked carefully around the room, noting the lack of any disturbance. He slid his hand gently along the fitted sheet to detect signs of dried semen but the sheet was smooth. He lowered his face to the mattress and inhaled deeply but picked up little beyond the floral notes of the detergent. He didn't want to touch the duvet in case he disturbed any evidence. Looking at the floor he noted that there were several pieces of train track scattered around, one of which had been crushed underfoot. After making one more visual sweep he joined the women in the kitchen.

"Did either of you open the window last night or this morning and stick a small wooden peg into the frame to stop it sliding down.

Both women shook their heads. "I left it slightly open last night because it was so hot. About six inches or so, no higher," said Rosheen using her hands to indicate the gap. "I pushed the stop in so it couldn't be lifted any higher... It was just so hot and we don't have air conditioning."

"You are *sure* that you didn't open it to the position it's in now."

"No, we'd never do that," said Siobhan quietly.

Timms nodded, "You've given a full description of what Thomas was wearing to Detective Wadesky?"

The two women nodded. "Tommy... He's Tommy," said Rosheen.

"Mom, I want you to come into the room with me and take a look for a moment," said Timms holding out his hand to her.

Rosheen got to her feet, wobbling a little with the effect of the sedative. Timms took her arm and walked her into the bedroom, turning her to face him. "You ready for this? Are you strong enough for me to run some ideas past you or shall I talk to grandma?"

Rosheen began to blanch. "You think he's dead?"

"What I'm about to tell you is what I believe but *not* what I know. You understand that? And this could all change when Crime Scene get here."

"Yes... I understand."

"You are going to feel scared and sick but I need you to stay as strong and co-operative as possible, if I'm going to stand a chance of getting Tommy back."

She began to shake violently. Timms gripped her arms firmly and drew her closer to him. "You ready?"

Her breathing made a rasping sound and unconsciously she grabbed his arms, squeezing desperately.

"Ok, this is what I believe," he said steadily, his eyes fixed on her. "At some point last night, when you and grandma were asleep, someone, male most probably, pushed his arm through the gap and prised out the wedge you'd put in and pulled up the sash. He then jammed it open with the wedge and went over to the bed. He must have lifted Tommy into his arms and climbed back out of the window.

Rosheen was nodding her head vigorously, her eyes wide and unblinking, her nose streaming. Her teeth began to chatter noisily.

"There is no sign of a struggle and –" he paused momentarily "– I have no evidence to suggest Tommy was sexually abused.

"I'm so cold," she whispered.

"It's because you're going into shock but I need you strong for a little longer. Can you do that?"

"Yes," she managed.

"I need to know if there's something missing from this room."

Rosheen began to look wildly around, her arms still gripping Timms' arms.

"Don't rush. Just look."

"I don't know... I don't..." She stopped and stared at the floor. Timms supported her as she sank to her knees and reached out for the track. He stopped her before she could pick it up. "The trains are gone."

Timms nodded. "Are you sure?"

She looked under the bed and then all the surfaces. She nodded, confused. They were here last night. He was playing with them before he went to sleep. I trod on one when I tucked him in and was going to put them in his toy box but he liked the arrangement. He asked me not to." Timms let go of one of her arms and opened up the toy box lid.

"Can you see them there?"

She peered into the box and shook her head. "Why would the man take his toys?" She cocked her head to one side, her shaking slowing to occasional shudders. "Because he wants Tommy to play... not to be scared?"

Timms watched the glimmer of hope take fire. He felt angry at having to keep this alive in her but she was the only hope he had to get the child back alive. "I don't know why the trains were taken. Maybe for that reason."

She tried to smile. "He's alive? You think he's alive?"

"Rosheen, I need you to go to the station with Detective Wadesky and talk to a friend of mine. He's called Mo and he will show you some photographs and try to build up a picture that might help us. Will you do that for me?"

She nodded and then pushed herself into his arms. "He's our life. Bring him back safely won't you? I'm begging you."

Timms held her tightly. "Tommy is my life now."

"Raven!" bellowed Samuelson, from somewhere in the corridor.

Eleanor rose from her desk and headed for Samuelson's office, trying not to catch her partner's worried gaze as she went.

"What the fuck sort of asshole beats up a member of the press?" he hissed, raising his eyebrows to emphasise his disbelief.

Eleanor opened her mouth but Samuelson shot a finger up as in indication that now wasn't the time for explanations. She nodded and listened. "But you are not an asshole, are you Raven?"

There was a pause before she responded. "Generally not sir."

"Now I don't think Smith has ever made an arrest without someone receiving some sort of injury, which is why he works the lower IQ spectrum of crime. That's not your MO is it?"

"Not usually, no."

"So what triggered yesterday's diplomatic coup?"

Eleanor thought for a moment. "I felt put upon."

"Put upon? I feel put upon from the moment I haul my ass out of bed in the morning. But I am allowed to feel that because I am the boss and it comes with the territory. You are not allowed to feel put upon because you are carrying a gun and some sort of emotional baggage that is converting one of the best cops in homicide into an asshole!"

Eleanor nodded. "I agree sir."

"You agree because I'm talking sense or you agree because I'm your boss?" Samuelson rocked back on his seat, his lips pursed. He lowered his tone to barely that of a whisper. "You aren't ready to be back at work Raven. That's not just my opinion either but here's my problem I've got a probable child abduction come in this morning and Wadesky and Timms aren't going to look at anything *but* that case until the child is safely back home. I have to believe that you can handle your caseload with the help of your partner Detective Whitefoot. Neither of which I'm convinced you are able to manage."

Samuelson leaned back in his chair, rocking slightly. "These are the rules Raven. You will not be pissed off or put upon by any member of the public until this clusterfuck is solved. You will endeavour to get on with your partner, until I see fit to transfer him to another department. You will attend every single fucking psychiatric consult they want you to attend and you will listen to what they are saying. They want you to see the Virgin Mary in an ink-blot, you see her and all the heavenly choirs. Are we on the same wavelength?"

"Yes sir."

Samuelson sighed heavily. "You have to give Claddis McAvoy his interview."

"That's not happening," she said slowly.

"I can hold it off till the end of the case but that's the deal. McAvoy presses charges you will be cover on every media outlet in Canada. You'll be treated as a pariah and shunted into cold case and evidence logging – a slow and painful death by anyone's standards.

Eleanor rolled the concept around in her mind for a second or two before delivering her final thought. "You can have my badge at the end of this case then."

Samuelson looked at her, shaking his head slowly. "For the sake of throwing a bone to some hack, you're willing to throw ten years of hard labour into the trash?"

She stood up and nodded. "Yes sir."

"How'd it go?" asked Laurence distractedly, as he sifted through mounds of paper on his desk.

"Terrific."

Laurence switched attention to Eleanor. "Terrific huh?"

"Yup," said Eleanor flicking the switch on the coffee machine. "It's just us two until Timms and Wadesky have cleared the Thomas Banks abduction."

Laurence nodded unhappily. "Mo?"

"Sharing him and Johnson but we have Smith all to ourselves and access to patrol, at Andy Harrison's discretion. On the brighter side, we can leave the landfill coordination to the radar guys and cadaver search. Any news and they'll call us in."

"We got a plan?" asked Laurence.

Eleanor nodded. "How about we take our coffee and go stare at the board?"

There's something I'm missing," said Eleanor grimacing.

"*We're* missing," Laurence said firmly.

Eleanor glanced at his profile, unsure whether he was making some sort of political statement, but his expression appeared to be that of stumped rather than confrontational.

She relaxed slightly. "I couldn't speak for you," she said quietly.

He turned to her, puzzled. "No, I've no ideas either," he said.

"Something connects all of these murders to the same guy but..." Her voice trailed off as she immersed herself in the collage of photographs, map printouts and forensic sketches, all laid out in a linear manner. "What?"

"Communications... Try that," said Laurence grabbing his notebook and pen from the desk.

"Okaaay... Parminder knows Giselle and let's assume she knew her murderer, as she arranged to meet him in TTP." Her eyes ran over the board.

"So, she had to have contacted the guy who killed her. She didn't have a landline at the apartment and every one of her calls from her cell pan out as legit. "

"She couldn't use the cell at work and she didn't use the restaurant landline, so where did she call from?"

Eleanor peered closely at the map, placing her finger next to the pin that marked The Orient Express. "She called from a public payphone. There must be one nearby. Let's get the number and run the calls for her work hours."

Laurence jotted down the instruction. "Shall I send patrol?"

"No, I'd like to suss that one out and then let Johnson grab the data."

"Did you call Dieter about the...?"

Laurence cut in smiling. "He really couldn't say that the skulls were those of conjoined twins, as he could barely remember them anyway. He did seem rather keen to help you in any way he could and felt that if you'd care to interview him again, possibly over a dinner, he might just remember a little more."

Eleanor smiled. "I'll bear that in mind." She stared at Lucy's sketch of the old-fashioned hair decorations, as described by Lula-Bell and then at the photographs of the wooden snake.

"He likes to give presents, unique presents."

"We're definitely lumping Tara in with Giselle and Michelle Brown, as murdered by the same guy?'

"I've no proof yet but everything's pointing to that." She looked at Laurence's expression. "You don't agree."

He shrugged and furrowed his brow. "We've nothing to link them. We haven't got a body for Tara."

"We're unlikely to get one, unless he messes up the preservation. Have we heard back from Isabel Drake yet?"

"No, shall we drop in?" asked Laurence, as he grabbed his jacket from the chair.

"Let's run these past her as well," Eleanor said, unpinning the comb sketch off the board.

Before either of them could make it to the door Andy Harrison opened it, a sympathetic expression on his face. "Not planning a good day were you?" he said.

"Apparently not," replied Eleanor, waiting for the spoiler.

"I've got Tyler Baxton due for release this morning, according to Mo, and I've just had a call from Toronto General informing us that Marcus Baxton passed away an hour ago."

"Shit," intoned Laurence.

"You want me to get someone from patrol to take Tyler to the hospital?"

Eleanor shook her head and sighed. "No, it's my call."

Andy nodded appreciatively and waved his cup. "I'll just grab a coffee, if there's one going."

"Help yourself," she said turning to Laurence.

"You want me to come too?" he asked.

She smiled. "No this shit's on me. Text me updates and press Isabel Drake on the skulls. She's had enough time to check on her stock."

Laurence nodded. "Roger that. You going to make the meeting with Doc Hounslow and Susan this afternoon?"

"Here's hoping."

Tyler Baxton sat in resolute silence, during both his release from custody and the subsequent explanation of his father's death. His eyes had remained slightly unfocused, as if he wasn't quite listening and his jaw was clamped tightly closed.

"Tyler, I'm going to take you over to the hospital now, to see your father," Eleanor had said slowly and placed a hand on his shoulder. "Are you ready?"

He looked at her with astonishment. "You said he's dead."

"He is but we thought you'd like to see him," she replied, carefully.

"But I'm not allowed near the dead! I had to promise!"

Eleanor sighed. "I'm going to be with you. This is your chance to see him again. Ok?"

Tyler looked unconvinced.

Toby had been pleasantly surprised at how effective the chloroform had been. Little Tommy had slept throughout the night and was still asleep as he prepared to leave for work. Realising that the boy would be able to squeeze through the bars of the 'crush' with some youthful manoeuvring, he had reinforced the frame with some secondary steel bars. It made the crush mechanism slightly more sluggish and less aesthetically pleasing but he didn't want to run any risk of Tommy being injured in any way. He had placed the child in the crush, his legs drawn up to his chest and head balanced on his knees. He thought that Tommy would be able to stand up, which meant that he could be cleaned more easily but if he couldn't, he would figure that out when he got back from work.

Today, Toby thought, was going to be a good one.

CHAPTER SIXTEEN

"Thank you," said Laurence appreciatively, as Isabel Drake poured him a glass of iced tea.

She pushed several sheets of paper towards Laurence. "It was as you'd said. I've run through the cataloguing system and can confirm that there are thirty-five items of museum property that can't be accounted for or located."

"That's a lot," replied Laurence, as he leafed through the list.

"It appears that the wooden snake you have in your possession was, most likely, part of our collection. If you look here…" She opened a file to a tagged page and pointed to a highlighted list and then compared it to the catalogue booklet, which documented the artefacts with images. "The listings, prepared by my department, describe each of these items including the snake but the corresponding catalogue makes no mention of it. Also, these specimens are no longer on display but are archived in the children's Saturday Club and Schools' materials boxes. I've found every one of these wooden toys but not the snake."

"How about the conjoined skulls?" he asked tentatively.

"No, they can't be found either," she sighed.

"How long have the thefts been going on for?"

Isabel shook her head. "So far I've only been back three years. It's an enormous operation to go back further because we changed the system three years ago, from a basic single entry one to, ironically, a more accountable double entry." She pushed herself back in her chair and rubbed her brow. Laurence waited. "Due to the complications of setting up another system and the time-consuming nature of the project, we decided to take on an extra set of hands."

Laurence raised his eyebrows and flipped open his notebook. "His name?"

"Enda Miller," she said uncomfortably.

"And this is the person you suspect of squirreling away these artefacts?"

There was an embarrassed pause before Isabel nodded. "All roads appear to lead back to Enda."

"Explain how?"

She sighed. "He was responsible for the cataloguing system and had free access to all materials both actual..."

"As in, keys to the vault?" interrupted Laurence.

She nodded and continued, "... and the paper chain. His laptop, as far as I'm aware, was password protected and if it was accessed by someone else they would have been doing it without him noticing over a three-year period."

"Does he have access to the entirety of the museum's collection?"

"Not really. My section employs Enda and fifteen other individuals and it deals mainly with the history of mankind, the bird displays and is predominantly situated on this floor."

"Can you give me his personal details please?" asked Laurence.

"Yes of course." Isabel opened her laptop and began to access her personnel files. The printer at the back of the room began to shudder into action.

Laurence placed the forensic sketch of the decorative hair combs in front of Isabel. "Is it possible that these could have been part of one of the museum's collection?"

Her brow wrinkled as she scanned through the sheets, running a finger along the list. Suddenly the finger stopped and paused. Laurence held his breath but the finger carried on. "Sorry no, nothing like that." Isabel frowned. "Could you tell me why these items have been brought to your attention?"

"Is Mr Miller in today?" Laurence asked.

Isabel shook her head. "It's his half day. Do you wish to speak to him?"

"Not quite yet. Both Detective Inspector Raven and myself will be doing that in the very near future. Until that time I'd be very grateful if neither you, nor any colleagues that you may have included in this matter, mention anything about our intentions."

Isabel shook her head. "Of course not."

Laurence stood up. "Thank you for all of your efforts. If you discover any other items that may have gone missing over the past couple of years, or even before that, please call me immediately."

Isabel took his card with a worried expression. Noticing the sketch she picked it up as Laurence opened the door. "You've forgotten…"

"Keep hold of that. If you could run a discreet check for me I'd be grateful."

As he reached for the door handle again there was a knock. Laurence opened the door to reveal a heavy-set man dressed in off-white linen trousers, a pale blue short-sleeved shirt buttoned up to his throat and held there tightly with a navy blue cravat. His features were pudgy and unnaturally pale for a Torontan summer resident. He was overly doused in eau de cologne, which made Laurence recoil slightly.

"Do come in Toby," said Isabel with a slight tightness in her voice. "The gentleman is just leaving."

Laurence nodded to Toby politely, noting that his eye infection would probably respond well to a course of Chloramphenicol.

"Where are you?" asked Laurence.

"I'm just driving Tyler back from the hospital and then I'll head over to see Susan," Eleanor readjusted her headset as she manoeuvred through the sluggish lunchtime traffic. "News?"

"We got a definite on the snake and skulls by the look of things... and a name."

"That's fantastic."

"It gets better. There were two phone calls from a public call box fifty feet away from her workplace, on the date Parminder Kaur was murdered, to the museum switchboard. Both calls correspond to her working hours but can't be traced to any specific department. They could have been tourist enquiries though."

Eleanor felt a heaviness lifting off her chest. Things were beginning to slot into place. "What about the combs." She glanced at Tyler but he was staring out of the window, his face a blank.

"No joy I'm afraid... Listen, I'm going back to run this name through the system and see you later."

"What is the name?"

"Oh, Miller. Enda Miller."

Noting that the street directly in front of Tyler's house was occupied by a group of teenagers loafing around, Eleanor drove round the corner and pulled in out of sight. Tyler didn't move. "You ok?" she asked. He turned to look at her with incomprehension. "Will you be ok?" she asked.

"Did you kill him?" he asked, slowly.

Eleanor's earlier lift in spirits took a plunge back into the darkness. "No. His heart gave out... but no doubt the stress of you being taken into custody didn't do him any favours."

There was a long silence.

She stared ahead. "I'm sorry that he's gone. Will you be able to manage without him?"

He shrugged and resumed his waiting.

"Tyler, I need you to help me. There's something I don't understand."

He looked at her. "I didn't do it."

"I know."

"What do you want to know then?" he said slowly.

"When you prevented Laura's body from being buried and had relationships with her. What did you feel?" she asked carefully.

Tyler sat in silence, working his jaw. He then quietly opened the door and stepped out into the sunshine, closing it behind him. Eleanor was about to restart the engine when he put his head through the open window and stared at her angrily. "I felt love," he spat.

Isabel closed the lid of her laptop and placed a book on top of the papers she had been looking at. "Yes Toby," she asked irritably. "How can I help you?"

"It's our weekly meeting," he said, uncomfortably.

Isabel looked at him for a second or two. "I'm so sorry, of course it is."

Laurence and Susan Cheung were deep in technical conversation when Eleanor arrived. "How are you?" asked Susan.

"Good," replied Eleanor, as breezily as she could.

Susan scowled at her. "There are a couple of those protein drinks in the fridge."

Eleanor was prepared. "I'll help myself then."

Susan's expression softened. "Ok, first thing is that Tyler Baxton's macaw is preserved in nothing more dangerous than household dust and anti-mite spray. I'm only just getting back results from the Michelle Brown trace evidence haul. Most of it is indistinguishable from the surrounding landfill, apart from a small collection of dog hairs. These were only found on the body and none in the surrounding debris. I've run a trace and feel fairly confident that she came into contact with an Irish setter post mortem and here's the really interesting bit. Those dog hairs register pretty high on the arsenic scale."

"Where did you find the arsenic specifically?" asked Laurence.

Susan smiled. "None in the medulla, all on the cuticle."

"The hair was dusted with arsenic?"

"That's how you could interpret that," replied Susan.

"So whoever embalmed Michelle Brown had an Irish setter that had been taxidermied and treated with arsenic, to prevent parasitic infestation?"

"It's a possibility," said Susan. "I've finished with the Richard Leslie Baker boxes and have compiled a list for you. Nothing of particular interest, you've already had the confirmation of a DNA match between Richard's skeletonised remains and his mother. Oh the photographs…" Susan disappeared into an adjoining room and brought in a tray with ten photographs on it. "This was the one you were most interested in." She selected a rather blurred image, that now had a more clearly defined bandstand in the left hand corner of the frame and in the foreground the outline of a thickset man his features obscured by his hand, which he'd thrust in front of him just as the shutter snapped. "Guess he didn't want to be photographed," said Susan. "Anyway, that's all folks! Got a deadline to meet, anything else I'll buzz you."

"Thanks Susan," said Eleanor, her brows knotted tightly.

"You think that's him?" asked Laurence.

"Well if it is, his secret's safe for a while longer," replied Eleanor, peering closely at the image.

"What've we got on Mr Miller?" asked Eleanor, as they headed over to her car.

Laurence skim-read the pages Johnson had handed to him, shaking his head. "He's never been arrested...had a couple of parking fines..."

"Anywhere interesting or sensitive?" interrupted Eleanor.

"No. He recently renewed his Vulnerable Sector Police Screening and it went through unchallenged. He's clean. Ideas?" said Laurence, rubbing his beard mechanically.

"We've got nothing to link him with either the thefts or the murders, so it's pointless even trying to get a warrant. However, an unexpected visit to his apartment might be enlightening don't you think?" said Eleanor. "I want his fingerprints, so let's get the images we want explaining in plastic document cover and see if any match the ones we've got so far."

Toby was a little agitated. It had always been a possibility that his casual pilfering over the years would either be discovered or curtailed in some way but he'd laid plenty of evidence to inculpate Enda. This would have the added benefit of ensuring that Enda would be axed from his position and may also face the possibility of criminal prosecution, a win-win situation. To that end, he imagined that the young man who had been in Isabel's office had been an investigator of some description. That was all fine, nothing he hadn't prepared for but now the thing was real he was concerned that he may have left a loophole

He'd been so preoccupied with these matters that when he opened the front door and stepped into the cool of the entrance hall, he was momentarily confused by the muffled screams emanating from the basement. His acquisition of Little Tommy had completely vanished from his conscience and it took him several seconds to adjust to circumstances. Suddenly, the whole notion of becoming a parent felt exhausting. He had planned originally to keep the child alive for a couple of days, in order to reduce the burden of keeping Tara's acetone saturation topped up and filtered. If he embalmed Little Tommy before finishing Tara's preparation, he would be constantly switching the filtration system from the freezer unit to the tank and with the best will in the world he didn't think it was up to that challenge. One at a time would be the best way forward but this new turn of events was making him nervous and unhappy. Only one thing would clear his mind and soothe him. Taking his jacket off and placing it carefully on the coat stand, so it wouldn't crease, he made his way up to the bedroom where Olivia was sleeping. He tiptoed in not wanting to disturb her. She looked so serene and perfect, her hair spread across the silk pillow. Toby knelt at the bedside and lowered his lips to hers, waiting for the stresses of the day to melt at her touch but there was to be no relief as the unmistakable sharp tang of putrefaction greeted him.

"Mr Miller? Enda Miller?" asked Laurence politely.
Enda nodded nervously. "Yes, who are you?"

"Detective Whitefoot and Detective Inspector Raven," said Laurence gesturing a hand in Eleanor's direction.

"Uh-huh. How can I help you?" he asked, puzzled.

"We'd like to ask you a few questions with regard to your work at the museum," said Laurence, making a move towards the interior of Enda's small apartment. Eleanor noted with some interest that Enda drew back protectively against his front door, pulling it slightly closed as he did so.

"Mr Miller, I imagine that you'd prefer the conversation we are about to have taking place in the privacy of your home, rather than have your business conducted in the middle of shared space where your neighbours can hear," said Eleanor, raising her voice slightly.

Enda hesitated for a second and then ushered them in. "Please..." he said, nervously beckoning them into the living area. As they passed him he surreptitiously pulled his bedroom door to, which wouldn't completely close, due to a couple of cables running from a power point in the corridor into the room. A gesture not lost on either detective.

"What do you want?" he asked, licking his lips and hopping from one foot to another. "Is there a problem?"

"There have been some inconsistencies in your cataloguing at the museum," said Laurence calmly.

"Huh? What sort of inconsistencies?"

"The sort that accompanies theft," said Eleanor slowly. For a brief moment she registered a flash of confusion, followed curiously by relief on Enda's face.

"I don't know what you're referring to," he said quickly.

"There have been thirty-five items that have disappeared from the museum, all of which were your sole responsibility to catalogue and monitor," said Laurence, reaching into a folder and drawing out the list of items. He handed the plastic wallet over to Enda, who hesitated briefly before taking it. "I don't understand what this means," he said, thrusting the list back towards Laurence.

"Are you saying that you were not responsible for those items Mr Miller? Dr Drake thinks you are. In fact if you look at the header on the top left you will see that it has your name and personal ID clearly written."

Enda squinted at the page. "But what are you saying? I catalogue thousands of items every year. I can't remember each and every one of them."

"Mr Miller, have you misappropriated these items?"

Enda curled his lip and made a snorting sound. "Of course not!"

Eleanor let the silence run on.

"How do you know these are missing? Have you looked for them?" he asked.

"Dr Drake has and she's sure that they are gone," said Eleanor.

"Well, it could have been anyone!" he replied, becoming notably more flustered.

"Explain how? You are the only member of Dr Drake's team that has responsibility for the cataloguing of items. Isn't that true?"

"Yes – but only onto the computer system. Anyone could steal something before its initial paper logging..." his voice trailed off as he thought through the possibilities. "Someone could have seen the thing brought into the basement and then just pocketed what they liked. I'd be none the wiser.

"So, there's no paperwork indicating an object's origin from or arrival in the museum?" asked Laurence with surprise.

Enda was flailing. "Look, where's there's a will there's a way," he offered hopefully.

Eleanor leaned forward slightly. "Mr Miller it looks to us and to the powers that be at the museum, that you have been spiriting away items of great value over the past three years."

Enda shook his head vigorously, his eyes wide with fear. "I haven't. I look after the collections I don't steal them!"

"Perhaps you'd let me and my partner look around, so you can prove to us that you haven't got any items stashed away," said Eleanor with quiet authority.

Enda began to sweat noticeably. "No. I... I want a lawyer."

"We're not arresting you yet Mr Miller."

"If you are innocent, then inviting us to look around your home would be the first step towards exoneration," coaxed Laurence.

"No!" shrieked Enda. Then more quietly, "I think you'd better get a warrant first."

Eleanor smiled politely and then stood up, reaching for the list. "Thank you, we'll be in touch."

"What are you thinking?" asked Laurence, as they both climbed into the car.

"He's behaving like a guilty man who's hiding something but I don't think it's anything to do with the museum thefts. Let's run those prints and see whether we've got enough to get a warrant."

CHAPTER SEVENTEEN

A t first glance the crush appeared empty and it was only when he was several feet away that he saw the child curled foetally at the bottom. The smell of vomit and urine clung tartly to the boy but Toby never let these more visceral issues bother his sensibilities. He couldn't tell whether the child was dead or not and held his breath, as he pushed a finger through the bars and poked the flesh on his back. The child began to groan and tried to lift his head but immediately began to shake and dry heave. Toby watched with interest as the boy held his head in his hands, his stomach lurching in and out with the effort. A faint sugary smell cut through the vomit and he could only assume it was the chloroform being ejected from his system. Toby placed the small, ten-millilitre syringe on the floor carefully and spoke reassuringly to the child. "I don't want you to feel concerned anymore Tommy. I am here to look after you. The child's body became rigidly taut and slowly he lifted his face. Toby took several involuntary steps backwards in shock. "What have you done?" he gasped. "What happened to your face?"

The boy stared at him in horror and disbelief. "Where's mummy?" he sobbed. "Please…"

Toby couldn't understand what was wrong with the child's face. He had been perfect when he arrived the night before, his skin unblemished; pure. Now it was blistered and bloody, as if acid had been poured on him. Toby took a step closer and peered at the child, who was pressed against the back of the crush, his eyes and nose streaming. "Where's mummy?"

"She's asleep upstairs," he answered vaguely, as he scrutinised the face.

"I want to see her now," he sobbed, his body trembling with shock.

"Toby realised that the blistering was the result of the child lying face down in his own vomit, as there were still small pieces of food attached to his chin and T-shirt.

"I want mummy!"

His voice was becoming shrill and penetrated Toby's sensitive hearing, putting him on edge. "Be quiet!" he shouted. He was pleased to see the immediate effect this had on the boy. His eyes grew wide and his mouth clamped shut. "Good boy," he said in a soothing tone. "I'm going to wipe your face for you…"

"No!" screamed the boy and covered his face with his now dirty hands.

"If you want to see mummy, you have to do as I say. Do you understand?"

Tommy nodded slowly, his lips trembling.

Reaching for the bucket of warm water and flannel he'd brought down for a different purpose, he wrung it out and cautiously put his hand through the bars. Tommy cowered in the corner, his back pressed against the bars. But the crush was small enough to allow Toby to reach the child's face and rub it. "Keep still," he hissed.

"Please can I see mummy now?" he pleaded.

The child was no longer beautiful or desirable. No amount of scrubbing was going to improve his skin or appearance. Balling the flannel, Toby flung it at the wall, showering them both in acrid water.

Tommy began to cry.

The summer storm had been anticipated and, to a large extent welcomed as a concept, if not the reality. Clouds roiled around the CN Tower at unnatural speed, looking more like a movie effect than a natural phenomenon. The downpour, when it finally began, was almost biblical in its ferocity, lifting drain covers and turning the roads into a watercourse. Sarah Wadesky had left her umbrella in the car and was now experiencing the lack of any meaningful public help with saturated hair, clothes and spirit. She glanced up and down the street, watching as uniformed officers carrying photographs and notepads knocked on houses and entered shops in an effort to find someone, anyone who had seen who had taken Tommy Banks. In a futile gesture she twisted the dial on her radio and checked her phone, just in case something had come in and was being missed. How, she thought, could a child vanish so completely and un-witnessed?

Timms looked at Ethan Banks and felt a hot prickly sensation rise beneath the collar of his shirt. Determined to keep a hold on any counter productive statements or gestures, he tried to conjure up an image of baby Tess and the boys, which was guaranteed to shine a light on any difficult day. Unfortunately, this image was marred by the looming figure of Grandma Wadesky and her perpetually humourless expression. So, gritting his teeth, he yanked the chair out and sat down heavily.

Ethan Banks, was, in many respects the adult version of his son. Pale skin, wispy blonde hair and blue eyes were the outward marks of shared genetic inheritance. Where the adult Banks differed was in the mean twist of his mouth, eyes that reflected little light and a penchant for prison tattoos. The uneven swastika that spanned his neck and the large breasted naked woman, legs opened invitingly on his bicep, made Timms want to grab him by the throat and throttle him. "You've been informed that your son has been abducted?" said Timms, as empathically as he could.

Banks lifted his eyes and stared back insolently. He placed a cigarette in his mouth and lit it, inhaling deeply.

Timms swallowed and soothed himself. "Do you have any ideas on who might have taken him?"

"Now how the fuck would I know that? As you can no doubt see –" he gestured expansively to the room "– I don't get out much."

Timms cleared his throat and loosened his collar. "I understand that. But, as we all know, being inside is no deterrent to making enemies and that can lead to families being involved. Now! As we are all desperately trying to find your son, I'm sure that you'd like to give us as much help as you possibly can. Is there anyone you can think of, or even hint at, being involved in your son's abduction?"

There was a slight pause as Ethan Banks picked a small piece of tobacco from off his tongue. "All the help I can give you is this." He leaned towards Timms, a hint of a smile playing across his face. "Go fuck yourself."

Timms closed his eyes and inhaled. Slowly he stood up. When he opened his eyes he saw Ethan Banks leaning back nonchalantly in his plastic seat, his legs apart and a scowl on his face. Silently, Timms turned his back on him, nodded to the guard and left the room. Pausing only to listen to the sound of the key turning in the lock.

Milo Cresswell had been crying for the last fifteen minutes and Smith had been unable to get anything out of him, other than the statement that 'he was not to blame' and 'knew nothing'. Smith suspected that this was probably correct but the grey area existed because Milo had served eighteen years, in various prisons, for the sexual abuse of thirteen boys all under ten years of age. This, in itself, proved that nothing Cresswell said was to be believed. The elderly man had ushered him into the small, city-owned apartment and encouraged him to look round for himself. Smith had taken in the piano, checking that the stool had not been raised above the level Cresswell would use himself and done some casual rifling through magazines. He also checked that the man wasn't using a password to enable himself to use his ancient pc and that there weren't any signs of an internet cable being utilised. Satisfying himself on these levels, Smith had proceeded to ask the paedophile whether he had any information regarding the disappearance of Thomas Banks. The man had instantly dissolved into tears and a mantra of innocence.

Smith had had enough. He was tired, upset and making no progress in trying to gather sufficient information to bring Tommy Banks safely home. So, having to listen to irredeemable bastards like Cresswell blubbing and carping was beyond the tipping point for Smith. Which was why a silent Milo Cresswell was being taken, in handcuffs, to spend the next forty-eight hours in a holding cell, with a probable visit from the duty doctor.

Dr Blackmore ushered Eleanor in with a smile and pointed to the patient chair. "Good evening detective. How are you?"

"I'm in the middle of a case so I'm tired and there aren't enough hours in the day to follow up leads and catch the guy responsible. So I'd appreciate if you'd bear that in mind next time you feel the need to drag me in here on a whim."

Seb Blackmore nodded and sat himself down. "I'm working a case as well. The difference being that your clients are dead and mine is still alive and savable. There are few 'whims' in my line of work."

Eleanor twisted the corner of her mouth with irritation and sat down heavily.

"You look tired," he said quietly. "Have you started eating more?"

There was a long pause before Eleanor started speaking. "Yes, I believe I have."

He nodded and repositioned himself. "I want to try something a little different this session."

Eleanor narrowed her eyes.

"I need you to be more relaxed and without the use of class A drugs or a DUI conviction I only know one other way."

"I am *not* being hypnotised, if that's what you're about to suggest."

He smiled. "Forget everything you've seen or read. You will be completely aware of everything I'm asking, just a little less inhibited."

"I can't imagine a scenario where I would accept that happening."

"Ok, how's this? I will use a technique that will relax you and make you less distressed with the interviewing process. I won't make any attempt to take you into anything deeper than a drowsy state. At no point will you feel helpless or violated in any way."

"I've arrested people who've used that as a defence strategy."

He laughed. "Then I'll come quietly officer."

She scrutinised the face in front of her. There seemed to be a dichotomy between the youthful, open features of the man and his ability to set her nerves on edge and undermine her confidence and carefully constructed barriers. She spread her hands in a gesture of defeat and made herself comfortable. "Do it!"

"There's a lever on the right-hand-side of your armrest that will tip the chair back slightly."

In seconds she found herself lying comfortably and staring at the expanse of ceiling, noting with interest that where there should have been a central light fixing, there was a nothing but a small grey dot. She focused on the spot with interest, surprised when she heard Dr Blackmore's liquid tones mentioning the importance of doing just that. The 'spot' he explained through an increasing aural mist, was a way of relaxing her tired muscles and mind. A voice in her inner self was about to question the relevance or even likelihood of this being so but a calmer Eleanor shushed it. She had been so tired recently and just looking at the little grey dot made her feel as though she were lying in soft warm sand on a foreign beach, the sounds of the waves being the only disturbance. A warmth was cradling her and the snatches of voice that drifted into her consciousness were imploring her to sleep. She would, just for a little while and let all her worries and concerns drift into the ocean, to be swallowed and digested by the currents.

She didn't need to turn her head in order to know that she was no longer alone on the beach. A man was walking towards her, he seemed unthreatening but his presence was intrusive and unwanted. She wanted to tell him to leave but decided to ignore him, even when he sat a little to her right, shading his eyes from the sun.

"Eleanor, can you hear me?" he asked. "I need to talk to you about some things that happened to you recently. Would that be alright?"

She wanted to explain that she needed to be quiet and just take a few moments to relax but his presence was authoritative and persuasive. "Yes," she replied.

"Is there anyone else next to you Eleanor?" he said quietly.

"No," she replied, raising her head a little and scanning the horizon. "It's just us."

"Maybe you need to sleep a little deeper then," he said quietly.

The sand seemed to rise and engulf her, leaving only her face above the grains. It felt heavy and protective. "Look again," came the insistent voice from further away now. She opened her eyes and allowed them to adjust their focus onto the horizon. There was a shape, a dark corrupted shadow that flickered like a mirage. She pushed herself a little further into the sand. "Can you see him?" asked the voice more insistently.

"Yes," she murmured. "He's there but I don't want him. Can you send him away?"

"Not just yet Eleanor. We need to talk to him before we can do that. Who is he?"

Eleanor was beginning to feel uncomfortable.

"A child," she whispered, hoping the figure wouldn't hear or see her. "He's dead." Her voice sounded metallic and brittle in her ear.

"How can you tell he's dead?"

"His skin is swollen and black. There are flies moving in and out of his eyes and nose."

"Are you a child Eleanor?"

"No," she answered puzzled. "I can't be a child."

"Look at your hands," said the voice firmly. "Can you see them?"

Eleanor lifted her hands from the sand and looked at them. They were smaller than she remembered. The nails were pink and the skin freckled and unwrinkled.

"You're a girl Ellie," he said kindly. "You're just a child... Caleb's been hurt. Do you know who hurt him?"

"Yes," she whispered. "The man who lives there."

"What has he done to Caleb? Will he tell you?"

She wanted the voice to stop because the boy was moving closer to her, the buzzing of the flies overwhelming the soft lap of the waves.

"Ask Caleb what happened."

She hesitated before asking, her eyes locked onto him. "What did he do?" she heard herself ask the figure, which lurched towards her.

"He has to explain to you what happened Eleanor, it's very important," said the man's voice.

The boy was very close to her now. She could see the eyes were flat and milky, incapable of focus. His skin was slipping from his hands and he made small scooping gestures to try and pull it back, like an ill-fitting glove. The grossly swollen belly and genitals were lined with green bands that spread like webbing across him.

"Caleb?" she asked tentatively. "What happened to you?"

The figure stopped moving and then began to topple towards her. She let out a scream as the boy's full weight lay upon her chest.

"I can't breathe," she gasped, struggling in the sand.

"Breathe slowly Eleanor," said the man's voice. "Nothing can harm you while I'm here. Caleb wants to speak to you. He can't leave you alone until you've asked the question."

She was panting, desperately trying to suck air into her lungs. She screwed her eyes tightly shut, trying not to let the milky, lifeless eyes meet hers. "I'm scared!"

"Ask him the question Ellie," said the voice firmly.

"You wanted to tell me!" she choked. "Before you died. You wanted to tell me something..." she was aware that a groaning sound was emanating from somewhere deep within her. The warm sand was beginning to cool around her and it no longer felt nurturing but cloying and dangerous. "Please tell me."

The boy opened his mouth and filled her world with darkness. "I felt love."

There was a noise, a heavy mechanical chugging sound that made her chest hurt and her eyes water. Caleb was gone now and she wanted to go home. She looked around her and saw the man sitting next to her. He was staring at the ocean, his face a mask of fear. Why was he afraid? He said he wouldn't be. She sat up and looked to the horizon. There was a figure but it wasn't Caleb. It was someone that trailed death behind them and he was watching her.

She screwed her eyes tightly shut, making them hurt with the pressure.

"Has Caleb gone?" asked the man's voice, barely audible above the chugging roar.

"He has but..." She didn't want to talk anymore. She was scared and missed the warmth of the sand.

"Eleanor. Listen to me. Is there anyone else there?"

She groaned and tried to get further into the sand, rocking her body from side to side, like a snake escaping from the desert heat.

"Eleanor it's time to wake up now," he said kindly. "You've been very brave."

Something about that phrase triggered a panic and she began to thrash around in the sand. "I don't like it here!"

A clock was ticking and reminding her that it was morning and she had to get to work.

"Eleanor, are you awake?"

She looked at the man's calm, friendly face. It took her several moments to name him and understand where she was. She opened her mouth to speak but her lips were uncomfortably wet and salty. She'd been crying.

"I'm awake." She took the tissues he held out to her and wiped her face.

"Tell me how you feel?"

She grimaced and thought about it. "I'm tired." She smiled. "Like running a marathon tired."

He nodded. "It will have released of lots of hormones. You did well. Can we talk about it for a minute or two? It will help when you mull things over tonight."

"Yes," she said resignedly. "We can talk."

"You confronted Caleb."

She scowled. "That sounds aggressive. 'Confront'."

"You *confronted* your fears. Your fear of letting down your friend, of not understanding what was happening to him, of not being there for him. That's what you've dedicated your adult life to: not letting people down and being there for them. The victims of violent crime are avenged by you aren't they?"

"'Avenged' makes me sound like a comic book hero… I do my job."

"Your job was selected so that you can bring justice to those denied it."

She shrugged, uncomfortable with praise.

"You spoke with Caleb."

She nodded and fixed her gaze on him.

"Did he explain what had happened to him? Did he give you the sign that you missed?"

She leaned forward. "Where are we going with this? I didn't commune with a dead child's spiritual emanation. I spoke to *myself*. The dead are gone."

"But the guilt lives on inside us, like a cancer. I don't believe in ghosts either detective. I believe we haunt ourselves."

She rubbed her face vigorously with the damp tissue and then balled it and threw in neatly into the bin. "Are you performing an exorcism on me Dr Blackmore?"

He pursed his lips, as if pondering this concept. "You could call it that."

She sank back into the seat and let her eyes close as she thought. "Can I be healed through this process? Can I let go of Caleb?" she asked quietly.

There was a moment's silence before he spoke. "I believe so." He sighed and she sensed him moving closer to her. "I think you hate yourself. You punish yourself for not saving Caleb, for allowing yourself to be captured by Lee Hughes and not being able to bring him to justice. You have a deep and chaotic anger inside of you and I am afraid that we are going to lose you again… Maybe for good this time."

She snapped open her eyes. "Is there an 'unless' in that scenario?"

"Unless," he emphasised, "you can learn to forgive yourself and understand that none of us is a god."

She swallowed painfully and pulled the lever that reset the chair into an upright position. "I need to go now."

It was after nine pm when she staggered into her apartment. Eleanor knew she should have gone back into homicide and helped Laurence with the warrant but she felt so exhausted she headed home, not even bothering to text him. As she paced her bathroom, waiting for the water to fill the tub, she tried to settle the surges of emotion that started in her belly and spread wave-like through her chest and throat, ending in a band of pressure that wrapped around her temporal lobes like steel. She was agitated and confused, not quite able to rationalise the events of the past couple of hours. She wanted the distress to end, for thoughts and fears to be buried deeper again, locked away but it seemed too late for that. The dead were rising inside her.

Eleanor lifted the carriage clock that squatted heavily on her desk and picked up the card she'd secreted there, smoothing it between her fingers and tracing the yin/yang symbol with her thumb. She could call the number and taste the contrition and release that anonymous sexual encounters brought.

CHAPTER EIGHTEEN

L aurence knocked loudly and repeatedly on Enda Miller's front door. It was seven thirty in the morning and emerging from the stairwell Smith looked as if he'd encountered a tornado en route. His clothes were creased and sweaty, his face red and expression pained. Laurence hammered again. "What happened to you?"

"What do you mean?" asked Smith warily.

"Yes?" said Enda, opening the door fractionally. Laurence held the warrant at eye level before giving the door a meaningful shove.

"Can you confirm you are Enda Miller of Apartment sixteen, Bantock Estate, Toronto?"

"Yes," he replied, licking his lips nervously. "I thought we'd established that yesterday."

"This is a warrant to search your premises and confiscate your computer and any other item deemed appropriate in our investigation into missing items from the Royal Ontario Museum," said Laurence, stepping past Enda.

"But I've not stolen anything from the museum!"

"Then you have nothing to worry about. Look at this as the first step in clearing your name and enabling us to move on with our investigation and locate the culprit," said Laurence, walking into Enda's bedroom.

If Laurence had expected a pile of incriminating evidence, he was to be disappointed. He turned to face Enda, whose expression slipped fractionally into one of smugness before regaining its default setting of nervous indignation.

"Where's your laptop?" asked Laurence, irritated.

"Unfortunately, I had a small accident last night and managed to knock a full cup of coffee over the keyboard. It's completely dead. Everything lost!" He shook his head to emphasise his disbelief in this turn of event.

"Where is it?" snapped Laurence.

I put it in a box, ready to take to a friend's to see if anything could be retrieved."

"Well maybe our forensics team can help you with that problem. They've retrieved data from all manner of broken and seemingly destroyed machines." He noted with pleasure that Enda's smile didn't seem quite as confident as it did earlier.

Toby was so distracted this morning that he walked straight into his office without registering the presence of Isabel Drake and a uniformed officer. "Toby, this gentleman is here to collect Enda's computer. Is this it?" she pointed to the machine on Enda's desk.

"Yes. Yes it is," replied Toby. "I'm afraid I haven't seen him this morning."

The patrol officer ignored him and began to pack the machine into a box.

Isabel moved towards him and said quietly, "You won't for a while. He's on extended leave until matters are concluded."

"I see," said Toby, with a suitably worried expression on his face.

"I'll be in my office," said Isabel, off the patrol officer's expression. She ushered Toby into the corridor and closed the door. "Goodness me what an awful business," she said unhappily. "Of course we can't be sure that Enda's been... pilfering but it seems as though it's probably him."

Toby nodded sympathetically.

She was just about to walk towards the stairs when she turned back to him, conscious that he seemed rather shaken by the events taking place. "Did you read about the police finding a second body on the Westex Landfill site?" she said in a conversational manner.

Toby jerked his head up. "I didn't know they'd found a first!" he said astonished.

"*Really* Toby, it's been headline news for the last week. There's not a paper or news channel not broadcasting it. Have you still not got a television?"

"I'm not really very keen on televisions or radio broadcasts," he answered weakly.

"But surely you take a paper?"

"I don't actually."

"How strange you are Toby," she said as lightly as she could. "I'd thought for a moment they might have found that girl who used to work here. You must remember her, Olivia something or other. She was on an exchange with Vancouver wasn't she? Lovely girl but it must have been nearly six years since she disappeared. Very sad."

"I don't recall her."

Isabel looked at him with astonishment, raising one eyebrow. "I'm surprised. I do recall you were rather attached to her." With that she turned and walked away. His heart racing, Toby began to feel sick. He put a hand against the wall to steady himself. It had never occurred to him that anyone would find them.

The board had been neatened since yesterday, all the connectives had been redrawn with a straight edge and the photographs evenly distributed and aligned. She smiled when she saw that Johnson had even taken Ruby Delaware's 'Fuck You' note and placed it below the line in a section marked 'Tentatives'. Eleanor drew up a chair and began to focus her energies on seeing connections. She hadn't slept particularly well last night, despite her exhaustion. Her dreams had been filled with chasing, drowning and darkness. She'd taken several painkillers when she woke up and was glad to get into the car and come to work. She let her eyes work the board.

"What can you see?" asked Mo quietly behind her.

She let her mind make another sweep before throwing out ideas. "Enda Miller isn't part of this but I know that the objects he's believed to have stolen are."

"The only one you can link is that toy wooden snake and that could have been bought off Enda when he acquired it from the museum," proffered Mo. "Did his fingerprints match any of the unknowns?"

She shook her head. "No, but chances of there being baby skulls…" she began.

"Neither Parminder nor Dieter mentioned they were conjoined. That's the only link to the museum. Tara's hair combs weren't on their list of missing objets d'art."

"There were two calls to the museum from a public call box next to where Parminder worked."

"But there were hundreds of enquiries that day. Why couldn't a tourist have been calling about opening times or directions?"

"I think I'm going to have another chat with Enda Miller. Can you call forensics and see what the time scale is?" said Eleanor thoughtfully.

"You betcha," Mo replied, pulling over one of the phones. Eleanor was dimly aware of her stomach rumbling noisily. When he finished dialling Mo pointed a finger at her belly and then stabbed it at the second room, which adjoined hers. She got up and sauntered in. Timms was on the phone and using a pen nib to puncture holes in an erasure on his desk, while he negotiated with the caller. The empty room was littered with papers and the remains of abandoned fast food, as officers had tried to snatch a mouthful before going back out to work the case. She noted that several spouses had brought in protein bars, snacks and left little messages willing them to find the boy.

She took a seat and waited for Timms to finish his call, noting that Johnson had applied his visual skills to the Banks Board as well. She cast her eye over the information and felt a pang when she saw the little boy smiling in his school photograph. She stood up and walked towards the board, her attention drawn to a photograph of some old-fashioned toy trains. The photograph had been printed off a website and it contained a detailed description of the Hornby trains and their estimated value in dollars, both with and without their original packing. Her stomach gave a lurch.

"Hey Raven..." said Timms stifling a burp. "Have you..."

"Why'd he take the trains?" she asked curtly.

"Huh? We don't know... Thoughts are that he may have taken them to comfort the boy or maybe as a trophy. Why?" he said suspiciously.

"Did he take *anything* else?" she said deep in thought, her eyes never moving from the board.

"No, not as far as we know. What are you thinking? 'Cos we are happy to receive any ideas, however fucking left of field, at the moment."

"It says there was track left behind. Was the track antique?"

"I don't know... Hang on, mom said he'd been given the track as a birthday present but the trains had belonged to his grandfather, so probably not. What are you seeing?" he asked, moving closer to her and following her gaze.

"He took the trains along with the boy..." she mused.

"Yeah, he did."

"I think it's him... The Collector."

Timms looked astonished. "I don't get how you think it's him? He didn't take anything when he snatched Giselle or killed Parminder. How have you gotten to this? Give me the thread."

"Objects... antiquities, matter to him. They're his currency."

"But taking a seven-year-old boy. That doesn't fit the MO." He shook his head. "This isn't working for me. He takes women and embalms them. That's *women* and every book and brain confirms that psychopaths stick to gender, race and type. Where does this kid fit in?"

"I think –" she turned to Timms and met his gaze "– he's making a family."

"A *what?*" said Timms with horror.

Wadesky walked in and lifted a hand in greeting.

"Come listen to this one. Raven thinks the perp that took Tommy Banks is the same guy responsible for Giselle, Parminder and Michelle Brown. *None* of which, I hasten to add, have been definitely linked as killed by the same guy."

"Okaaay," said Wadesky warily. "Let's hear the whys and hows."

For a brief moment Eleanor doubted her judgment. As soon as she'd vocalised her theory it sounded crazy, even to her. She cleared her throat and focused her thoughts.

"I believe there might be a connection between Tommy Banks' kidnapping and the murders of Giselle, Parminder, Michelle and…Tara."

"Tara?" yelled Timms. "You have no fucking *body* for Tara Roques. She's a missing prostitute who *happens* to look like a dead transsexual prostitute!"

Wadesky's eyebrows shot up. "Hey when did we stop listening to ideas Timms? Because we are drowning in fucking theories and leads at the moment!"

There was a silence broken only when Laurence and Smith walked in closely followed by Mo.

Laurence looked around expectantly. "We missing something?"

"Raven here's got a new theory on Tommy Banks," said Timms, waving his hand as if to introduce her.

Eleanor stood by the board and looked at the exhausted faces. She braced herself. "Whoever took Tommy took his trains but nothing else. The trains were antique Hornby ones by the look of it; collectible and quite rare." Eleanor looked at the sea of disbelief surrounding her but ploughed on. "I think there's a possibility that Tommy was taken by the same killer and that he's going to kill and preserve him."

"Urm, why?" asked Laurence sceptically.

"He's creating a family for himself." Her throat felt tight and she was finding it difficult to swallow but she had crossed her Rubicon and carried on. "That's why he replaced Giselle with Tara, she is a type and I imagine there are more bodies, maybe a lot more. We know that he has an Irish setter that was probably taxidermied years ago, as it registers high for arsenic used prophylactically."

"Huh?" said Smith.

"Used to prevent infestations of mites," said Laurence.

"I thought arsenic was a poison," said Smith, surprised. Laurence looked at him and then back at Eleanor. "Go on," he said encouragingly.

The ensuing silence in the room could be sliced.

"So all this is based on the fact that the perp who took Tommy took his train set?" said Smith, shaking his head.

"It fits the profile." Eleanor said flatly.

"How?" said Timms. "I'm listening but I gotta tell ya I've not heard anything that convinced me yet." He waved his hand expansively.

Eleanor glanced at her feet before taking a deep breath. "If I stole a child from his bed in the middle of the night I wouldn't stop to pick up four trains which are ill-suited for just slipping into a pocket. It was hot and the kidnapper wouldn't have worn lots of clothes, particularly as he had to climb through a window. It's unlikely that he had a bag or would want to come back and grab them. If I was taking the child with the intention of keeping him alive and wanted to grab a comforter I'd take a teddy bear or soft toy. I could put it under my arm or let the child hold it. I wouldn't select four trains." She paused and noted that only Laurence and Mo were nodding at this point but neither with any degree of conviction. She carried on. "A paedophile would find only value in the child, not the trains. So, I think it's worth pursuing..."

Timms cut in, "...Pursuing what exactly? You haven't managed to find a link between any of *those* murders yet!" he said loudly, pointing his finger in the direction of her murder board. "You haven't anyone lined up as a possible candidate, *neither* have you one single piece of evidence that links any of the women. Hell, you don't have a body for Tara, and Parminder Kaur wasn't preserved. It's just supposition! Tell me I'm wrong?"

She stared at Timms for several moments, thinking carefully. "You're not wrong. But… I believe I'm right."

Timms flung his hands up in despair. "I need facts not wishful thinking. If you can get me some concrete evidence that links your caseload to mine then I will consider it and come on board and let you lead. Until then…"

Eleanor suddenly realised what Timms was thinking. "I'm not looking to take over your case!" she said with astonishment.

"Honey, you're welcome to this shit. We're past forty-eight and as far as me and Wadesky here are concerned, we're most likely looking at taking Tommy to Doc Hounslow, not his mom when we find him! But listen it was interesting and anything more substantial I'm all ears." He pointedly reached for the phone, after first catching Wadesky's eye.

Eleanor made her way back to her own office and closed the door.

What the hell was she thinking? She hadn't even given herself five minutes of thought processing before jumping in with an opinion. She rubbed her neck and head and tried to clarify her thoughts, why had she jumped to the conclusion that The Collector had kidnapped Tommy Banks? There wasn't a shred of proof or even a hint that could be communicated clearly to another person. It was just a belief, a gut instinct. Maybe, she surmised, every single above the board fact and link could be relocated below the line into 'Tentatives' and the only thing that was a solid, fact-based concept was that Timms should 'go fuck himself'!

She sank into her chair and hoped that she'd said enough for everyone to steer clear of her for the next couple of hours. Mo and Laurence entered and closed the door behind them. "Maybe," said Laurence firmly, "you could have run that little theory past us first. You know, just to see if there were any holes in it." He lifted his hands in a gesture of defeat. "Because if you had I think we could have refined it a little more and not just stated that there was only the one guy responsible for every body between here and Nova Scotia!" He sat down heavily and sighed.

Eleanor rubbed her eyes. She felt an overwhelming tiredness. " I agree," she said.

"Do you regret what you said?" asked Mo carefully.

She thought for a moment. "No. Not what, just how I said it."

Mo nodded and then added simply, "Then find him." Mo answered the phone after a couple of rings. He nodded. "Be right down." He picked up a notepad and pen. "Bob Brown's just arrived."

Mo ushered Bob Brown into 'Interview Three' and pulled a chair out for him. "Mr Brown, we met on a couple of occasions three years ago."

Bob nodded and held out his hand, "I remember. It's Detective Morris?"

"Just Mo," he shook Bob's hand and gestured to Eleanor. "This is DI Eleanor Raven and she is in charge of the investigation into Michelle's death."

Bob took a seat.

"Neither Mo nor myself worked your daughter's case three years ago but we have read through all available materials and are being supported by Detective John Smith, who will be working closely with us," said Eleanor, positioning her notebook and pouring three cups of water.

"Can you tell me if you've got any suspects yet?" Bob asked carefully.

"We are following several lines of investigation but were hoping that by talking to you, there may be something you could add that might help us," said Mo, taking over at the prearranged nod from Eleanor.

"Christ, I told them at the time everything I knew about her plans that day."

"The day she disappeared?" clarified Mo.

"Yes. And I can't be one hundred per cent that anything I tell you again wouldn't have been altered by the years passing. I kinda knew the day off by rote, as I'd been through it so many times with the officers." He scratched his head and fidgeted.

They waited. Bob began to wring his hands uncomfortably, reluctant to embark on the journey again. He cleared his throat. "She…" He took a deep breath and started again. "Michelle, was already up that Thursday with her mother Liza when I got downstairs. She'd been accepted at the Nursing School and was making some extra money over the summer to help with the costs, so she'd been helping her mother clean.

Mo consulted his notes. "She helped clean over at the morgue."

Bob coughed and nodded. "Not the morgue itself; she cleaned the offices. Her mother used to work for the city cleaning services but they'd brought in some legislation that allowed the morgue to go to private tender. So, Liza set up her own sort of one-woman company and cleaned the office suites because Doctor Hounslow, bless her, wouldn't have anyone else do it. She trusted Liza…" He pulled a handkerchief from his pocket and rubbed his face, emptying the cup of water before resuming his account. Eleanor filled it up again. "So, she paid Michelle to help her there and with some of her private clients. She had about five houses she'd go and clean for when she'd finished at the morgue."

Mo selected a sheet of names and addresses and placed it in front of Bob. He looked at the list and nodded. "Yes, that's them."

Mo took the sheet and passed it to Eleanor, who read through the list as Bob carried on.

"She went with Liza to clean and they finished at around four and according to her mother she had a shower and then went out to meet her friends at a bar. I was at work and didn't get home till round seven-ish. Michelle said she'd be back at eleven but by twelve she wasn't home. I called her friend Esme Randall, who told me she'd never shown." He shook his head and looked at his hands.

"What did Esme and her friends think when she didn't show up?" asked Mo quietly.

Bob shook his head. "They had tried calling, as we had, but the phone was dead."

"It was never found."

"No, the phone never showed up, neither did Michelle or any trace of her," he cleared his throat. "Until now." He shuddered and when he began to speak again his voice was slightly louder and higher in pitch. "I saw her. She was... recognisable... as Michelle." He focused his gaze intently on Eleanor. "Doctor Hounslow swore to me that whoever killed her did it quickly; straight away." He was beginning to get agitated. "That she hadn't been alive all these years and locked up." Bob Brown turned away, his shoulders slumped and his eyes and face wet. "Because I couldn't bear that she was alive and I hadn't found her."

"I think she was murdered around the time she was taken. There were no marks on her body as far as Doctor Hounslow could see, which means she didn't die a violent death. She was…" Eleanor chose her words carefully, "…gone and unaware of the abuse that followed. Do you understand what I'm saying?"

He stared at her, eventually nodding slowly.

"There's a possibility that Michelle's murderer selected her. Perhaps he'd seen her on a previous occasion. Maybe she knew him, however vaguely."

"A friend?" he said horrified.

"No, an acquaintance, maybe not even that. All of her friends were checked and rechecked and she didn't seem to lead a secretive life."

"No, she was open and friendly and liked people, that was why she wanted to be a nurse." He looked away. "She knew she was different, with having the Marfan and all but she'd laugh about her height."

"She was six foot two wasn't she?" said Mo.

Bob smiled. "Her mother was tall but Michelle towered over everyone." He leaned forward conspiratorially. "She said that people would think she was a tranny when she wore heels." He laughed. "She was a good sport." Suddenly Bob stopped smiling and looked at Eleanor. "It was a joke," he said with an apologetic edge.

"Mr Brown did your daughter have any connection to the museum. The ROM?"

He shook his head. "I don't think so… Hang on, how'd you mean?"

Eleanor felt her stomach tighten. "Had she any connection to the city museum in any capacity?"

"She went for an interview there about a week or so before she died. It was a cleaning job but she didn't get it… Is that what you mean?"

CHAPTER NINETEEN

"**D**o you remember interviewing her?" asked Eleanor hopefully, writing notes with her right and cradling the receiver in her left.

"I'm sorry I really don't recall her that well," said Isabel Drake. "There were two candidates for the cleaning job and we offered it to Mrs Perkins because she was happy to take the full contract. I think Miss Brown only wanted the contract till the end of the summer." She paused for a moment. "Detective Raven, I really feel as though there's something more going on than the stealing of a few artefacts. You're a homicide detective aren't you?"

"I am yes."

Suddenly Isabel Drake let out a gasp, "I recognise the name...from the papers this morning. Michelle Brown was one of the landfill victims wasn't she?"

"Yes she was."

"Do you think that someone working here is responsible for those murders?"

"I have no idea," replied Eleanor. "Do you?"

Toby was taken aback by the cost of the *Toronto Sun* and his natural reticence for spending made him almost tempted to reject the purchase but he desperately needed to know how much information the police had and whether or not they had linked Little Tommy's disappearance to him. He sat down in the quadrangle and read. He wasn't entirely sure how to sift the facts from journalistic hyperbole but noted, with a degree of comfort, that Tommy held the front page and that the two detectives in charge of this investigation weren't the same as the two allocated to Giselle and Michelle's case. Something that wouldn't have been plausible if the cases had been deemed connected. As for the disposal of Parminder Kaur, there was only a small mention on page eight, which appeared to conclude that the detectives were stymied as to the motivation. Toby took a deep breath and relaxed. He had wound himself into a state of distraction over the whole business and needed a few moments to calm down and get matters into perspective. Of Tara, there had been nothing. No mention however oblique had been made to her disappearance and this was the best news of all. When he thought about things in the clear light of day he realised that he'd jumped to conclusions. As it was, Enda would be found guilty of stealing objects and would lose his job, a scenario that suited Toby just fine.

Laurence was troubled. He had found an excuse to go and investigate on his own, leaving Eleanor to pursue a different line. It wasn't the most effective way to conduct an investigation but he had no idea what was happening to the woman. She seemed incapable of rational thought at the moment and after having announced to the whole department that she knew who had taken Tommy Banks, he felt the need to distance himself from her. He'd popped in to see Marty Samuelson earlier about whether or not the transfer he wanted was going to be sanctioned but the short shrift he'd received from his boss put that thought on hold for a while longer. He had been so desperate to win Eleanor over and shift her dogged allegiance from Mo to himself, that he hadn't really considered that her methods were, at best, unorthodox. It was undeniable that she had the best solve rate in the department and, some considered, the city itself but where the hell was she dragging him with these ideas? It was as if her encounter with Lee Hughes had killed all the sense in her. He mulled over these thoughts, as he pulled into a spare parking spot outside the forensic labs. Monster began to whine, presumably in anticipation of getting out and stretching his legs. He'd promised Kate on reception that he'd bring him and no one ever denied her a request.

Monster trotted through the automatic doors and headed straight over to Kate. Laurence winced as he saw the huge creature put both forepaws on the edge of her wheelchair and tower above her. Kate responded by flinging her arms round him and burying her face in his fur. A gesture both seemed happy with, as it was sustained for several moments. "Every time he does that my heart leaps into my mouth," said Laurence as he signed in and helped himself to a visitor's badge.

"He's fine, he's never going to knock me over and if he does I get a good-looking cop to lift me back in," she giggled.

"I'm not seeing any of those round here," said Laurence.

"You tease," she said, examining Monster's re-stitched head. "Aww, it looks so sore!"

"Well, he shouldn't have pulled out all the stiches with his foot should he?"

"I guess not," she said stroking him. Monster had caught a glimpse of a couple of patrol officers arriving with several boxes. "Go on," she said shoving him gently. Monster trotted off happily to pursue more attention.

"You ok with him while I pop up and grab my report?" he asked.

"Of course."

Laurence headed for the stairs. "How'd you know he's not going to tip you over?"

"Because he's smart. When he walks towards the door, he never stops or slows down because he understands how fast the doors open and where they register him as approaching. Never seen any other dog that can do that. Hell, most people can't do that."

Laurence turned to face the glass doors, noticing that several people had approached them too quickly and had to stop and wait for the mechanism to catch up with their movement. "You sure?" he asked. "He seems like a bit of an asshole to me."

Kate smiled. "You need to have a little more faith in others."

He looked at Kate and then at Monster, who had adopted the 'tickle me' position, managing to bring all work and traffic in the building atrium to a standstill. 'Hmm," said Laurence non-committedly.

"We are doing our best but there's a backlog and your case isn't a priority," said Dr Andrews, as he identified Enda Miller's personal laptop as having arrived in the holding pen. He turned over the page. "However, the laptop brought in earlier from the ROM has been printed and suctioned. It's due for system analysis later."

"How much later?" asked Laurence.

"Well let's measure that concept shall we," said Dr Andrews acidly.

Laurence tapped lightly on Susan Cheung's door and slipped his head round. "Hey Susan, just in the neighbourhood..."

"The hell you were Whitefoot. You're hoping to bully your caseload through."

"Yup. Any news?"

"Funny you should mention but look at this." She beckoned him over to the adjoining room, where several plastic tubs, all bearing labels, barcodes and evidence tags were piled on trolleys waiting for attention. She opened a plastic tub after checking the label and slipping on latex gloves, picked out a small plastic wallet, sealed and barcoded. She held it up to eye level. It contained about a teaspoon full of dust and hair. "This was suctioned out of the laptop you sent in this morning. It's got a rather interesting hair in it."

"Go on," said Laurence, wondering where this was going.

"I haven't started processing this yet but I took a quick look under the microscope just to confirm I was right." She jiggled the contents and then pointed to a hair that was clearly distinguishable by its colour."

"Shit!" said Laurence excitedly, seeing the three-inch-long red hair.

"I'm going to try and do this properly later on this afternoon. But unofficially it's a hair from an Irish red setter."

"That's fantastic. I can get a warrant on that basis as soon as you've confirmed that it's –"

Susan interrupted. "But I took this from the museum laptop and what's even more interesting is that there weren't any fingerprints on the keyboard."

"What do you mean?" asked Laurence confused.

"Plenty on the case but someone wiped the keypad clean."

"When can you run them?" he said, struggling to make sense of the information.

"I can't today but will as soon as I can. I had to dust and suction so the IT guys could start whenever. I'm not sure how the home laptop is going to be tackled as it will be dried out first, which can take several days."

"Ok," he said, waggling his phone at her. "Call me as soon as you…"

"Yeah, yeah," she waved her hand dismissively and carried on with her work.

Monster was lying contentedly next to Kate's wheelchair keeping a careful eye on all the comings and goings. "He behave himself?" asked Laurence.

Kate smiled. "Of course!"

Monster caught sight of Timms approaching from the steps and bounded over to greet him. "Hey Kate," said Timms, as he ruffled the dog's ears.

"How's it going?" she asked. Timms grimaced and shook his head.

"That good huh?"

"You know it," he replied glumly. "Hey Whitefoot, you leaving?"

"Yup. Listen…" said Laurence, manoeuvring Timms away from reception. "I wanted to say that I wasn't aware Raven had been thinking in those terms and if I had, I would have got her to think it over before announcing it to the whole department."

"Uh-huh…" said Timms, his eyes narrowing. "You just told me this or anyone else?"

"What do you mean?" said Laurence, confused.

"I'm not sure what the point is you're making here but if my partner blasted a theory outta her ass and God knows that's a monthly event, I'd be backing her up one hundred per cent…in *public*! You getting me? You disagree with the shit your partner's coming out with it's a *private* matter." Timms moved closer to Laurence and examined his face as he spoke.

"The second thing is that however bat-shit nuts the thinking is behind Raven's ideas, she is generally right. You and me," he said poking him in the sternum with a finger, "we don't think outside of the box. We just keep digging and bullying till something sticks. Raven thinks *creatively* and remember that next time you want to apologise for her doing that. Now I think her latest idea's a big bag of shit but I wouldn't be overly surprised if there was some grain of truth there."

Laurence stared back at him, his lips pursed and jaw clamped tightly shut.

"Loyalty Whitefoot, that's the key to a partnership."

Irritated, Laurence headed for the door. He gave a low whistle hoping that Monster wouldn't require a second. He paused momentarily as the doors opened, noting with satisfaction that Monster trotted past obediently.

He turned to look at Kate who smiled and nodded. "See," she said.

"Where are you now?" asked Laurence, pulling into the traffic. He heard a sigh on the end of the line.

"I'm in the office but will be heading over to the museum shortly."

"Well wait, I'm coming with you," he replied.

"Okay," she replied.

Eleanor drove swiftly and a little erratically through the stagnating traffic. If the car journey had been intended as an opportunity for Laurence to discuss some of Eleanor's recent statements on possible links to suspects, it wasn't to be. There had been a steady stream of incoming calls to Laurence and Eleanor was finding his laid back conversational phone manner increasingly irritating.

"Fantastic... Thanks for that... You too," he replied, scribbling a couple of notes in his pad. "Okaay... How does this sound? That was the waitress from The Libertine and she managed to chat to one of the guys she recalled hung around with Giselle from time to time. She thinks he might remember the boyfriend. I'll follow that one up."

There was a pause, as Eleanor manoeuvred the car into a bay, careful not to scratch the beautifully preserved Oldsmobile to her left. In the unforgiving summer sun, Laurence noted that her skin looked dry and grey, her eyes rimmed with dark shadows. As she pulled the key out of the ignition she caught his expression. "What," she snapped. "Are we about to discuss whether I'm fit enough mentally and/or physically to do the job?"

"No, I was just wondering how you are?" he said lamely.

"Fabulous," she replied indifferently.

Eleanor walked slowly through the cool atrium of the museum, stopping to show her badge to the receptionist who nodded and waved her in. "What are we looking for?" asked Laurence, contritely

She sighed. "A sign."

Laurence nodded. "Any idea of what form this will take?"

"Signs have a habit of being retrospective beacons unfortunately." Then in a lighter but lower tone, "What we have, apart from gut instinct, is a series of links to this institution. Giselle had kept a brochure of a ROM 'Animals in Art' exhibition amongst her possessions. She had a snake that originated from here and possibly a pair of skulls. Parminder may have called the museum hours before her murder and Michelle Brown had attended a job interview in the museum days before her disappearance."

Laurence pondered and nodded, determined at this stage not to point out the discrepancies and vagaries of the links.

"Michelle Brown's body had trace evidence of dog hairs, the same as the one found in Miller's work laptop. That's solid evidence, unless there's been a breach of handling protocol. There was no dog found in Enda's apartment was there?"

Laurence shook his head. "So, what are we looking for?"

She smiled and shrugged. "We're looking for a Collector and a museum seems as good a place to start as any."

Isabel Drake knocked lightly on the door and turned the handle when no response was forthcoming. Frowning, she selected the master on a small keyring and opened the door to Enda and Toby's shared office. "I'm really not sure where Toby is at the moment," she checked her watch. "I suppose he might be taking an afternoon break in the canteen… Shall I page him?"

"Yes please," said Eleanor, walking into the room and absorbing the ambience.

"Has Enda Miller been arrested?" asked Isabel cautiously.

"I take it you have no objections to me looking around?" asked Eleanor.

"Of course not," responded Isabel. "I'll just…" she waved her phone and tiptoed back out into the corridor. Seeing an opportunity, Laurence closed the door carefully behind her. Eleanor slipped on a pair of latex gloves and began to run her fingers along Enda's table, pulling out the drawers and looking through them. Laurence turned his attention to the bookcases on the peripheries of the room. "Anything?" he asked.

Eleanor had replaced the bottom drawer and was pulling out the top one. "Check the other desk," she said, nodding towards Toby's. With a furtive glance at the door, Laurence scanned the tidy desk, notable for its absence of personal objects. There were two pens and a pencil in a small jam jar and two trays marked 'in' and 'out', positioned at one end. He pulled out a drawer and began to leaf through the meagre contents. A roll of what looked like picture hanging wire was uncoiling messily in the back of the first and a collection of jewel beetles preserved in resin sat in a small ceramic bowl alongside various papers and photocopies bound together in a clip file in the bottom drawer. Flicking through the papers, Laurence noted that most of the subject matter seemed to be concerned with a new paper on Occupational Health and Safety Regulations, an area that drew yawns from all but the heartiest of jobsworths.

Toby really needed to get home. He wasn't due to leave for another three hours but decided that no one would notice if he disappeared a little earlier than usual. To be more precise he didn't really care if it was observed. Now that Enda had been removed he had all the scope he needed to move around the museum with the minimum of detection. Who would be able to find him or deny his presence in the labyrinthine corridors and vaults of the museum? He had taken a back exit to the staff car park and slid into the Oldsmobile, without attracting a single glance.

Tamping down his excitement, he managed a double check on the garage locking mechanism before heading quickly into the main house. He stood still and listened to the unbroken silence. That worried him. Little Tommy had definitely been alive when he left in the morning, as he could hear his monotonous wails for his mother. He approached the basement with a degree of trepidation. It really wasn't the end of the world if the boy had passed but it would mean that his plans to start the final stages of Tara's transformation would have to be put on hold. As he turned on the light he was greeted by a squeal. "Good evening Tommy," he said warmly. The boy stared at him with dull eyes. "Did you eat your bread?" Toby peered critically at the child's face. He noted with a sinking heart that the blisters and open sores were little improved, if anything they seemed worse. He tutted. "Have you been scratching your face? I told you…"

"I know who you are," said Tommy, glaring at him. "You're the ugly man from the museum."

Toby bristled and began to prepare the bowl of water and flannel in order to clean the child.

"I hate you," he hissed. "I hope you die!" Tommy sank back into the crush, his filthy arms wrapped tightly around his skinny frame. Toby was used to being abused but hadn't expected it from the child. Maybe this was a salutary lesson for him in the essential corruption of the human spirit. Just when an individual should have been striving for some dignity and elevation they were generally bad mouthing, carping and behaving like guttersnipes. He tutted again. "I'm a little surprised by that last remark Thomas. Only really horrible children would say something designed to make another person feel unhappy and uncomfortable."

"I'm going to chop your head off!" said Tommy, with slow deliberation. His fists were now balled and his mouth pursed with anger. "When I get you, I'm going to chop you into little dead pieces and stamp on your face."

Toby relaxed and allowed himself a little smile. The child was feisty and determined, just as his son should be. Turning his back on the child he made his way up to the landing, snapping off the light. He noted with satisfaction that the child let out a little whimper of fear.

Tara's body rotated slowly and gracefully in the tank as he prodded it with a staff. Toby had checked that the pump was working and that the bubbles released by the acetone were sporadic rather than regular, which indicated that the preliminary stage of the process was pretty far advanced. A less impetuous man would have given it a few more days but Toby was feeling a pressure to complete matters. He had long since recognised in himself the tendency to maintain the status quo for months, sometimes even years and then go on into a frenzy of family expansion. It generally followed the death of a family member and their subsequent removal and burial. He would have preferred to continue burying those lost loved ones in the garden but he had filled the small plot years ago and felt that attempting to squeeze in any more would be disastrous.

Right, there was to be no more brooding, he had work to do and it was complicated and technical.. Once the acetone had been drained to the bottom couple of inches of the tank he carefully extracted the body of Tara and laid her gently on several towels. Her body was pliable, her skin toughened and slightly puckered. He examined her carefully, running his gloved hand over her flesh with all the desire and satisfaction that ownership brought. He gazed at her face, the eyeless sockets gave her depth and mystery and the compliant body made him rage inside. Pulling sharply at his belt, he lowered his trousers and pants, letting his hands slowly and firmly work at the tightness between her legs.

Quickly and heavily he pressed himself onto and inside the body of his new mistress.

Laurence spoke quietly and briefly into his phone. "That was Dr Andrews," he said. "He's started extracting data from the Miller hard drive and thinks we should probably call in and see."

"Any hints at the flavour of the data?" she asked.

Laurence shook his head. "He didn't sound particularly happy though."

Eleanor looked around the room, reluctant to leave. There was a tentative knock and Isabel opened the door cautiously. "I'm sorry but Toby hasn't responded to my page. I've called up various likely haunts but no one's seen him."

Eleanor looked interested. "Did Toby know we were coming here today?"

"I don't think so," replied Isabel. "He's a little... vague and is probably lurking in some dim and distant vault in the basement. I could run another check for you."

Eleanor thought for a moment. "I'm afraid we're both rather pushed today but I do want to speak to Toby...?"

"...Adams. Toby Adams. He's worked here for about twenty years, started before me and I've been here since the Ark..." her voice trailed off. "I'll tell him you'd like to speak to him."

"Is he working here tomorrow morning?"

"Yes."

"Perhaps you could call us when he gets here and keep a tab on his whereabouts."

Isabel nodded. "Of course."

Laurence watched, with grim determination, the unpleasant sight of Enda Miller jacking off to a karaoke version of 'I Can't Get No Satisfaction' and hoped that this vision wouldn't haunt him every time he considered indulging in a similar activity himself. "That is truly horrible," he said to anyone who was listening. "Dare I ask if there's more?" he asked Dr Andrews cautiously.

"You bet there's more," he sighed. "There's the section we've entitled, 'Mr Miller with various root vegetables'. 'Mr Miller and the cat'...Oh, and Mr Miller indulges in 'water sports'." Dr Andrews drew air quotes to illustrate the figurative nature of the latter.

"How much and how gruesome?" asked Eleanor deflated.

Dr Andrews sighed heavily and consulted his notepad. "No kids but I suspect the Humane Society will consider bringing a prosecution. Particularly the Small Mammal League," he grimaced.

"Could there be anything darker in there?" queried Eleanor.

"This guy's not data savvy in the slightest. His password for both work laptop and home was 'password'. It could be a double bluff but he doesn't seem to understand basic encryption either, so I'm guessing what we see is all that's there. However, I shall extract Mr Miller' back catalogue and present it to you on the morrow, where I hope you've got someone with a strong stomach prepared to sit and watch."

"No snuff, no necrophilia?"

Dr Andrews held up a hand. "One ground squirrel definitely didn't make it. Does that count?"

Laurence grimaced. "What an asshole! Where was he posting these Oscar winners?"

"All uploaded onto a site called, 'Amateur Sexploits'. Well, now we're all scarred for life, how about you guys leave me to it and I'll be in touch tomorrow?"

"Thanks," said Laurence, rising.

"So, you think that was what Miller was so reluctant to let us see?" asked Laurence, as they sat in the office drinking coffee. "His salubrious collection of mono-porn?"

Eleanor grimaced. "I'm not sure. He didn't seem all that concerned about being accused of theft, which could effectively lose him his position and prevent re-employment."

"If he didn't steal anything from the ROM, maybe he felt he had nothing to worry about?" suggested Laurence. "His stuff's in bad taste but not particularly criminal."

"Apart from the ground squirrel I'm guessing," said Eleanor grimly.

"Hmm."

Mo opened the door and smiled. "You chewing over Enda Miller? If so you might like to know that he was about to be appointed as a Methodist lay preacher."

Eleanor looked up. "Where'd you get that info from?"

"Ah," toyed Mo, helping himself to a coffee. "It was a good idea letting Smith conduct the interview. Three minutes into Smith's rant on paedos, sodomists and individuals capturing their abilities on webcams, and Miller wanted to confess immediately and requested the presence of his pastor. But he's still adamant on not having had anything to do with stolen artefacts from the ROM."

"So where does that leave us?" asked Laurence. "There's nothing to link him to any of the murders, or the stolen snake and skulls for that matter. Even if we do prove that he's been acquiring items from the ROM, there's nothing to say he's the direct link. The items could have passed through several hands."

Eleanor rubbed her neck and stretched. "There's a link, we just haven't got to it yet. If Enda didn't do it, someone at the museum did." Mo tapped his watch and nodded at her, a gesture not missed by Laurence. "Tomorrow, after we've interviewed Toby Adams, we're going to run through their employment records."

"And we'll know the perp by his name?" ventured Laurence his eyebrows raised.

"Perhaps by his address," smiled Eleanor, picking up her bag and neatening her desk.

"Clocking off?" said Laurence.

"I've got a therapy session."

"Ok, so I guess it'll be tomorrow morning then?" asked Laurence, looking at his watch critically.

"I'll try and meet up with you afterwards ok?" she said quietly.

"Excellent, well give me a call when you're done and in the meantime you want me to get a warrant for the records?"

"Prep the DA but so far Isabel Drake's been pretty co-operative."

Chapter Twenty

Eleanor sat quietly next to Seb Blackmore and stared at the sea. She let her fingers carve lazy circles in the sand and counted the waves with him, as they lapped around her feet. "How are you feeling?" he asked slowly, his voice coming from a distant point.

"I'm tired," she heard herself reply.

"Is Caleb here?" asked the voice.

"No, he's not here anymore."

"Eleanor, is there anyone else here?"

She heard herself groan as she scanned the horizon. A silhouetted figure stood with his back to her facing a tree. Something was twisting and flailing in the tree but she couldn't get a clear line of sight. "I can see... him."

"Is it Lee Hughes, the man who killed you?" asked Seb Blackmore.

Eleanor needed to see what was in the tree but she was afraid. Seb seemed to understand this instinctively. "What is he hiding from you Eleanor?" She could see the dark outline of Hughes flickering intermittently, as the hidden thing flapped and struggled behind him. "You have to take a look Eleanor, it's your job!" he said firmly.

Suddenly, she felt herself walking towards Hughes. His back was naked and scarred, covered in strange indecipherable markings. As his hand dropped to his side, she could see that it held a small paring knife. Eleanor was beginning to understand now what hung from the tree. She wanted to skirt round Hughes and see the object, without having to pass him but as she tried to clear a distance between them the ground fell away from her step, leaving a rope of sand that lead to where he stood. She placed her foot behind her, in an effort to regain some distance but felt the ground dissolve away. There was only one path and it lead to her death.

"Tell me what you can see?" said Seb anxiously.

"There's a tree... An oak tree standing by the water and something's hanging from a branch," she whispered.

"What is it?"

"I think it's me."

"Then you have to save yourself Eleanor," said the doctor firmly. "You can't let Hughes murder you. This is your chance to survive. If you fight, you can live."

Time's passage was difficult to gauge and Eleanor wasn't sure whether it was the past or the future that stood with his back to her. Quietly and deliberately she moved towards Hughes, her hands spread, ready to defend herself. As she crept forward, Hughes began to mirror her actions. He twisted round and looked directly at her; his bland features conveying the same fanatical expression he'd worn when he dragged her broken body into the ghost train, ready to present her as a macabre sacrifice to future artistic endeavour.

"You've been so brave," he hissed. "But now's the time to end it." As he leaped towards her, he drew his hand back and made a slashing gesture towards her face. Instinctively she pulled back, letting her weight drop onto her back foot. Using the momentum she launched herself forwards, grabbing his right hand, just as he raised his and using her left to create an arm lock. Kicking as hard as she could at his leg, he fell backwards, allowing her to land on top of him heavily. She held firm as he thrashed and bucked beneath her, looking into the empty pits of his eyes. She *could* kill him. There was so little life left in him; he would expire in an instant. Applying more pressure to his hand, she used his counter-pressure to enable her to press her elbow into his throat. The more he pulled away from her grasp the deeper her elbow penetrated, closing off his windpipe. She lowered her face so she could hear his last breath but there was nothing. He couldn't be killed because he was already dead. She stood up and stared at him sadly.

"Is he dead?" asked Dr Blackmore from somewhere close by.

"He always was, wasn't he? I kept him alive."

"It's time to wake up now Eleanor. You're going to hear me counting back from twenty..." His voice began to grow distant as she turned to look at the body wrapped in plastic that hung from the oak tree. She had believed absolutely that the figure swinging lazily from a meat hook would be hers; with horror she saw it was too small. She took a step towards it, her feet sliding deeply into the loosening sand. Desperate to see the face of the child, she tried to cut out the steady count down that brought her back. In the moments that straddled her dreams from the reality of the therapy room, she saw the dead face of Tommy Banks pressed against the plastic shroud.

As she opened her eyes she could see Seb Blackmore's smiling face. "You have done incredibly well Eleanor... How do you feel?"

What she felt was a deep well of anxiety and desperation but couldn't face analysing these feelings. "I feel... tired but okay," she answered lamely.

Blackmore narrowed his eyes. "Go on..."

She shook her head and tried a smile. There was a pause while Seb Blackmore's body language changed. He folded his hands onto his lap and straightened his back, then, realising she was watching and assessing this, he modified his position. Eleanor looked at him critically and waited.

"There's something we need to discuss," he said carefully.

She stared at him, wondering what he was preparing himself to say.

"I noticed your wrists," he said. "The first time you came in."

It took her a split second to understand his implication. She felt her face tighten and her chin lift.

"I think you are...self harming," he said cautiously.

She relaxed a little at this surmise.

"And...I think you have someone that helps you."

"Why do you think that?" she answered.

"Because you had, what appeared to be, rope burns on both wrists. Something that is difficult and...unsatisfactory for one person."

"My sex life," she said coldly, "is consensual and nobody's business but my own."

"I am not judging you Eleanor. I'm trying to enable you to forgive yourself."

"I'll call your secretary." Eleanor stood up and grabbed her bag, turning to him as he stood. "Thank you."

Eleanor lay in the bath and tried to work logically through the unconstructed emotional narratives her brain had flung up during the therapy session but felt frustrated and confused. Seb Blackmore appeared to be working on the premise that once faced, fears could be conquered but did she really fear Lee Hughes? He was dead, cremated and dumped in Potter's Field. Her eyes strayed to the images of Tess, and Rosalia Lombardo and wondered to which category Tommy Banks' picture should be added. She poured herself another glass of wine and closed her eyes. Tommy was dead and they wouldn't find him for years probably, because she'd managed to alienate the whole department by not processing her statement on The Collector being the likely kidnapper, through any rational section of her brain. She groaned, what the fuck was wrong with her? She stepped out of the bath and, snatching a towel, walked into her sitting room and began to pace. She felt stifled and a steady sense of outrage began to well up inside her. What she needed was not for some patronising asshole to help her find an inner forgiveness but for everyone to back the fuck off, stop judging her and let her get on with solving her caseload.

She reached for the card.

The man was early and this threw Eleanor slightly. She had expected sufficient time to prepare and control the environment but the knock came before she'd had time to compose herself mentally and physically. She hesitated before opening the door to a man, whose jumpy demeanour did little to assuage her own nervousness. For a moment she considered calling it off but on closing and locking the door he notably relaxed, even rewarding her with an apologetic smile. He was tall, expensively tailored and had a band of pale skin on his fourth finger. This made her uncomfortable; it had always been an unwritten rule of the club that members were single and no other person would be harmed, other than those seeking it.

After scrutinising him for several seconds Eleanor handed him the sheet of paper, which listed the tolerances of the encounter. All equipment used was to be hers and a blindfold would only be permitted after a verbal agreement from Eleanor herself. He read the list a little too quickly but redeemed himself by asking her to repeat the 'safe word' to him. She cleared her throat and articulated the word carefully. "Caleb." She wondered if he was going to question her choice or comment on its relevance but he didn't.

"Caleb," he repeated, as if that would somehow ensure that it had been stored in his memory. "Would you like a few moments to prepare yourself?" he asked quietly.

"Yes," Eleanor replied. The man nodded and turned his back to her. She undressed to her underpants and lay down on the bed. The hotel had supplied sheets of laudable vintage with a faint brown stain in the middle, which gave the event the rather sordid vibe she secretly loved. The hand and ankle cuffs had been supplied by Eleanor herself and were designed to allow the wearer an unscripted escape if the narrative wasn't going according to plan. "I'm ready," she said simply. The man turned to her, his breaths increasing as he took in her appearance. It was immaterial to Eleanor whether the man did or didn't find her attractive and as he took in her slender frame and small breasts she wondered if he found her as repulsive as she often found herself.

The man shrugged off his jacket and hurriedly slid it over the back of a metal chair, loosened his tie and slackened his belt. His fingers trembled fractionally, as he placed his hand onto her stomach. For a moment he was completely still and silent, as if mesmerised by the scene, then with a halting fumble he grabbed her wrists and fastened her to the uprights of the headboard. Her acquiescence must have given him more confidence, as he cuffed her ankles together in a fluid motion and then sat back onto the bed to take in her vulnerability. His trousers bulged tightly at the crotch in a tasteless display of arousal. Eleanor glanced away; she didn't want to see evidence that her selected partner was sexually stimulated by the act. It was etiquette that the majority of men or women that she shared these events with remained stolidly indifferent to the process. The right to a climax was hers, for the dominant partner, retrospection in the privacy of his or her room was the ideal.

The event began calmly and predictably with some gentle stroking, interspersed with slaps and squeezes. The man had managed to vary the rhythms so that she wouldn't be able to anticipate when a blow or pinch would occur. Eleanor didn't writhe or pull away from the blows she let them purge her. Nothing she'd felt whilst sitting in Seb Blackmore's office had been as cathartic as this. She allowed her mind to drift as her body made and wasted endorphins. Sensing her ease the man flipped her onto her belly, causing her arms to twist across each other, pressed to each side of her head. He pushed her face into the mattress, while slapping her legs and buttocks. She was conscious of being uncomfortable and restricted by her position but more concerning was that she could no longer see the man's expression. She pulled her head back sharply in an effort to free her face from suffocation but sensing this he pushed it down again, pressing so hard she felt the cartilage in her nose begin to crack. Before she could make a decision regarding the aborting of the event, the pressure was released and gently he turned her onto her back and let her recover. He had stepped away from her, as if taking time to calm himself. She examined his face and noted with a rising panic that he was no longer able to meet her eye. With a sudden lunge, he leaped onto the bed, straddled her and slapped hard at her face. That in itself wasn't particularly distressing, it was her glance at his left hand that sent a warning pulse through her. He was fishing in his pocket for something.

"What are you doing?" she hissed, bending her middle finger and pinioning it with her thumb in preparation to release the emergency catch. The man looked puzzled and then pulled out a white cotton handkerchief, which he used to mop his brow, shrugging off her concerns with an eye roll. The man was still, as if deep in thought. Eleanor waited, her breathing hard and ambivalent. He cleared his throat and began to speak haltingly. "I want to blindfold you."

Keeping her eyes firmly on his face she slowly rolled her head from side to side. He took a couple of seconds to mull over this reply before grabbing her hips and twisting her onto her belly. He pushed her face between her arms and into the mattress with his left hand, dropping his weight on top of her. Her finger was beginning to twitch under the pressure of holding it against the catch. Just as she felt his penis push between her legs she unclipped the cuff, releasing her hand. 'Rule One' stated clearly and categorically that no attempt at any form of penetration would be tolerated. The rage that suddenly began to boil inside her had a detached, almost clinical quality to it. In fact she could have been lying in Seb Blackmore's chair, focusing on the little grey dot for all her conscious self knew.

Eleanor grabbed his left wrist with her free hand and twisted it as hard as she could, using her right hand to push her away from the bed and embed her elbow into the soft tissue of the man's neck. Rotating her hips, she shoved her knees into his groin causing him to drop his raised fist and roll off the bed in a rictus of silent pain. As he fought for expression, she unfastened her right hand and not waiting to free her ankles, rolled off the bed and onto his chest. The first couple of punches broke his nose and snapped his bridgework. The second volley was less emotionally satisfying but the monotonous delivery, despite upbraiding the knuckles of her right hand, were a succinct reminder that rules were there for both party's protection.

She really wasn't sure how many seconds or even minutes had passed before she decided that some sort of external help was required. The man sobbed and cowered in the corner of the room, his erection long since deflated in contrast to that of his face and neck. His eyes were sealed with blood and haemorrhage and his spat out bridgework gave his collapsed features an ageless misery.

"Laurence?" she whispered into the phone.

"Yeah?" he said sleepily.

"I need you."

Laurence made a cursory knock as he opened the door to Eleanor's apartment and marched in.

"He *insists* on not pressing charges," he said angrily. "What the fuck are you doing? This is the second guy you've hospitalised in a matter of days!" He was struggling to modulate his tone and decibel level. "This is insane!" He began to pace in an effort to control his frustration. He pointed a finger at Eleanor and then withdrew it. "I am sick of being reminded that I fail you as a partner…"

"I have never said that," responded Eleanor, calmly.

"You don't need to *say* anything! The whole fucking department feels as though I let you down and that I don't support either your ideas or methods of policing."

"I don't feel you're alone on that one." She tried a smile but Laurence was on a roll. She watched his body language change as he revved himself up for the argument.

"Hughes had put you in a plastic body bag and was hanging you off a meat hook when I found you and how did *he* find you?" Laurence's cheeks were red, his pupils dilated with anger. Eleanor suspected that this was rhetorical and kept quiet, waiting for the inevitable answer. "He was gifted this information by a guy you met casually for abusive sex! But not having bothered to learn anything from this near death experience, you are still contacting random guys using the same card!"

Eleanor was feeling considerably less calm. "You have no right to…"

"I have every fucking right to!" he bellowed. "Because it wasn't just your life on the line when I went in to save you!"

"Would it have been more acceptable if Hughes had located me using his own initiative and not that of a casual sexual encounter?"

"You're a detective and you exposed yourself to unnecessary danger by your actions!" he hissed.

"I do that every day I put on a badge. You are objecting to my sex life, which is not yours to scrutinise or judge, " she said quietly.

"This relationship was killed, once and for all, when you accused me of arranging to have you kidnapped and tortured…I'd say that you do a pretty good job of arranging that yourself," he said, opening the door and slamming it shut behind him.

The silence settled heavily.

CHAPTER TWENTY-ONE

Samuelson looked tired. He hadn't shaved and was worrying his sleeve cuffs. "Your partner came in earlier to see me. He was very upset." He waited for her to say something but when nothing was forthcoming he carried on. "It is his belief that you are no longer fit for work."

Eleanor nodded, aware that Samuelson was scrutinising her hand and the bruising around her face. He leaned forward, his voice lowered. "I *knew* you weren't ready to come back." He looked away and sank back into his chair. "I don't know what has happened and –" he put up a warning hand "–don't want either to be told or given a hint of the reason because if you do that I *have* to investigate. Do you understand what I'm saying?"

She nodded.

"I am recommending that you accept the decision by this department that you require another three months' further sick leave, *with* a period of psychological assessment and probation before resuming full time responsibilities. Is that acceptable to you?"

Eleanor slowly shook her head. "I accept." Her career in homicide was over now. If Seb Blackmore deigned to provide an endorsement of psychological fitness, she'd be considered too fragile or jumpy for front line crime. They'd give her a pay rise and extra stripes but she'd be desk bound till retirement.

"I'm putting Whitefoot in charge of the case and Smith as his second. Mo will supervise unofficially. Give a debriefing before you take your leave."

She thought about this for a moment.. "Of course." She got to her feet.

"I'll need – " he began but she was already placing her badge and firearm on his desk.

Smith seemed particularly unhappy about the change in leadership. He stared grimly at Laurence as he explained that they would be running the case together for the foreseeable future with help from Mo. "I don't want this shit," he said with conviction.

Laurence shrugged.

"I don't want it because I don't know what the fuck we're dealing with and those connections you see on the board..." he looked pointedly at Eleanor. "I don't *see* any of those. I do not *excel* at these sorts of investigations," he said, choosing his words carefully.

Eleanor nodded. "I'll be ready to read through any material and advise. I would suggest that you start..."

"This is something to do with you, isn't it?" he said, scowling at Laurence. "You think you can do this without her. That you're going to ride in like the fucking cavalry with the perp roped behind you, like Jesse fucking James. Well –"

"Laurence is right. I'm not ready for work," said Eleanor quietly.

"The fuck! You were alright yesterday!" said Smith.

"You need to interview Toby Adams today." she said calmly. "The link is the ROM. It's important that you put that in the centre of the investigation."

Laurence nodded, grabbed his jacket and headed for the door. "You coming?" he glared at Smith. Taking sufficient time to register his reticence, Smith snatched up his pad and gave Eleanor a last growl. "You'd better pick up!"

Mo walked passed them, his cheeks flushed. "What the hell's going on? Samuelson's just told me that you're on sick leave and Whitefoot's in charge."

Eleanor got to her feet. "I need a little time, that's all." She gathered some papers together and put them into a box.

Mo rubbed his head. "Something's happened. Is it... Can I help in any way?"

"I fucked up but it'll be ok," she smiled.

Mo shook his head. "Not on this you haven't. I just popped in to see Timms. Tommy Banks can be linked to the ROM. The Saturday morning class he attends is held there."

Eleanor's body language changed in an instant. "What sort of class?"

"Apparently. It's for ages five to fourteen. They draw stuff and learn about it. He's been going there for about six months."

"I need a list of anyone who helped out there. You need to make sure Whitefoot gets all the employees' names and addresses. Our killer's name is on that list," she said emphatically.

"Keep your phone on you," said Mo anxiously.

Eleanor took a final wistful glance at her office and headed towards the stairs.

"Mo!" barked Samuelson, on seeing Eleanor depart.

"Boss?" Mo replied, walking into his office and closing the door behind him.

"You run *everything* past Raven you understand. Whitefoot and Smith have no fucking idea what they're doing. It's unofficial though. Anything she touches now will be thrown out of court so don't use any official channels; that includes work cell phones."

Mo smiled and tapped his forehead with two fingers in salute.

"Toby Adams?" asked Laurence, peering at the worried looking, middle-aged curator.

Toby nodded cautiously. "Is this about Enda Miller?" he asked meekly.

"You share an office with Mr Miller?"

"I do, yes."

Laurence waited but Toby seemed reluctant to offer any further enlightenment. "You've worked with him for the last three years. Have you noticed anything out of the ordinary with either his behaviour or work?"

Toby shook his head slowly. "I'm terribly sorry I haven't. I feel awful about being so half-witted about matters. Isabel confided in me that Enda was... suspected of having acquired certain items from the museum but I saw nothing to indicate that his behaviour was anything but noble."

Smith pursed his lips and rolled his eyes. "So while all this was going on, you'd have us believe that you saw nothing?"

Toby's cheeks burned as he considered this. "I'm sorry, no."

"Okay, okay." Laurence scratched his head, aware that Smith was growing bored. He ran through the print off that Isabel Drake had handed to him. "I see you live over in Little Portugal."

"That's right," he brightened.

"On your own?" asked Laurence.

"No, with my parents," he said relaxing more.

"This is your address and current phone number?" Laurence pointed to the information sheet. Toby narrowed his eyes, examining the list of names, job titles and addresses.

"Goodness, everyone's down here." Then, seeing Smith's expression, "Yes but the landline is currently not working, as they're laying some new cables down there. So we have mobiles."

"Would you mind writing that number down please?"

"Of course," said Toby, laboriously writing down a number in fussy italicised print.

"Do you drive in?" asked Smith.

"I occasionally drive here in my father's car but it's much quicker to use public transport."

Smith checked his phone. He read the text from Eleanor and then addressed the question to Toby. "Do you help run the children's club on Saturday?"

Toby pinched his lips together and looked embarrassed. "Very occasionally but only when they're short of hands. I'm afraid that working with children is not to everyone's taste. I tend to leave that to my colleagues." replied Toby, with feeling.

Smith nodded sagely. There was a moment's silence as Laurence contemplated matters. Smith tapped his foot and raised his eyebrow, much to Toby's satisfaction.

"Thank you, Mr Adams, we'll be in touch," said Laurence. Toby opened his office door for the two officers and nodded politely as they left.

"That guy's a perv," said Smith emphatically, as Toby closed the door firmly behind them.

"Based on what evidence?" snapped Laurence, irritated.

Smith contemplated this. "That cravat thing he wears, it yells perv to me."

Laurence sighed.

"Where are you?" asked Eleanor, checking the call number.

"At work," replied Mo.

"Uh-huh," she responded, lying back down on her bed. "So, Samuelson wants you to unofficially run the case past me, gather my thoughts but make sure the case sticks by not having any trails to me?"

"That'd be about right. What are you doing?" he asked.

"Staring at a spot on the ceiling," she answered.

"Well no fucking good will come of that!" he snorted.

She smiled. "I agree. What news?"

"Whitefoot and Smith spoke to Toby Adams but he claims not to have known what Enda Miller was doing."

"Where does Adams live?"

"Little Portugal with his parents."

Eleanor thought for a moment. "How old would his parents be; seventies, eighties?"

"Urm, guessing so."

"So, how come a couple with a surname like Adams settled in Little Portugal fifty plus years ago?" she said excitedly, grabbing a pair of jeans off her bedside chair.

Laurence ran through the address list, occasionally glancing at Smith as he shovelled in ROM café cheesecake. "You should chew," he noted dryly.

Smith glared at him. "What's your plan now?"

"Raven thinks there's a link between the victims and here. There's also a probable link between Giselle and the Annex. If we can find someone working here that lives there, it's worth looking into."

Eleanor slipped on a reflective tabard and attached a radio to the belt of her jeans. Holding a clipboard with a printed sheet she found in the glove compartment, she approached the front door of a neatly appointed terraced house. After several knocks an elderly woman of obvious Mediterranean stock opened the door cautiously. Glancing quickly at her clipboard Eleanor asked, "Mrs Adams?"

The woman looked suspiciously at her. "Yes."

"Hi, my name's Lucy Fernandes and I work for the Park's Commission."

"Oh yes," replied Mrs Adams, notably relaxing at her choice of surname.

"Just doing a little survey into local residents' views on park amenities. Have you lived in this house for long Mrs Adams?"

"Forty-three years," she replied proudly.

"That's incredible. Have you any grandchildren that would benefit from an improvement in park facilities?"

"Yes," beamed Mrs Adams. "I have three."

Eleanor rewarded her with a smile. "So you have a son or daughter either living with you or nearby. "I have two daughters and they live over by the school," she replied happily.

"No sons?" said Eleanor smiling.

"Three grandsons!" she chirped.

"I only say that because I used to work at the ROM and there was a lovely guy there called Toby Adams. I wondered if he might have been your son."

Mrs Adams shook her head and smiled. "No, I'm sorry I don't know him."

"Now tell me I'm being nosy but Adams isn't a Portuguese name is it?"

Mrs Adams laughed heartily. "My husband's family were from England to begin with."

"Ah," laughed Eleanor. "That would explain it. You have been extremely helpful Mrs Adams," she said, as she quickly ticked a couple of boxes. "Have a good day now."

"I want to see this guy."

"You *can't*," said Mo. "Give me something so I can bring him in."

"He lied about where he lived," she replied.

"You lied about who you were to the resident too, I'm guessing."

Eleanor sighed. "Get Whitefoot to interview him again."

Mo was frustrated. "I can't before I've sent a patrol officer to check out the address and for that I need grounds for suspicion."

"Then do it!" snapped Eleanor. "I'm sorry I –"

"Don't! I should be finding ways to help you, not putting up more barriers..." his voice trailed off. "You're sure this guy took Tommy? It's a gut instinct?"

She wasn't sure how to talk to Mo about these matters. She'd hoped he'd understood over the years, accepted why she could get into the minds of the dangerous and the insane. "Mo, it's not a gut instinct, a hedged bet or a psychological evaluation... It's because I look into the mirror."

There was a pause before Mo cleared his throat and asked quietly. "Is Tommy alive?"

"No, I don't think so," she said carefully and disconnected.

Eleanor slumped back into the driver's seat and closed her eyes. She debated calling Whitefoot but without a more considered approach and some degree of evidence what was she going to say? That a man she hadn't met yet was the likely murderer and preserver of several women known and probably several yet to be unearthed and, in her opinion, the probable kidnapper of a seven-year-old boy. Eleanor tapped her hands against the steering wheel and for a brief moment an image of a car flashed into her mind. A classic car: an Oldsmobile Deluxe 88, just like the one her uncle used to treasure; and then she saw it clearly as she pulled in next to it in the ROM car park. She'd been told exactly what car Giselle's new boyfriend had been driving by Chantelle; she just hadn't listened. He drove an old car, Chantelle had said several times but what she'd meant was an *Olds*mobile. What else had she missed? That his eyes had made Giselle feel sick. Steering the car through the late afternoon traffic she reached for the phone. "Susan?"

"Hey honey? What's up?"

"I need help on a technical question."

"Uh-huh."

"Would exposure to arsenic in powder form affect the eyes?"

"Absolutely, it's an irritant and usually doesn't cross the dermal barrier but it does affect the eyes. They'd be red, crusted, maybe constantly watering. Probably would appear like a common bacterial infection such as conjunctivitis."

"You're a star!" said Eleanor.

"I am indeed."

"What do you mean he doesn't live at that address?" asked Laurence.

"Ellie checked it out and he doesn't and never has lived there," said Mo, as he scanned through the long list of names and addresses thrown up by the data search.

"Shit!" Laurence replied, climbing out of the car. "We're just picking up the Parminder Kaur and Giselle boxes from forensics and will get back over to the museum as soon as we've dropped them off with evidence."

"How long? Don't let this guy go without talking to him again. Did he offer his address or just confirm it?" asked Mo, rechecking the museum listing again.

Laurence glanced at Smith's back as he disappeared into the atrium of the Forensics building. "Shit," he muttered under his breath.

"Huh?" said Mo on the other line. "If he lied to your face there's a reason. I'm not going to have time to send down patrol, so you're going to have to bluff."

"Okay. Find out where he actually lives and I'll get back before he clocks off," replied Laurence sprinting up the steps to the building.

"It's five now!" snapped Mo.

"I'll be there!"

Timms opened the fridge door and looked at the empty shelves glumly. "Where's the food and where's Raven?" he asked.

"Gone," answered Mo distractedly, as he hovered over a pile of print outs, marker pen poised.

"Why and what the fuck's going on?" asked Timms, slamming the door.

Mo looked up. "She was deemed unfit for work."

"By who?" snarled Timms. "You implying that there's a fitness standard that has to be adhered to, to work here?"

"Not if you're the poster boy for recruitment," quipped Wadesky, stacking three polystyrene containers on the table. Timms grabbed a box and tucked in, pushing one over to Mo. "We got you a salad," he said meaningfully, raising both eyebrows. "So explain to me and my overworked partner here, why the only thinking member of this squad is on sick leave?"

"You are shitting me!" said Wadesky, letting her mouth drop.

Mo shook his head and sighed. "Samuelson considered her unfit for work."

"The fuck he has! What happened? Was it that asshole Whitefoot?" Timms put up a hand. "Don't bother! So you running her case now?"

"I'm helping," replied Mo. "You got news on Tommy Banks?"

"Christ there's nothing! No one saw shit. There's no evidence and we've ruled out every possible lead. It's like he vanished." Timms clicked his fingers together, magician style.

Mo looked up. "You've got nothing huh?"

Timms looked at him suspiciously. "Where are we going with this?"

"Give Raven's idea a go."

Timms shook his head slowly. "There is no idea! You've pulled in one guy who fucks squirrels and unless Whitefoot's uncovered some new evidence since yesterday, that's all you've got him on. You don't even have any proof that he's been peddling museum shit either!" Timms arranged a mouthful, in much the same way as he would a Tower of Hanoi. Mo watched him with a sour expression as he chewed.

"Tommy was at the museum on the day he vanished, wasn't he."

Timms growled. "For fuck's sake! Who do I go interview?"

"Toby Adams," said Mo carefully.

"And who the fuck is he?" snapped Timms, pushing his half eaten tray away.

"He shares the same office as Enda Miller, the squirrel guy." Mo ploughed on, despite Timms leaning back in the chair, his arms crossed. "He fits Doc Delaware's profile and he gave Whitefoot and Smith a false address." Mo let this sink in before resuming his argument.

Timms knotted his brow. "Go on…"

"He was asked to confirm the address provided by the museum and he did. But when it was checked out…"

"… By Raven I'm assuming," Timms interrupted.

Mo nodded. "It was the long-term abode of a Mrs Adams and her husband. They were neither related to nor knew a Toby Adams."

Timms glanced at Wadesky. "What you thinking?"

"Museum curator's not the right job to be giving false details," she replied.

Timms nodded. "So Whitefoot's bringing him in?"

Mo shook his head. "They're over at forensics on a box drop." He was almost there. "Tommy Banks went to the museum on the morning of his disappearance didn't he, for his Saturday class?"

Timms checked the clock. "You send me what you've got, ok?"

Mo made sure it was an inward smile, as he watched Timms and Wadesky leave.

Laurence was about to blow. He'd collected the boxes, signed for them and was now waiting in evidence while Smith negotiated a location for them and caught up with the hockey results from the uniform on duty. Slamming the boxes onto a shelf he quickly checked off the contents on the four boxes and signed off on them. "I'm going now!" he announced and stormed out. If Smith wanted to stay then fuck him! He'd made it to the bottom of the stairs, pleased to hear Smith's heavy trot behind him when he stopped dead.

"I thought we were in a goddamned rush," snarled Smith.

Ignoring him, Laurence hurried back into evidence and pulled from the shelf the Parminder Kaur evidence box. Using his knife, he sliced through the tape and rummaged through the sealed bags until he found the one that contained the garrote. Holding it up to the light he carefully studied the wire. "Fuck!"

"What you found?" asked Smith.

"I think I've seen this same wire in Toby Adams' desk drawer."

"He's not responding to his pager I'm afraid," said Isabel Drake anxiously.

"When is he due to clock off?" asked Wadesky.

"About now but he has a tendency to be elusive."

"Elusive how?" asked Timms.

"Hard to locate, rarely answers a page and I suspect, though have no proof, that he is not always in the building when he should be."

"Ok, this is the puzzle. When he was interviewed by Detective Whitefoot a couple of hours ago he confirmed that he lived at the address in Little Portugal that you have down on your records. He doesn't."

Isabel looked ashen. "He lied?"

"I'm guessing that's what that means. Now, can you take a look at your files and give me his SIN number and the address where his monthly salary goes?" asked Timms firmly.

She nodded, "Of course. I should be able to access them from here," she said logging on.

"Does Toby Adams have anything to do with the Saturday morning children's club?" asked Wadesky.

"Not really…sometimes, depending on how under-staffed we are."

"Does he drive a car? We could see if it's still in the parking lot?"

"Very occasionally I see him arriving in a beautiful fifties Oldsmobile but mostly, I believe, he takes the tram or walks."

Timms nodded to Wadesky, who slipped out of the room to go and check.

"Did he help out this Saturday gone?" he said, leaning in to see the screen.

She nodded. "I'm fairly certain he did."

Isabel adjusted her glasses and peered at the screen. "Ok, that should be all." She collected and handed three printed sheets over to Timms.

"He's gone and all the museum have got is a postal box number for Spadina, the decoy address and his SIN," said Timms.

"Spadina Post Office covers the University and the Annex doesn't it? Let me check his Insurance number and I'll get back to you," replied Mo.

Timms disconnected and was just opening the door to Toby's office when Whitefoot appeared, a breathless Smith in tow. Without further discussion, Laurence slipped on latex gloves and pulled open the desk drawer and placed it on the table top. Laurence put the evidence bag next to the wire, adjusting the plastic so that a comparison could be easily made. Timms leaned over and looked. "Fuck! Get Raven on the phone now!"

CHAPTER TWENTY-TWO

There had been absolutely no doubt in Eleanor's mind, when she saw Toby Adams slip out of the staff exit, that he was the man whose face had been obscured by his hands in Giselle's spoiled photograph. The fact that his eyes were red and crusted, with what looked like conjunctivitis, was a bonus to proof. She was too focused to feel frustrated or angry, just determined to keep out of his sight and keep him in hers. He hesitated momentarily at the tram stop, but then presumably decided to walk home. She kept several hundred feet behind at all times, keeping as many people in between them as possible. He walked quickly, but didn't show any sign that he suspected he was being followed, and it was with some degree of satisfaction when it became clear that he was heading for the Annex residential quarter. The last half-mile was more challenging, as other pedestrians thinned out and she was left pretty much the only person, other than Toby Adams, walking in that direction.

Noting that he had adopted a more alert demeanour, she slipped into the entrance of one of the houses. Giving it ten seconds, she peered out and saw Toby unlocking a gate next to a high privet hedge. Peering through the foliage she could just make out his outline as he walked towards the front door. He entered quickly and she heard the sound of a lock being turned in the quiet of the traffic-free avenue.

Skirting cautiously along the hedge line, she took in the features of the house. It was in poor condition, brickwork supporting a heavy creeper was missing large sections of its mortar, and where she could see the roof there were several broken and missing tiles. As far as she could determine, there was access to a detached garage through a wooden gate, which was secured with a heavy lock. The rear of the house was inaccessible, as it backed onto the fenced gardens of the adjacent avenue. She would have to enter via the garage and then make her way along the back of the house, hoping there was a less secure means of entrance. For a brief moment she toyed with the idea of switching on her phone and texting Mo her plans, or at least the location, but to what end? She had no official sanction for her actions and once she'd established that she was correct in her assumption of Toby Adams as The Collector, she would hand the facts over to the team. No one was going to follow up on any of her ideas, unless they were backed up with solid evidence. What she dreaded most was that she would find Tommy Banks floating in a tank of formaldehyde.

Swiftly, Eleanor vaulted the wooden gate and ran to the concealed edge of the garage. Squinting in the early evening sun, she could make out that the ground floor windows had all been shuttered from the inside and those of the upstairs rooms bore ancient, weather-stained net curtains. This was a house that hid its secrets. Peering through a small window, she saw the Oldsmobile parked next to what appeared to be a black and silver woman's bicycle. Unsure of whether Toby was watching her, she ran from the garage to the house. Keeping her back against the wall she moved methodically, trying each window as she made her way round to the back. Using her penknife, she pried at each frame but there was no give in any of them. Frustrated she slowly turned the doorknob on the kitchen door but it too was locked. To the right of the kitchen door there was a small basement window, just wide enough for Eleanor to slip through. The glass had, rather ominously, been painted on the inside with black paint, and was firmly locked. Despite her reluctance to enter below ground level, she couldn't see any other way. Leaning against the side of the house to minimise her profile, she gazed around the overgrown garden. The garden was unusual in that it was very uneven and unkempt. No effort had been made to restrict the rampant progress of wild rose, or poison ivy. Clumps of poppies and cornflowers flourished in a manner reminiscent of a battlefield. If there had been any doubt in her mind as to Toby Adams being the likely suspect, it was dismissed.

This garden was a burial ground.

Toby was irritable and unnerved. Why were the police hounding him? They had Enda in custody as far as he was aware, so why the constant bombardment of questions, and why had they a list of employees' addresses? He calmed himself with a glass of single malt and downed it quickly, pouring himself a second for savouring. The drink soothed him, pouring oil on the turmoil. It was standard procedure, that's all, he reasoned. They were running through the staff records because Enda had committed a crime against the people. So, no wonder the police were being vigilant: they had to have a well-documented case to present to the prosecution services. He really needed to relax. What were the chances of the police heading round to interview him at the address in Little Portugal? Maybe, the recent stress of becoming a parent had made him jumpy and irrational. Anyway, all that was in the past now. He would finish his drink, change out of his work clothes and begin the chemical procedures that would preserve Little Tommy for years, if not a lifetime. Tara was in the final stages of the forced impregnation. The acetone was being sucked out of her body, drawing in the active polymer. By his calculations, if he were to embalm Little Tommy this evening he could soak him in the freezer full of filtered acetone, and still have a large window of opportunity to position and harden Tara, while filtering the polymer ready for his son. It was hard work but the rewards would be worth every bead of sweat, and as a mark of his caring nature he would warm the liquid in the syringe, to make his son's passing more comfortable. Toby placed the loaded syringe in a steel kidney bowl full of warm water, finished his drink, and headed for the basement.

Eleanor suspected that the basement window had been nailed closed and any attempt to knock a hole through the glass next to the latch would prove fruitless. The paint had flaked away in several places, and lying on her belly and peering through a gap she could just make out a small storage room, with several large glass containers stacked against the wall. Suddenly, the room was illuminated and she could see with startling clarity the figure of Toby Adams as he moved around inside. She kept absolutely motionless; any movement on her part might draw his attention to the window where her silhouette, the sun low behind her, would be visible. She held her breath and watched. He had placed a small metallic object on a shelf behind him before lifting one of the liquid filled carboys. Eleanor noted that despite his pudgy appearance, Toby Adams was strong, lifting two of the full carboys with apparent ease. As he manoeuvred the huge bottles through the small door, she saw clearly what the metallic object was. It was a syringe suspended in a surgical bowl. A wave of nausea swept through her.

The door to the storage room opened once more, but she rolled quickly away from the window. She had minutes to get into that house and find the child before Adams killed him, and without a firearm she was powerless. She looked around desperately and saw, leaning against the side of the garage, a spade next to a small pile of broken bricks. Desperately raking through her childhood memories, as she sprinted towards the garage, she tried to recall whether her uncle's Oldsmobile possessed a motion alarm. Grabbing the spade and smashing it through the garage windowpane, she hurled one of the bricks at the car's side window. Lacking sufficient momentum, she saw the window crack, followed by silence. She put all of her weight into the second throw and was rewarded with a klaxon of ear numbing intensity. Turning on her heels, spade in hand, she ran back to the house and hunkered down behind a small partition wall to the left of the kitchen exit. She would give it thirty seconds only before having to make the riskier, more overt breach. The countdown tapered in her head, as she tried to gauge the most productive entry point to the house. There were two shuttered windows directly to the right of the kitchen, and smashing her way through using the spade would gain her access but would alert Toby and give him the opportunity to greet her on the other side. Twenty-seven, twenty-eight... She stood up and grabbed the spade, just as the kitchen door began to swing open. Dropping to her haunches and calming her breathing she waited, unable to see anything. Giving him several moments to move towards the garage, she peered carefully around the wall. Toby Adams, a butcher's knife held tightly in his right hand, was moving purposefully towards the garage. She hesitated, it was at least a twenty-metre dash to the kitchen door and he would be able to cover the distance quickly. So far, he was unaware of her presence, which gave her the advantage. If she locked the door behind her he'd know for certain she was in the house, and he may have another access she didn't know about. She glanced at Toby's hulking figure; the knife held at shoulder height gave little doubt that he wouldn't hesitate to kill her. Running as fast as she could to the kitchen door, she glanced at Toby at the precise moment that he turned to see her. She put her weight behind the door, slammed it closed and threw the locking mechanism.

The building reeked of volatile chemicals, ordure and decomposition. If she'd previously considered it to be a fortress she now amended that description to a charnel house. Eleanor calculated that she'd have between three and four minutes to find Tommy, and plan either an escape or a defence. She debated whether to turn on the lights, as it was so dark, but darkness was to her advantage. Yanking out several kitchen drawers she found a slim but sharp fish knife. The kitchen door rattled and then began to shake as Toby tried to open it. She reasoned that the carboys were heavy and, if filled with volatile chemicals, dangerous to manoeuver, so the basement was the most likely location. The door rattling stopped.

Time to move.

Eleanor's eyes were not entirely adjusted to the sudden change in light intensity and her lurch forwards caused her to crack her leg on the side of the huge oak table. The pain seared through the scar tissue reminding her that the last time she'd been alone with a killer, it hadn't gone well. Limping to the nearest door, she pulled it open to reveal a pantry. The second opened onto a corridor, which stretched off to either side.

There was no doubting the entrance to the basement and its purpose. She shuddered as she took in the noise-reducing polystyrene sheets that had been attached both to the door and around the frame. A clumsy hole had been cut, about halfway down the right hand side, and a key poked through. Once she entered this basement she knew that there would be no exit points, other than the way she came in. There was a splintering sound coming from somewhere off to her left. Decisively, Eleanor turned the key but the door was unlocked. The stench of unwashed flesh and fecal matter had an almost palpable quality as it surrounded her. Pocketing the key, she flipped on the light to reveal a small flight of stairs leading to a damp and squalid basement room. She could just about make out a steel cage in the middle of the room, and to its left a mattress covered in a pile of discarded and stained women's clothing. Closing the door behind her, she tiptoed down the steps, and stared with disbelief at the contraption. She took in the mechanism, noting the lock was still in place, and concluded that it must be used for caging and pinioning his victims. The familiar band of pressure circled her throat as she moved closer. There were signs of some recent modification to the design, with unmatched metal supports making the structure smaller, possibly so that a child couldn't escape. "Tommy?" she heard herself whisper. She peered into the bottom of the cage, hardly daring to look, but it was empty. A pair of soiled pyjama bottoms lay on the floor.

Tommy was gone.

There was a heavy running tread above her, and Eleanor knew she couldn't make it out of the basement without confronting Toby Adams and his butcher's knife.

Toby was incensed. Who the hell was the woman, and why had she smashed the window of his car and then locked him out of his own home? He knew of no one who held a grudge against him. She couldn't be police, as she wouldn't have behaved like a home invader. She definitely wasn't Tommy's mother, as Rosheen was pale, with short brown hair. He had never felt so violated in his life. But he wouldn't make a scene; he'd get back in and deal with the problem quietly and efficiently, just as he had with Parminder Kaur, the blackmailing bitch. He had been averse to hiding spare keys under plant pots, as they were the first place someone would look and decided that entering the house through its weakest link, as he had done over thirty years ago, would be the best bet.

Grabbing a crowbar from the tool kit he kept in the garage, he pulled back the ground ivy from the top of the unused coalhole and then slid it between the wooden cover boards. The slats were rotten and yielded easily to the pressure. Lowering himself cautiously into the dark pit, he felt along the damp walls till his feet touched the stone steps. The door that led up to the utility stairs gave out with the lightest of shoulder pushes.

Toby didn't bother adopting a stealthy approach, it was clear to him that the intruder had an agenda, and that it concerned a member of his family, he had little doubt. As he approached the basement door, he noted it was open and the key missing. Outraged, he yanked open the door and thundered down the stairs; she was going to pay long and bitterly for this. The crush was empty. His son was gone and only one thing could have happened; that woman had taken him. With a howl of rage, he hammered back up the stairs.

Dragging in a deep lungful of air, Eleanor flung the clothes off her and tried to steady her racing heart, as it made her clumsy and light headed. The exquisite torture of not knowing if a twelve-inch blade was going to be thrust into her, had taken a toll on her nerves. Did Adams think she'd taken Tommy? He must have assumed he was still captive, or he would have searched the only feasible hiding space. If he didn't know where Tommy was then she had a chance to find him first. Grabbing a cheap leather-look jacket from the mound, she wrapped it round her left forearm; it wasn't Kevlar but would give some protection. Cautiously, she mounted the stairs, trying to pinpoint where Tommy was, and praying that wherever he was, he would stay silent and secure.

Tommy was looking for his mother. He had finally managed to squeeze himself through a small gap in the cage and, despite his pain and distress, had opened the unlocked door and found the stairs that led up to where his mother was. He didn't understand why his mom would have been upstairs, and had to conclude that either the man was lying or she was in a cage like the one he'd been in. He heard slams and crashes downstairs, but had to find her. The first room was a bathroom, the second some sort of cupboard, with sheets piled in it. He tried the next door. It smelled awful in there and he thought it might be another toilet but the light was on and he could see a bed with a shape in it. "Mummy?" he whispered. He glanced behind him; perhaps he'd better shut the door. Tiptoeing closer to the shape, he saw that there was a lot of dark brown hair on the pillow. It couldn't be his mom, but it was a lady. Carefully, his teeth chattering, he pulled the sheet away, to reveal a big doll. He didn't understand. Why would the man have a doll in his bed? He touched the doll's face, it was hard and gave off a stink as he pressed it with his fingers. Suddenly there were heavy footsteps, without a second thought he slid under the bed, covering his face with his hands in an effort to screen out the terror. The footsteps paused outside the room. Slowly, the door swung open and covering his mouth, so a scream wouldn't slip out, Tommy looked at the large feet as they stepped into the room. He wanted desperately to close his eyes, or even make a dash for the door but he was frozen to the spot. The feet moved towards the bed, stopping inches from his face. The heels began to rise, slowly.

Suddenly, crashing through the silence of the house there was a loud, metallic ringing. The heels dropped, turned, and then walked briskly away from the bed and out of the room. Tommy waited for several moments before scrabbling forwards and pulling himself upright. Suddenly, a pair of hands encircled his mouth and a woman's voice whispered urgently into his ear, "Tommy, I'm a detective and I'm going to get you home."

His instinct was to bite and claw and get away, but the arms held him tightly and the voice soothed him. "Tommy I'm going to take you home to your mom Rosheen, but you have to trust me. I need your help."

The emaciated, filthy body began to lose its tension and allow her arms to take its weight. Gently, she turned him round to face her. His face was covered in open sores, and his skin loose and grey with dehydration. "Tommy, I think that's my police friends at the door and they're coming to help us. But we need to stay safe until they get into the house. Do you understand?"

"Why can't you shoot him?" he asked.

Toby stood in the corridor and stared at the front door, his lip curled with anger and disappointment, his fists clenched. He knew who was at the door. Only one type of individual would ignore the deterrents and clear messages that he wanted peace and privacy: the police. The bell was a strident reminder that his situation was poor, and his options apparently limited. Now, a hammering sound accompanied the cacophony. It wasn't as if he hadn't thought through the possibility that this may happen at some time in the future, or played with the idea that he may have to abandon his family and start again. He glanced at the stairwell and smiled. She could have the child. He knew now that he was never meant to be a parent. But his family existed for him and him alone. He wouldn't leave them to be owned by anyone else.

It was time to leave, his hands as empty as the day he'd arrived at Crowthorne.

Running into the basement, he pulled open the metal door to the chemical cupboard, lifted down three empty glass bottles and hurriedly filled each half-full of gasoline from the plastic fuel can, taking care not to splash himself. He'd long ago cut and rolled the linen to act as fuse, and quickly doused all three before wedging them into the tops. His hands shaking from the effort, he paused momentarily to ascertain where the police were now. Despite the incessant ringing of the doorbell, he could just make out a hammering on the kitchen door. He would have very little time to execute his departure but his was a prepared mind, and fortune would favour him.

Tipping over the first carboy, he stepped gingerly away from the flow, quickly uncorking the second. The flashpoint would be reached within seconds and that made his safe exit through the coalhole dependent upon exquisite timing. He ran out of the now saturated storeroom, along the corridor, and into his workroom. Pushing off the lid to Tara's tank, he allowed his eyes to linger momentarily on her perfect form and take in the lonely figure of Monty, his beloved dog but there was no time for sentimentality, his future was at stake. Placing the first Molotov cocktail by the storeroom and the second two by the workroom, he lit the first, shocked by the instantly expansive flame. He flung it at the far wall, delighted at the intensity of flame. Turning and fleeing down the corridor, he had just lit the second bottle, when he felt the impact of the flash point. It seemed to create an internal sound that compressed his lungs. A balloon of flame hugged the ceiling and rapidly expanded upwards. Hurling the second towards the sides of the tank, he turned and ran, taking the last unlit bottle with him.

Eleanor had no idea where Toby Adams had gone. She suspected, or rather hoped, that he had been unnerved by the doorbell, and was planning his escape. However, several other plausible scenarios, vied for a less optimistic outlook. She just had to make it to the front door and Tommy would be safe, but those stairs were beginning to resemble a snake pit. Darkness on both sides gave her little opportunity for stealth, and Tommy had used up all of his reserves and clung to her like a limpet. Keeping her back to the wall, she inched along the corridor, the child's legs wrapped round her waist, and his head buried into her shoulder. If Adams was waiting for her, she wouldn't see him until he attacked. Maybe she should just stay low and wait it out? Momentarily distracted by the sudden increase in noise and smell, Eleanor instinctively dropped to the ground, covering the child's body with hers. She could feel his chest heave with the shock of her weight, but any sound he made was lost as the explosion ripped through the building. Staggering to her feet, she was immediately hit with the impact of second and third explosions. Flames billowed from the stairwell and hugged the ceiling, and she knew the intensity would soon engulf the first floor. Pulling the terrified child into her arms, she ran to the end of the corridor and tried to open the window but a quick glance at the nails driven into the frames made it futile.

"Up!" screamed Tommy, pointing to a staircase that lead up to the second floor. Her instincts were to avoid being trapped by the fire but the corridor was filling with heavy, black smoke. A blast of flame igniting the curtains to the left of them, decided matters for her. The second level corridor was smaller and narrower than the first. Of the five doorways leading off from it she pushed her way into the first, slammed the door shut behind them and, falling to her knees, unwrapped the jacket from her arm to use as a smoke excluder. She'd chosen this room as it faced the front and any fire truck would be able to reach them. Flinging open the curtains, she tried to open the window, but like the others it was nailed shut. She needed a chair or something heavy. Spinning round she saw with horror the awful thing that Tommy was staring at.

Mo had arrived a full eleven minutes before Timms and Wadesky, and another four before Whitefoot and Smith drew up. He'd been rather circumspect about calling in the troops on such a tenuous lead but his unhappiness and frustration with recent events was sapping his usual reticence. He'd been unable to get through to Eleanor, and anxious about this had run through the residential lists for the Annex area. There were only two households that had the name Adams listed and both checked out. Warning bells had rung when he saw that an elderly couple, Mr and Mrs Godfrey Aspen were listed as living at 'Crowthorne', and had been since 1926. That, he had calculated, put them comfortably into their hundreds. So, his finger immobile on the doorbell, he waited.

Mo had been mulling over his options when the explosion kicked at the door. He felt his chest tighten alarmingly and made several involuntary steps backwards into the arms of Timms. This wasn't the time for supposition, Mo called for the Fire Support Unit, as Whitefoot ran round to check on Smith, who was trying to gain entry round the back of the house, Monster racing ahead.

"Who's in there?" bellowed Timms, above the noise.

"Mo!"

"Ellie. I think Ellie's in there."

The elderly couple lay, dressed in dated evening attire, side by side on the double bed. Their hands had been linked and they were surrounded by dessicated, floral arrangements. Tommy's small naked body began to shake, his unblinking eyes riveted to the sight. Saving his skin was her priority; his mind could be coaxed back later. Grabbing a small bedside chair she hit the window with all of her strength. The immediate increase in siren and shouting, gave her a flush of strength. "Here!" she screamed at the top of her lungs. "We're here!" Uncertain that she had been spotted she grabbed the child. "They're dolls Tommy," she said, sinking to her knees.

He shook his head. "They're…"

She gently turned his face away from the door; pulling him into her chest and wrapping her arms tightly round him. A small glowing spot had appeared in the centre of the wooden door panel and smoke seeped urgently around the casing.

"No, dolls… like the one downstairs… like the ones in clothes shops. *Nothing* more. Do you understand?"

The door bulged and cracked against the heat onslaught.

"Yes… dolls," he said faintly, as he wrapped his arms around her neck.

She scanned the room, desperate for escape but there was nothing. They were surrounded by death and its means. She closed her eyes.

Smith's internal alarm bells were ringing loudly as he tried to see into the house. He raised his torch but there were no entry points, or even gaps in the shuttered windows. What the hell was this place? Monster had followed him round to the side of the building and was sniffing enthusiastically, his hackles up. "You don't like this either buddy eh?" he whispered. Making his way to the back door, he gave it a try and then started to hammer on it. "Open up!" he bellowed. "Police!"

Suddenly, the dog was barking hysterically. Smith shone his torch on him and was horrified to see Monster was barking at him. The dog lunged forward, taking Smith off his guard and began to growl, jumping nervously around his feet. "What the fuck!" he managed before the explosion blew him and the dog fifteen feet into the garden, sandblasting them with glass and debris.

Smith was trying to focus on exactly who was down. He tried opening his eyes but they were wet and unresponsive. The 'man down' voice was speaking loudly into his ear, while running calm hands over him. "Smith? You with us?"

"Who's down?" he managed to croak.

"You are buddy. Keep very still and we're going to get you outta here," said the voice. "Officer down at rear of building. Needs urgent medical assistance, but area not secure! I repeat, area not secure," Whitefoot yelled into his radio. He could hear the sirens but couldn't make out much else. "Roger that..." came the reply.

In the intermittent light given off by the fire, he could see Monster limping furtively towards the house, growling.

His coat was alive with reflected light from the glass fragments trapped in it. Laurence watched as two cellar doors began to open, and flipping the safety on his Glock, stood up and levelled it at the spot.

Mo had been forced by one of the patrol officers to sit on the fire truck's footplate, while she took his pulse. He had managed to indicate to the fire crew, who were now extending the tower ladder and bucket, where Eleanor had been standing when she'd smashed the window and called for help. That entire floor had been engulfed in flame now and not even the urgency of his chest pains could detract him from keeping his eyes pinned to that window. Time and the motion of the ladder seemed to have slowed to a heavy crawl and it was only the sight of Eleanor, Tommy Banks in her arms, being helped into the bucket by the fire fighter that paced the clock again.

CHAPTER TWENTY-THREE

"Simon, I'd like you to take a look at these photographs," Eleanor said, selecting a handful of enlarged images from a file.

"I don't want to be called that," he said firmly, turning his head away from her and staring at the mirror.

"But Simon is the name on your birth certificate."

"I haven't got a birth certificate," he replied coldly.

Reaching into a second file, Eleanor took out a photocopy of a birth certificate and slid it towards him. "Simon Mantell, born 1959, at the Sisters of Mercy orphanage. Your mother's name was Martha Mantell, aged fifteen and there's a blank where your father's name should have been."

There was a pause while he mulled this over.

"Explain to me why you took the name Toby?" she asked quietly. "The Father in charge of the Orphanage was called Wainwright Adams, wasn't he? Did you feel he could have been your father?"

Toby turned to her, his face a mask of spite and anger. "He *was* my father!"

"Why do you think that?"

Toby was beginning to get agitated, his body language became twitchy and his temporal vein began to throb.

"Toby?"

"How is Detective Smith? Is he out of hospital yet?" asked Toby in a conversational tone.

Eleanor sat back and smiled at him. "He is well, thank you. He's out and you'll be able to see him next week, as he's back on the case."

Toby looked away again, staring at his image. "Who's behind the mirror?"

Eleanor looked at the two-way, catching their reflection as she sat opposite Toby Adams. "Sometimes it's Timms or Wadesky, sometimes my partner Laurence Whitefoot. Sometimes the Chief comes along to see how we're progressing...Does it bother you?"

"A little," he replied. "You and your partner are staying together?" he asked.

Eleanor looked at him, puzzled.

Toby smiled, coyly. "Detective Whitefoot came in yesterday and took my temperature. I felt a little under the weather and he said he was a qualified doctor."

Eleanor nodded, wondering where this was going.

"He mentioned that he was very interested in the bird display at the museum. Apparently, it was a trip there as a teenager that gave him his love of nature and medicine. I've always said that the bird display is the highlight of every child's visit." Toby flicked his eyes at the mirror and then leaned towards Eleanor, conspiratorially. "He told me that I'd have never been caught if someone as brilliant as yourself hadn't been on the case." Toby nodded at her. "He confided in me."

She raised an eyebrow and indicated he continue.

"He said he'd wanted to transfer to another unit but that even though you're difficult to understand and work with, he wants to stay and learn from you."

Eleanor glanced at the mirror and wondered if Laurence was watching them and listening. Some of the ease she felt must have shown, as Toby leaned back in his chair and smiled at her. Making the most of this connection between them she carefully spread the images in front of him and tapped each one. Toby had, so far, resolutely refused to look at the mortuary photographs of the bodies exhumed from his yard.

"Was she a lover, or a sister Toby?" she asked, pointing to the partially skeletonised body of a woman in her late teens or early twenties. "She's very pretty still."

Toby glanced at the photograph and gasped. "She *is* still beautiful, isn't she? That's Ariana. She was my third wife."

"Can you remember her last name?"

Toby smiled and ran his fingers across the paper. "Roscoe. Ariana Roscoe."

Eleanor breathed a sigh of relief, nodding imperceptibly at the mirror. "When did she join your family Toby?"

"In late ninety-eight. The summer," he said brightly.

"Can you remember where you met her?" she asked in a conversational tone.

Toby smiled and shook his head. "The museum, of course."

Eleanor sighed. "Thank you. You're being helpful Toby. Really helpful." She gathered the material together and stood up.

"How's Little Tommy?" he asked brightly.

She paused. "You know I'm not allowed to talk about Tommy."

He nodded sadly, studying her for a moment. "You look tired Detective Raven."

"I am a little."

"They're not going to take you off our case are they?" he asked, anxiously.

"No Toby, they know you prefer to talk to me."

"Will it be much longer?"

"They're still digging Toby," she said quietly. "There's still a way to go."

"I saw you were mentioned in the paper, the *Toronto Sun* I think. They said you beat a journalist to within an inch of his life," he said with wonder. "Did you?"

She headed for the door, nodding to the patrol officer who sat next to it.

"Detective?"

She turned and looked at him.

"I would have liked you to have been a family member, now that I've gotten to know you." he said earnestly.

Eleanor took a moment before answering. "Thank you."

ABOUT THE AUTHOR

 Karen Long is a former teacher who took up full-time writing ten years ago. She has written numerous screenplays and is currently working on the third novel in the Eleanor Raven series. Married to a film director she is fortunate to travel the world where she spends most of her time zealously flushing out and photographing reluctant wildlife. She lives in rural Shropshire with her three children, three dogs and a small but noisy collection of crows.

Book one in the series, *The Safe Word,* is available to buy at Amazon and other retailers.

It would be wonderful if you would consider leaving a review on Amazon to let others know what you think of *The Vault.* It doesn't have to be long, but it would be much appreciated.

Contact Details:
Website: karenlongwriter.com
Twitter: @KarenLongWriter
Email: karenlongwriter@gmail.com

Made in the USA
Charleston, SC
15 December 2014